Always Montana

Always Montana

Deb Martin-Webster

Cover Design & Photo: Deb Martin-Webster

Published 2014 by Shorehouse Books
Printed in the United States of America

ISBN 0-692-23968-5
EAN-13 978-069223968-1

For Jeremiah Ryan

Introduction

"I guess you could say I'm a small town sort of guy. Cities dwellers annoy me. Fancy, over-priced restaurants and flashy duds do nothing for me. All I need is my beautiful wife beside me, the big sky above me, a good horse beneath me and my favorite gray Stetson." - Lash Jackson Montana (Montana Joe)

Chapter 1

"Excuse me Ma'am, I don't mean to interrupt your bitch session; however, you do realize your hair is on fire?"

Joe's been dead for two years, and he still makes me laugh. He was so relaxed in front of an audience. Unlike me, who would panic at the thought of giving a five-minute PowerPoint presentation, Joe loved entertaining his fans for not only was he a renowned author and accomplished writer but a prolific storyteller as well. The video was from a charity event he attended in Princeton, New Jersey. Some affluent donors weren't very happy about the lack of seating. Joe was famous for drawing large crowds. He noticed a well-dressed, older woman sitting by the exit door complaining about the seating arrangement. Joe, being the gentleman that he was, excused himself and headed toward the back of the room. She was so engrossed in her own bitching that she failed to notice that he was standing directly behind her. Inadvertently, she leaned into the table's candle centerpiece and set the front of her hair on fire. Without blinking an eye, Joe gallantly grabbed a glass of water from a nearby table and doused the flames. Needless to say she was humiliated, but ever so thankful for his quick action.

Joe flashed his infamous shit-eating grin and said, "You're welcome, Darlin'. Now, how about you come up front and sit with me. And by the way, that'll cost you another thousand dollar donation for my heroic firefighting service."

The audience gave him a roaring round of applause. He informed the guests that his tip jar was in the back and that it was pathetically empty – nothing her thousand dollar donation couldn't fix. Joe knew how to work a crowd and please his fans. He was good at what he did, and he knew it.

I turned my computer off and continued to tidy his office. Funny, I still called it his office. *Has it really been two years since his death – seems like yesterday.* I thought if I left the room the way it was, it would in some way comfort me. Regrettably, it did just the opposite. It irritated me beyond belief. I'm a neat-freak, and he was an incurable pack rat. Receipts from gas stations, fast food restaurants, numerous coffee shops and illegible crib notes on discarded manuscripts littered his desk.

There was still the matter of scattering his ashes. I couldn't bring myself to do it, but I knew it was time to honor my husband's last wish which was to scatter his remains at the place where he proposed. In my mind, I knew I needed to let go and move on, but in my heart his untimely death still hurt like hell. I've heard people use the term heartbroken or heartache. I'd never experienced either – until Joe died. It was an endless, helpless, hopeless pain. I needed to let go. I needed to move on. No matter how painful the task, Joe's ashes had to be spread.

When the time was right, Raymond said he would accompany me to the spot Joe designated. He was very patient and understanding when it came to my grieving.

"Joe was a procrastinator in life so why would he change in death—always needing to be in control," Raymond would joke. "He still annoys me from the grave—arrogant son of a mangy coyote!"

I knew it was Raymond's way of expressing his grief and how he too missed Joe. To be honest, in some strange way, it made me feel better. I missed being referee to their incessant bickering. They had a lot in common. Their inimitable friendship was cherished more than they were willing to admit.

Charlotte was now in her terrible-twos and quite skilled at navigating herself around the house. She was becoming quite a beautiful little girl. I know all parents think that their children are beautiful and talented, but Charlotte was truly a beautiful child. I called her our little golden girl because of her glowing olive complexion and curly, sandy brown locks. She had my focus and temper and Lash's (Joe as his fans knew him) curiosity and smile.

She toddled into the office and climbed onto his rawhide leather chair. I remembered him gloating when he finished assembling it. He wasn't patient when it came to following directions or handling tools. He called it his one-and-only successful IKEA achievement. I didn't have the heart to tell him that if I'd given Charlotte an Allen wrench she could have put it together.

Lord, I miss him. I miss those final edit nights when I'd come in with coffee and sit in his lap. It saddened me to think I'd never see him sitting at that desk again. I picked up Charlotte and gave her a big hug.

I turned away to keep her from seeing my tears. She placed her small hands on my cheeks.

"Happy . . . h-a-p-p-y Mama," she whispered.

Her attempt to console me brought a smile to my face. I kissed her tiny palms.

"This one's from me and this one's from Daddy."

Charlotte instinctively knew when I needed her happy reminder. She was wise beyond her years. Raymond called her "Nadie". Blackfoot and loosely translated, it meant the wisdom of an old soul.

Keough cracked the office door and peeked inside.

"You gals okay? Both of ya' need to get some rest. It's long past your bedtimes."

Charlotte climbed off my lap and ran over to Keough and latched onto his leg. He picked her up and swung her onto his shoulders.

"It's time for this little cowgirl to hit the hay. Come on let's get you into your bunk. Lou and I will tell you a story about the time I tried to lasso and ride an ornery wild mustang. Would you like that?"

She bounced up and down on his shoulders squealing, "Pap-Pap, horsey!"

"Don't worry, Rose. It's a very short story. It took me three seconds to lose that man-versus-beast battle."

I chuckled at Keough's honesty and said goodnight.

"Okay, Baby Girl —a quick story then bedtime. That goes for you too Mama." He paused for a moment and whispered, "And don't think I haven't notice you sneaking into this office in the middle of the night. It ain't healthy for you to deprive yourself of sleep. And it ain't good for this baby to see you so dang sad all the time. Now, don't make me tie you up and drag your ass to bed."

"I promise I'll go to bed. Just a few more minutes, okay? Thank you Keough."

"You're welcome, Darlin' and goodnight."

I was leaving the office when I noticed something on the side of the door jam. Funny, I'd never noticed it before. There were two perfectly shaped hearts carved into the trim with the initials MJ loves R. I rubbed my finger over them. *When did he do this? What other little treasures has he left behind for me to discover.* I went back to his desk, picked up some paper and a pencil and rubbed it over the carving and then tucked it into my shirt pocket. *We miss you too, Joe.*

Chapter 2

One missed voice message? I looked at the phone number—it was from Paul.

"Hello Poppet, it's me Paul. Hope all is well. I'll be heading back from California and thought I'd drop by. Let me know if it's okay. I've got a gift for the bab'bee and a little something for you. Sorry, I couldn't attend the scattering of Joe's ashes. I know I haven't been in touch, but this new company has me doing my nut driving OTR, that's over-the-road, Luv. Be that as it may, it'll be good to see you, eh, you all – call me. Cheers."

It was good to hear from Paul. He was a huge help after Joe's death. His help on the ranch went beyond selfless. He'd use his flatbed to haul winter hay and load it into the barns. It took Joe and the ranch hands weeks to bring what he brought in a day. It would be good to see him. I enjoyed listening to him talk. His British accent amused me. So different from the accents I hear in Montana. I had to admit that most of the time I didn't know what he was talking about. What the hell does *doing his nut* mean? I saved his voice message and made a mental note to call him back tomorrow. He'll be curious as to why I haven't scattered Joe's ashes. *Was I subconsciously waiting for him to attend Joe's final farewell?* I guess I relied on Paul more than I was willing to admit. I didn't like relying on people; however, he was different. He never expected anything in return. They were simple acts of kindness on his part.

There was so much I needed to do. The matter of Charlotte's christening came to mind. After Joe died, I was so distraught I couldn't organize anything. I couldn't think straight – still can't. It's a challenge for me to cook or to do our laundry. Thank goodness for Cecilia or we'd have starved to death and gone naked.

I need to contact Morgan and Jannine. Both agreed to be Charlotte's Godparents. They would take care of her in case anything happened to me. Not that Lash Jackson Montana's kid would ever need or want for anything. The Montana Joe novels were more popular now than ever. Hanna stayed busy promoting his books. Before Joe died, he finished two series. One was entitled, *Gunslingers of Culver Silver Creek* and the other, *Outlaws of Burnt Canyon Crossing*. Fans continued to attend his book launchings and buy his novels which would soon be available online. His entire life's work could be purchased through his redesigned website—thanks to Hanna.

Keeping the Montana Joe legacy afloat was no easy task. He'd be pleased by Hanna's nonstop promotional enthusiasm. Joe's books continued to dominate the western genre. She was worth her weight in royalty checks. *Note to self: Remind me to give that woman a big raise! Second note to self: Ask Raymond if he would perform the christening.*

Raymond was fast becoming a beloved family member. There were times when I felt I was taking advantage of him.

He would say, "Rose, you could never take advantage of me. I would gladly give you my right arm if you needed it. Good thing I'm left-handed."

Keough stepped up and took on the roll of Montana patriarch. Keeping his promise to his son, he stayed on to manage the ranch. He also kept his promise to stay sober. Joe would be proud. He looked healthier and a tad younger since giving up the booze. In fact, I could now see the strong resemblance between him and Joe.

From time-to-time, his twin brother Kurt would stop by. It was difficult for me to tell them apart. I'd have to remember who was wearing what. Keough preferred denim shirts to Kurt's plaids. Both men were still exceptionally handsome. *I wonder if Lash would have looked as good in his seventies.* I must admit Montana men do age well.

The two years since Joe's death brought changes for my friends as well. Patrick and Daniel, who were the closest thing I had to family when I lived and worked in New York, left Manhattan and semi-retired to Seattle. A few months after their relocation, Patrick called and informed me they had gotten married. It was a small gathering with a few of their friends from New York. He jokingly said they would have invited me, but they were too afraid I'd sing at the ceremony. They expressed how much they missed me and how excited they were to live so close to Montana. I congratulated them on their recent nuptials and said that I loved they'd be able to visit more frequently. New York now seemed like the other side of the world to me.

Daniel bragged about Patrick buying him a real cowboy hat with matching chaps. "Can you image, *me* wearing cowboy clothes? Honey, I must admit I do look fabulous. Who knew being a cowboy could be so glamorous."

I had visions of him walking down a staircase like Scarlett O'Hara boasting, "As long as I live, I'll never wear Armani again!"

Their courage was admirable. Leaving their comfort zone was a huge step. Not many people would relocate such a distance to console a grieving friend. I was happy they did. Even now, I don't know what I'd do without them.

I decided to take Joe's advice and breed Daisy, the horse that Joe gave to me. She turned out a beautiful little filly that looked exactly like her. I named her Daisy Deuce, and I knew she would make a perfect ride for Charlotte.

Everyone was moving on with their lives – everyone except me. How does one move on after an epic love? The more I'd think about it, the angrier I'd get. *Damn you Joe for leaving me!* Perhaps going for a ride would clear my head. I wiped my eyes and put on my boots. It always helped Joe with his bouts of writer's block. He'd arrive back at the house with new ideas, shit-covered boots and an occasional bouquet of wild flowers. What I wouldn't give to smell them again – the flowers, not the boots.

A rapid knock at the door brought me back to reality. I noticed the small white van idling in the driveway. It was a young man holding a gold box.

"Morning Ma'am, I have a delivery for an Amelia 'Rose' Montana."

I signed for the package and rummaged through my jean pockets for a tip.

"Wow, THANK YOU—you have a great day. . . Thank you!"

I was in such a daze, I didn't realize I'd given him a fifty dollar bill instead of the ten – oh, well. Joe would have said, "Darlin', its only money. I'll just write another book. You are becoming an expensive habit, Mrs. Montana—one I never want to kick."

The box didn't weigh much. I didn't remember ordering anything either. Who could have sent me a gift? It wasn't my birthday. It was the middle of May. Maybe it was from Jannine and Morgan. I stared at the box for a few minutes – then opened it.

Inside were two daffodils and a petite strawberry cheesecake in the shape of a heart. Tucked beside the daffodils was a note. I slipped it out of the envelope.

"I know your heart. Happy Mother's Day Cuppy, and for goodness sake quit your droolin'! Love, Joe"

I dropped onto the couch. *He always told me he was a man of many surprises.* I'd been so preoccupied with my grief that I didn't realize it was Mother's Day. A few minutes later the phone rang. It was Lash's lawyer. He asked if I had received the delivery.

"Yes, it just arrived a few minutes ago. How did you know? Do you have hidden cameras in our house? Did Lash set them up before he died so you could keep an eye on me?"

"No, Rose he would never spy on you. Your husband was . . . eh, with all due respect, rather peculiar. Part of his will states that after his death, you are to receive occasional gifts. When he realized his condition was terminal, he provided me with a list of what to send. He also wrote a series of notes with specific instructions attached as to when and where to send them."

Hmm, I understand the when, but the where was very weird - even weird for Joe. Where else would I be? I know the ranch is huge but I haven't left it since his death. Maybe he knows something I don't. I decided to save the cheesecake for dessert. It would be good with my after dinner coffee. It's a good thing I wrote down Joe's cowboy brew recipe. Lord knows he's probably bitching up a storm complaining how weak the coffee is in heaven. I laughed to myself imagining him expressing his opinion to God.

"Excuse me Lord. I don't mean to be rude and with all due respect you're a pretty good miracle worker; however, you make a lousy cup of coffee."

It was time to wake up Charlotte from her afternoon nap. Just like Joe, she would lie down on the living room rug and sleep. She was a sound sleeper. I could turn on the vacuum and push it around her, and she would not stir.

I knelt next to her. "Wake up, Baby Girl. it's time for your lunch."

She rubbed her eyes, blinked and stared at me if to say, *Why did you find it necessary to disturb me while I was dreaming about toys?*

I sat her in her booster seat. She asked for diced fruit in her favorite *My Little Pony* bowl. It made me think of our honeymoon in Italy when the fruit bowl went crashing onto the floor while Joe and I were celebrating our love on the kitchen countertop. Charlotte poked me on the arm.

She picked out a strawberry and put it in my mouth.

"One for Mama."

She shoved another one in my mouth.

"One for Daddy." She pointed up towards the ceiling.

"Yes, one for Daddy in heaven; he loved strawberries."

She smiled and dropped one onto the floor.

"One for Lou!"

I picked the berry off the floor. "No, no, not one for Lou!"

"We'll give Lou a doggy treat later, okay?"

She took a deep breath and pouted. Lou looked disappointed as well. He lumbered outside to the deck to sulk.

It was a beautiful day—the kind of day Joe would call *Big Sky* beautiful. After lunch, we went outside to sit with Lou. He was such a sweet dog. Keough trained him to retrieve Charlotte's favorite stuffed toy whenever she'd say bear-bear. It was a present Joe bought for her during one of his book tours in Texas – a large teddy bear dressed like a cowboy. She wouldn't go to bed without it. The minute I tucked her under the covers, Lou trotted over with the bear in his mouth.

I reached down and stroked him on top of his head. He knew I wasn't myself. Everyone knew I wasn't myself. I lived and breathed for Joe. *Why did he leave me so soon?* I was barely a wife, and now I'm a widow with a child. Maybe this was my life—how my life was meant to be. I never thought I'd be married let alone a mother and young widow. Or perhaps this was the precise way my life was meant to be—to have married my soul mate and be left to carry on his legacy.

I could hear Raymond say, "Of course this is how your life is meant to be. From the day we are born we make our own path and some are wise enough to follow it no matter where it may lead. Is the path good; is it bad; is it neither? It's up to the person experiencing the journey to make that decision."

Raymond was always positive with his counsel. I called him my living spirit guide. I'd never been very religious or spiritual until I met him. All the woo-woo bullshit people would spout in my New York Yoga class about tapping into their inner-self and finding their higher purpose used to drive me crazy. I believed once a person was dead, he or she was dead and ceased to exist. However, I was not so sure anymore. Wherever I went, I felt Joe's spirit. His presence was strong and constant. From his hairbrush and toothbrush that remain on his side of the bathroom sink to his unopened bottle of lavender shampoo and not to mention his smelly old barn boot by the mud room door—his spirit lingered. I was not ready to have a séance just to ask him something silly like where he put the extra set of truck keys, but I did want to know if he's okay.

I picked up Charlotte and her toys and headed back into the house. It was such a beautiful day—too beautiful to stay indoors. *I think I'll go for that ride and I'll take her along with me.* Charlotte had no fear of horses and loved sitting bareback on Daisy. She'd bounce up and down on her shouting, "Go Daisy." Joe would be proud of our budding little cowgirl.

I sat Charlotte on a hay bale and finished saddling Daisy. Charlotte noticed a plastic object sticking out of a pile of old hay. She walked over, picked it up and handed it to me. It was an empty throat spray bottle. I stared at it for a few seconds then tucked it into my jacket pocket. There wasn't an inch of this place that didn't hold memories of Joe.

I lifted Charlotte onto the saddle first then mounted behind her.

"Okay, Girls . . . let's go!"

Daisy had a gentle and steady gait. Joe trained her well. His horse Bailey was too much of a ride for me. He was fifteen-and-a-half hands of ex-rodeo roping horse with two speeds – full gallop and quick stop. Both moves were beyond my riding skill. Maybe someday I'd try to ride him. But for now, Daisy would do. I couldn't risk being bucked off. Breaking bones was not an option—not with an active toddler in the house.

We didn't ride far, only to the end of the large pasture, which in itself was a half-hour ride. It took another ten minutes or so to get to the large stock pond. The smaller one beside the house was more decorative than functional being only about the size of a swimming pool. Charlotte loved throwing pebbles into the water and then watching the countless ripples they'd create. She would giggle each time they made the plopping sound. I sat in the grass and watched her play. *Joe, I wish you were here.*

Seconds later, a hummingbird whizzed by my face. At first, I thought it was a large bumblebee. It returned and hovered in front of me. I remembered what Raymond said about loved ones who have passed on sending animal spirit guides. The small bird remained in front of me for a few seconds then shot off over the pond.

I thought, *If that was from you Joe, stay around a little longer – I miss you.*

Charlotte ran over and sat in my lap. She pointed and said, "Mama look, horsey!"

In the distance, I could see a horse galloping toward us – it was Keough. He was riding Bailey.

"Hey there ladies, I thought I'd give old Bailey a much needed work out seein' that you don't have the guts to ride him, Rose."

I stood up to confront him face-to-face.

"Listen Old Man; it's not that I don't have the guts, I have a daughter to look after and pardon me if I want to do it from my home and not a hospital bed!"

Keough laughed, "Hah, I knew that would get you riled up! Lord knows you never pass up an opportunity to be right, do ya'?"

He handed me a small basket. "I thought you two could use a little treat. Now if'n you don't want my homemade biscuits and sweet tea then I guess I'll just have to throw it in the pond for the fish. What do you think about that Charlotte?"

"No, no Pap-Pap. Please, biscuit please!"

"That's my baby girl. You always know how to bring a smile to this mud-ugly face . . . and please no comments from you Rose!"

"Hey, you said it. I was going to comment on your excellent baked goods, however, now that you mentioned it . . . "

"Let's just leave it at that Rose. I'd hate for the baby see her mama splashin' around in the pond after I've tossed her in."

"Okay, you old crippled up old saddlebum – you've won this round. But next time, when the baby ain't around, it'll be you and me. You'd better watch your back, because you're goin' down."

"Lord have mercy, Girl. Now that was a threat worthy of a Montana! I'd better hide my six-shooters."

"Ha, all I'd need to do is hide your glasses, ya' blind old geezer."

"Okay, now you've hurt my feelings. What a terrible thing to say Rose! You know I don't wear glasses."

I laughed so hard I snorted. I had not laughed like that in a long time. Not since Joe died. It felt good. I thought back to the hummingbird. *Maybe Joe is around after all.*

Chapter 3

"I'll have a dirty martini to go and a bag of Doritos please."

The cashier was puzzled by Jannine's request. "Eh, Ma'am I'm afraid we don't sell martinis to go or otherwise, but we do have root beer."

Jannine took a deep breath. "I keep forgetting I'm not in New York City anymore. Okay, how about a Perrier? You do have Perrier?"

He seemed perplexed by her request.

"You mean that fizzy French water in the green bottle?"

"Yes, Goober that fizzy French stuff in the green bottle!"

"Yes, we sell it . . . but we're out of it."

Jannine mumbled, "Of course you are."

Morgan could tell she was about to implode. He put his arm around her shoulder and smiled at the clerk, "A bottle of water—plain water will do just fine, thank you."

The cashier took a bottle out of a barrel of ice and wiped it dry on his stock apron.

He was noticeably nervous by Jannine's east coast bluntness.

"That'll be fifty cents even; would you like this in a . . . eh, s-s-sack?"

Jannine lowered her sunglasses staring over the top. "A sack, what the hell is a sack?" She shook her head and headed toward the exit.

Morgan nodded, gave him a dollar and told him to keep the change. Jannine impatiently paced by the door.

"Pardon me for sayin', but she's a fiery one ain't she."

"Yep, she's got a mean streak alright, but a very kind heart. Once you get to know her she'll grow on you."

The cashier mumbled, "Yeah, like kudzu."

Morgan handed Jannine her water.

"It won't be long, honey. We'll be at the ranch by sunset. I know Amelia will be happy to see you."

"It'll be good to see her, I miss her so much. She is my only true friend. Not that you aren't my best friend and the love of my life, but I can't see you going to an all-day-spa treatment with me. Although, seeing you naked in a mud bath would be sexy hot."

She leaned into Morgan and gave him an affectionate kiss.

"We can go skinny dipping in the horse pond and I'll make as much mud as you like."

"Okay, okay, cool down, Cowboy. Remember there will be a child at the house, and I don't think Amelia would appreciate us going at it hot and heavy in her guest room."

Jannine chuckled to herself.

"It feels so odd calling her Amelia. She will always be Joe's Rose to me."

"Yeah, Dad loved her so much. I still can't wrap my brain or heart around the fact that he's gone—and gone for almost two years!"

Jannine hugged Morgan.

"I know Baby, I can't believe it either. Amelia is still grieving for him, and it breaks my heart."

Jannine uncapped her bottle of water and took a long sip.

"Why is it so damn dry in Montana? For God's sake a little rain wouldn't hurt!"

Jannine noticed they'd passed the Welcome to Montana sign. She took a deep breath.

"We're finally in Montana."

"Just a couple hours, and we'll be there and you can take a nice long shower. I'll even scrub your back."

"You'll need to do more than that to make me forget how long of a ride it is from New York to Montana! And please remind me again why the hell did we not take a plane?"

"Because you wanted to see the country from the passenger's seat—remember? You're always complaining about how we never do anything adventurous. Well, now you can brag to your city-folk-divas that you drove cross country with an honest-to-goodness cowboy."

"Okay, you've made your point! But for goodness sake, break the speed limit why don't you and let's get moving."

"Yes, Miss Jannine; whatever you say Miss Jannine. Thank goodness I love you as much as I do or you'd be camping with the coyotes tonight."

It was almost 7:40 PM. The sun was starting to set when they turned onto the road leading to the ranch. Morgan nudged Jannine.

"Wake up, Honey. We'll be at the ranch in a few minutes."

"How long have I been asleep?"

"I think the more important question is, how long have you been snoring? My Lord, Girl, truckers were asking me if I was towing a broken reefer unit."

"What, huh, WHAT . . . what are you talking about Morgan? And what is a reefer unit?"

She leaned over and pinched is arm.

"Ouch! What was that for?"

"For the snoring remark!"

Morgan laughed, "I guess I deserved that. But to answer your question, you've been out like a light for almost four hours and a reefer unit is truckers' lingo for a refrigerated truck—you know the kind of truck Paul drives when he's hauling frozen foods."

"Oh, well that was a painfully boring answer. I thought it was a drug runner's truck that hauled marijuana from Mexico. Now, that would make more sense. Why do men find the need to make up cute little names for common things?"

"Oh, so I guess mani-pedi is so much more sophisticated."

"Hey, don't mock the mani-pedi!"

Through the thickets, Jannine could see the house. She squirmed in her seat like a little kid.

"Damn I missed this place. It's so majestic and so . . . freaking smelly. Was it always this smelly?"

Morgan put the car in park. "Yes Jannine, it always been smelly. It smells like horse manure. Hence, all of the horses running around in yonder pasture."

"Hmm, I don't remember it being this bad. But I used to drink a lot back then."

Morgan laughed, "I loved you back then, and I love you now." He gave her a quick peck on her cheek and continued driving.

Lou was the first one to hear their car. He jumped up and ran to the door.

"Careful Lou, you almost knocked over Charlotte. What's got you so excited boy? I'm not expecting a delivery, and no one comes out this far unless they're lost." I picked up Charlotte and headed toward the window. I didn't recognize the vehicle at first, but as it got closer I definitely recognized the occupants.

OH MY GOD . . . its Aunt Jannine and your brother Morgan!

I ran to the door almost tripping over Lou and started waving like a mad woman. Charlotte waved too.

She pointed, "Mo'-Mo', Mama. Mo'-Mo'!"

I didn't remember Jannine getting out the car. One minute she was in the passenger's seat, the next we were locked in an embrace.

"Girl, Girl, Girl, I've missed you so much; how are you?"

Morgan pet Lou on his head and picked up Charlotte.

"Howdy Lil' Sis, how's my favorite cowgirl?"

She gave him a big wet kiss on the cheek.

I told them to leave their stuff in the car and come sit down. We instinctively went into the kitchen. It was the place we would gather when Joe was alive. Joe loved entertaining guests over a cup of his infamous cowboy coffee. There were times I thought he loved coffee more than me. But if it weren't for our abnormal obsession with wicked brew, we wouldn't have met.

"Why didn't you two tell me you were coming? I could have had supper ready or at least tidied the guest room."

Jannine rubbed Rose's arm.

"Honey, you know why we didn't tell you. Because you would have come up with some lame-ass excuse for us not to come, and you know it."

Jannine was right. As happy as I was to see them, I would have made up some reason for them to reschedule their trip. I was still grieving and truthfully, I didn't want to stop. My pain reminded me that Joe was gone. In some surreal way, the pain made me feel closer to him. It didn't make any sense. Somehow my pain was the only physical feeling I had left of Joe. I didn't expect anyone to understand – to be honest, I didn't want anyone to understand. It was my private sanctuary of unresolved emotions – safe and impenetrable. I didn't want to waste time explaining it, so I kept my emotions locked inside with everyone else locked outside.

My focus and consciousness came back to Jannine. I asked her how their lives were now that they were living together. It seemed like yesterday that they could barely stand each other. It didn't seem like two years had passed since Morgan thought she was an obnoxious, overbearing Prada-wearing New Yorker and Jannine thought Morgan was a dumb rodeo hick. But they grew on each other, and a serious romance blossomed. Their relationship reminded me of how Joe and I met. *It seems lately everything reminds me of Joe.*

Morgan retrieved the rest of their luggage from the car and took it into the guest room. Jannine and I went into my bedroom for a bit of girl talk while Morgan went back into the living room to play with Charlotte.

Jannine curled up on the bed.

"Amelia, okay between me and you how are you holding up? You are putting on a brave face, but I know you too well to believe that everything is okay."

Jannine was right. Nothing was okay. Nothing would ever be okay. "Honestly Jannine, I feel nothing . . . absolutely nothing! My heart and soul are numb. I miss Lash. I miss his Montana Joe character. If it weren't for Charlotte, I would climb into a hole and stay there. She's my only reality check. Knowing that our daughter needs me keeps me from falling apart."

Jannine slid over and hugged me.

"Honey, I wish I could say I know how you're feeling but I can't. You and Lash had something no one I know has EVER experienced; an eternal and epic love. I know you're hurting, but I know that Joe wouldn't want you doing this to yourself. He loved life, he loved you and you were his life. It's the kind of stuff romance writers thrive on. Hell, it would make a great Lifetime or Hallmark movie. Oh my God, you could ask Halle Berry to play you! But you are so much prettier than Halle, minus those atrocious bags under your eyes and by the way, nothing a little cucumber can't fix. I'll ask Cecilia to put them on her shopping list."

Jannine's comments made me smile. But I had to admit that Jannine spoke the truth. Joe would be livid if he saw me sitting around the ranch grieving, re-reading his old emails, thumbing through his old rodeo albums and from time-to-time drinking a cup or two of instant coffee. In his eyes, the instant coffee would be a crime against humanity, and coffee growers all over the world.

I could hear him ranting, "LORD HAVE MERCY GIRL! Haven't you learned by now instant coffee from a jar is an unforgivable abomination – it's evil, pure evil! "

To which Raymond would reply, "In the name of the great spirits, Joe, why don't you shut the hell up! You would drink liquefied buffalo shit if it were brewed long enough!"

My daydream gave me a giggle.

"It's good to see that Amelia-Rose smile again. Let's see it more often during our visit, promise?"

"I promise."

She started to hop off of the bed and then stopped.

"Now I understand why Lash called you Rose. Your smile accents your gorgeous bronze blushing rosy cheeks – minus the dark circles of course." I didn't have the heart to tell her that Lash nicknaming me Rose was just a random choice on his part. "Okay then rosy cheeks, how about you and I raid Cecilia's pantry and get dinner started."

I stopped in my tracks.

"You . . . cook?" I held my forehead faking a dizzy spell.

"Yes Amelia, I can cook. I never saw the need to cook when I lived alone. But my God, Joe's son can eat. So I started watching those cable cooking shows, and the rest is culinary history. My specialty is grilled American cheese on white bread."

"Eh, grilled cheese, hmm, that's . . . eh, fantastic Jannine. I'm so proud of you!"

Jannine shook her head. "My God Amelia, I'm joking. Actually, I'm becoming a rather good cook. If you have chicken, I make mean chicken parmesan. It's Morgan's favorite."

"Well then, I'll have to break open a bottle of our best ranch house wine. This is a special occasion. I think I can make the salad if that would be okay with you, Miss Child."

"Hey, don't think I don't know who she is. She's the one Meryl Streep played in the film, Julie & Julia—am I right? I think she won an Oscar . . . for the film, not the cooking."

I moved over on the bed, "You could cook anything and I would eat it just because you made it."

"And that's why I love you Amelia Rose."

"Of course you do Jannine. Because I'm so loveable, talented, beautiful . . ."

"Okay, let's not go crazy. I seem to remember Lash saying something about a drooling-and-snorting-when-you-laugh problem."

"All of it is a tissue of lies Jannine. Well maybe the drooling stems from a bit of truth, but only when there is strawberry cheesecake involved."

Morgan peeked in. "If you two are done with this mutual admiration love fest, can you fix something to eat? I'm starved."

"What did I tell you Amelia? He's got an insatiable appetite just like his father."

He pulled Jannine toward him playfully kissing her nose and neck.

He whispered, "And that's not the only insatiable appetite we shared."

Jannine giggled and push him away.

He's more like his father than he'll ever know.

We'd started fixing dinner when the phone rang. It was Paul. He was an hour away from Malta and asked if it was still okay for him to visit. I told him that I was looking forward to his visit and that Jannine and Morgan had arrived as a surprise as well. Paul seemed genuinely excited at the prospect of seeing everyone again. *What a sweet man.*

Jannine had just set the timer on the oven when the phone rang again. It was Raymond. He happened to be in the area was making a stop to check in on everyone and to bring a little gift for Charlotte.

"Yes, of course. We are just getting supper started," I told him. "And Paul will be here shortly. It'll be like a homecoming."

Raymond was happy to hear Paul was coming. He liked Paul. To Raymond, the British bloke as he called him, displayed great character strength, and he enjoyed his company. Jannine and I set two additional places at the dinner table.

Chapter 4

We could hear the rumble of Paul's 18-wheeler a mile away. I never understood why anyone would want to drive something that large. It was the size of our hay barn. Morgan moved the horse trailer so he'd have a place to park the rig. The trailer kicked up road dust and gravel as it made its way through the thickets.

I found myself primping in the mirror by the door. It was a habit I developed whenever I saw Joe's truck pull into the driveway. I guess old habits never die even though the person you're primping for is no longer around. The unmistakable hiss of his air breaks and air horn announced Paul's arrival. Whenever Charlotte heard those sounds, she knew Paul was here. She loved to climb into the cab so she could sit in his big captain's chair and pretend to drive. He would let her pull the air horn even though trucks weren't allowed to honk their horns within city limits; however, it didn't matter because there were no neighbors in a four-mile vicinity of our ranch.

A few minutes later, Raymond's truck pulled behind Paul. They exchanged hugs and handshakes. Morgan came out of the kitchen with Jannine and Charlotte in tow. After so many months of unhappiness, it finally felt as though the house had come back to life.

Lou and I greeted them at the door. They both looked good. Paul had grown a beard, and Raymond—well, Raymond always looked good. He'd just celebrated his 62nd birthday and he didn't look a day over fifty. He'd boast the secret to looking and feeling good is to never stress over the small things and to make time to go fishing. One keeps you focused, and the other gives you good food to enjoy.

Raymond's wisdom never ceased to entertain me. He enjoyed making me laugh, and he always said humor is good medicine for the soul.

Charlotte adored them. Both were more like family than friends. They never came empty handed which thrilled Charlotte to no end. Paul knew that Charlotte—or as he called her, *the bab-bee* loved cuddly toys. He gave her a cute stuffed doggie that looked just like Lou. She immediately named it Little Lou.

On occasion, Paul would bring a gift for me. He handed me a bottle of Napa Valley Merlot and a dozen state magnets for Charlotte to put on the refrigerator.

"Here you go, Luv. These are the places I've been and maybe someday you can take the bab-bee on a road trip. I remember how much you loved to travel. If I'm not mistaken that's how we met. You feeding me that horrid line of rubbish about donating a kidney or liver or what have you."

I laughed at the image of me flagging him down like a deranged mental patient to use his internet. He chuckled at the fact it led to a wonderful marriage and a beautiful daughter.

Morgan announced that dinner was ready and thanks to Jannine's over zealous chicken parmesan recipe, there was enough for everyone. We sat at the table laughing, eating and talking as if nothing had changed. But something HAD changed – Joe was missing. I zoned out for a second hoping to hear his voice joining the conversation. But all I could do was cry. I left the table and ran to the bedroom. Raymond, Morgan and Jannine started to follow me but Paul said he'd check on me.

He knocked on the door. "Are you okay, Poppet? Was it something we said? Did Lou pass gas or perhaps it was Jannine's cooking? To be honest it was dreadfully overdone, but I'm so completely frightened of her, I thought it best to remain silent."

His concern and honesty was soothing; it took me a few seconds to respond.

"Yes, it was terribly overdone. I'm okay, Paul. However, seeing you plus the reminiscing overwhelmed me – I'm sorry."

"Oy, hang on. What do you mean *seeing me*? I know this beard makes me looks a bit dodgy, but I certainly didn't think it looked that bad."

Paul sat beside me.

"Amelia, there is absolutely nothing to be sorry about. You just loss your husband, the love of your life and you're still grieving. It's okay to be sad, angry and even scared. It's bloody painful. Joe was a brilliant man. To say the least he was, eh . . . unique. I never understood his obsession with coffee. Be that as it may, I guess I'm the same way about tea. I'm a bloody horror when I haven't had my cuppa."

I wiped my eyes and turned to Paul. He had kind eyes – familiar eyes. But I'd never met Paul before until the internet incident. He handed me a wad of tissues.

"There you go, Luv. What say we go finish dinner? To be honest I haven't had a home cooked meal in three weeks and I'm still hungry. "

"You do remember that Jannine cooked it, right?"

Paul stood up and rubbed his chin.

"Poppet, all I've had is bad truck stop food. I could eat roasted road kill if it had enough salt on it!"

Jannine knocked on the door.

"Okay, Rose I know my cooking isn't THAT bad. Get your butt out here and finish eating."

We walked back to the table and sat down. I apologized for my outburst. Morgan said there was no reason to apologize.

"If you didn't come back I had first dibs on your plate – I'm still hungry."

Jannine rolled her eyes, "You see what I mean. He's a bottomless pit!"

Raymond and Morgan reached for the last piece of chicken. Raymond stabbed it with his fork and flicked it onto his plate. Morgan backed off.

"I was afraid that boy would take a bite out of my hand if I lingered. You know I carry a tomahawk, Morgan and I'm not afraid to use it. I swear there are times you remind me of your father – loony bastard with a single buffalo turd for a brain."

The entire table laughed. Charlotte laughed along with us even though she didn't have a clue what she was laughing about. It felt like old times at Casa Montana. All that was missing was my husband.

It was getting late. Jannine and Morgan offered to give Charlotte her bath and put her to bed. They knew Raymond, Paul and I had to discuss the subject of scattering Joe's ashes.

Raymond held my hands, "It's time Amelia. The only way you can move on is to let go. Joe would want you to move on. You know this; your heart knows this."

Of course Raymond was right. I had to let go. We decided we'd spread them first thing in the morning.

Jannine had set her alarm for 7:00 AM and was already dressed. She tipped into my bedroom and opened the curtains. The sun was bright and hurt my eyes. I pulled the quilt over my head.

"Amelia . . . Amelia, Honey, wake up. It's eight o'clock, time to get up."

She handed me a cup of fresh coffee and sat at the edge of the bed.

"Did you sleep well? I came in to say good night and you were out like a light."

I didn't remember falling asleep. I didn't want to wake up. But I had to face the fact that Joe's remains had to be spread.

Morgan knocked on the door and asked to come in. He wanted to know if Charlotte would be attending and, if so, he would get her dressed. I nodded yes. She would be coming along. I needed her to be there with me to say goodbye to her daddy.

Jannine suggested I take a quick shower. I loved showering with Joe. Some of our best times together were making love in this shower. I never realized there was a bottle of his lavender shampoo still sitting in the shower rack. The scent overwhelmed me. Sliding down the shower wall, I muffled my cry. *WHY? Why did you have to leave me Joe? It's not fair. We never had the chance to dance on our anniversary or sing Happy Birthday to Charlotte on her first birthday. So many memories, holidays, birthdays celebrated without you.*

I toweled off, collected myself and grabbed a pair of jeans and boots from the closet. The location was on the far end of our large pasture. It was easier to reach by horseback. Although it was roughly a three-mile trek, Paul insisted he'd rather walk, and he would meet us there. I told him we had more than enough horses and to pick any one he wanted to ride.

He muttered, "I eh, I've never ridden before. I'd look-a-right-chuff bouncing around in a western saddle."

"You can ride Daisy. All you need to do is hold on. She is a very gentle ride. In fact she's the horse Joe started me on. I promise you'll be fine."

I put on the necklace Joe gave me when we first met. It was one of the most extravagant gifts I'd ever received. He did have excellent taste in jewelry. I clipped it around my neck and admired it in the mirror. I imagined Joe behind me lifting my hair out of the way so I could fasten it.

Don't lose it now Amelia – hold it together.

Raymond had already retrieved Joe's urn from its long familiar resting place on the mantle. He cradled it in his arms like a newborn.

"He was a good man, Rose – an honorable man. A man I was privileged to call friend and brother. Now it's time to honor him."

I took a deep breath and nodded in agreement.

It was time to leave. Everyone was waiting in the paddock area. Keough and Morgan had the horses saddled and ready. We all mounted and rode to the site. Morgan and I led the group. Jannine, Paul, Keough and Raymond followed us.

Charlotte sat in front of me holding onto the saddle horn. Joe would have remarked how she sat tall in the saddle—just like her mama. I was so proud of her. She was not afraid to mount up on a horse 15-hands tall. Montana blood definitely ran through her veins.

About five minutes into the ride, I thought about our wedding vows and how it was three years ago I married this amazing man. I never thought I'd be saying goodbye so soon. I bit my lip to keep myself from crying.

I could hear Keough's horse galloping behind me. He slowed down and asked, "You okay, Honey?"

I choked out, "As good as can be expected."

He leaned over and kissed me on the cheek and rode ahead to catch up with Morgan.

Morgan and Keough arrived first and helped to tie up the horses. This spot held countless memories for me. Joe called it, "The Great Wide Open." The sky was just as blue as the day he proposed and just as clear as the days we sat and talked about growing old together and raising a family. Our time together was short, but we lived a lifetime of amazing moments.

Raymond walked over and handed me the urn. I hadn't held it since the funeral.

"It's time, Amelia to say goodbye – are you ready?"

I would never be ready. However, I had to let go. His ashes needed to be spread.

Raymond asked if I wanted him to say a prayer or words of spiritual comfort. "I'll respect whatever you and Joe want. "

Reflecting back, I remembered what Joe had said – keep it short and sweet. I told them I knew exactly what he wanted me to say and I'm going to honor his final wishes. Raymond and Keough carefully removed the cap from the urn then handed it over to me. We walked over to the clearing where Joe requested his ashes be spread. The mesmerizing scenery of the Montana prairieland lay before us. I caressed his urn in my arms and cleared my throat.

"I'd be the first to say that my husband was peculiar and at times downright loony. He lived between the realms of reality and fantasy. His sense of humor was quirky and irritating. And let's not forget his abnormal obsession with coffee. Never understood it – never will I guess. Nonetheless, in the short period of time we had together, I learned to love the random idiosyncrasies that made Joe, Joe. He was the kindest, most generous man I've ever known. He held my heart and soul in his hands so much so that it has taken me nearly two years to let him go. So – my beloved, my precious Lash Jackson Montana, my very own Montana cowboy, I'm setting you free to soar forever amid the prairie winds, and as you requested, I say these two simple words . . . Adios, Joe."

I waited for a strong breeze then flung his ashes. They traveled over the creek, beyond the prairie brush. They glistened in the sun. I watched as they finally disappeared. Everyone was in tears—everyone except me and Charlotte. I was determined not to cry because I knew Joe would somehow conjure up a way to call me a crybaby. Charlotte smiled and waved goodbye to her daddy. She held her palms up to the sky waiting for Joe to kiss them. It killed me knowing she would never experience her daddy kissing those hands or giving her a bath or reading her a bedtime story or rocking her to sleep. I picked her up and walked back to the horses. The ride back to the house was quiet. No one knew what to say. There was nothing left to say. Joe was gone, and for the first time I felt like a widow. My husband was dead, and I'd never see him again.

Chapter 5

Three weeks after spreading Joe's ashes, Raymond asked about Charlotte's christening. To be honest, I'd forgotten about it. Morgan stayed on as moral support while Jannine headed back to New York. She'd already used the bulk of her vacation time and had a backlog of work to finish. Morgan tried to convince her to stay, but Jannine needed to leave. With all of her quirks and diva attitude, she was a conscientious worker and took pride in her position. That's why she outlasted all of my administrative assistants. At times, I felt as if I worked for her. Her delegating skills were far better honed than mine. She'd say I was a pushover and seriously needed to develop my NYBAB (New York Bad Ass Bitch) attitude. She was right. As tough as I thought I was, I could be easily swayed by a hard luck story. My dad used to say I had a hard head but a soft and sweet heart, and he was right. *Maybe that's why Joe called me Cupcake.*

A few days had passed. I was about to call Jannine when the phone rang. I recognized the number as her cell phone.

"Hey Sweetie, I don't have much time, but I wanted to let you know that you'll be getting a phone call about a freelance gig. Remember the rich bitch that dropped a big wad of cash to fund that new state-of-the-art arts center last year? She wants you to write an article about her Montford-Wellesley collection of Remington sculptures. Can you believe it? She specifically asked for you! And get this – she was born and raised in Dodson. Before marrying Monroe Wellesley, you know that billionaire dude, she lived in the same town as Joe's mother. Her son, Jameson Montford-Wellesley is also a Fortune 500 guy. They are old money people, Amelia – not that you need the money. But hey, it'll get you back into writing. I know you miss it. You are still one of the best art columnists in the business. Listen Sweetie, I've got to go. But I wanted to give you a heads up. Tell my honey I miss him and I'll call him later tonight for a little phone sex. Love ya', bye."

Her conversation left me dazed. I wasn't writing anymore. In fact, I hadn't written or published an article in more than two years. And more importantly, I never got the chance to ask Jannine about being Charlotte's Godmother.

The name Montford-Wellesley seemed vaguely familiar. I did an internet search and found pages of information about them. Meryl Montford was originally from a little town called Dodson near Malta and Wagner. She left Montana to attend college in California where she met and married Monroe Wellesley. He made his billions in the software industry in Silicon Valley.

The town of Dodson was all too familiar. It was the town where Joe's mother was buried. *I wonder if Meryl knew Charlotte.* I continued with my research and took copious notes. I had to admit that it felt good doing research again. It also kept me from grieving. Maybe Jannine was right about getting back into the writing saddle again. I was about to walk away from my laptop when I saw an email message pop up. It was from Jannine.

To: Amelia
Fr: Jannine
Re: YES!

LOL, sorry I totally forgot to tell you, of course I'll be Charlotte's Godmother. Who else is going to teach her how to walk in red stilettos? Give her a big kiss and I'll see you soon.

Love, Jannine

That's what I loved about Jannine. She knew what I needed before I asked. I started a desktop file for my notes and waited for Meryl's phone call. Two hours later she called.

"Hello, Mrs. Montana this is Meryl Montford-Wellesley. I'm sure your assistant gave you advance notice that I'd be calling—I hope?"

"Yes, hello and please call me Amelia. I appreciate your call. As honored as I am, I'm surprised that you chose me to write this article. May I ask why you asked me?"

There was a brief silence then, "If you're as talented as everyone says you are, you already know why I chose you. I'm sure you've done your research and know that I'm from Montana. To be precise, I was born in the small town of Dodson—not far from where you live."

She's good! I like this woman. She went on to confess that one of her guilty pleasures was reading Montana Joe novels.

"I loved the way he captured the heart and soul of Montana. His characters are reality based and believable. My husband teases me about reading them, saying I'm just a misplaced cowgirl with a champagne-filled canteen." I chuckled at her attempt to lighten the conversation. "And please let me express my condolences for your loss. Mr. Montana will be sorely missed in the western genre."

Her comment softened the mood. I'm sure she was able to sense I was still grieving. We continued talking about some of the pieces in the collection, how they were attained and how many of them were handed down to her by her father.

"My husband is not as interested in my western upbringing as I am. He indulges me, and I take full advantage of it."

I asked, "Do you ever get an opportunity to visit Dodson?"

"No, I haven't visited or thought about Dodson since I married Mr. Wellesley. He's more of an ocean and sand creature – preferring seashells to tumbleweeds. But from time-to-time I do get homesick for Montana. I do miss that Big Sky country."

My silence prompted her to ask how I was adapting to my relocation.

"I fell in love with the state and the man. It was an easy transition. My heart will always be here in Montana."

There was a long pause. I believe we both felt a twinge of sadness. She still longed to revisit Dodson, and me, I missed Joe. Glancing at the clock, I realized we'd been on the phone for an hour. Charlotte needed a nap, and I needed to eat. Eating meals without Joe depressed me. I'd lost ten pounds since his death and I was not a person who could afford to lose much weight. Joe used to say if I got caught in a good prairie wind I'd end up in Utah.

Meryl said her personal assistant would forward me my contract and an advance.

I thought, *Advance? I'd never received an advance for doing an article before.* We wished each other well, and we both said how we looked forward to working together.

Charlotte had fallen asleep on the floor again. I knelt next to her and rubbed her back until she opened her eyes.

"Wake up Baby Girl – time for lunch."

She rubbed her eyes and pointed to the window.

"Happy sun, happy sky, happy Daddy," she cooed.

"Yes baby, happy sun, sky and Daddy. He's now a part of that big blue sky."

She hugged my neck and toddled off into the kitchen with Little Lou clutched in her arm.

During lunch, I reviewed my notes and made some personal notes about Meryl. She was nothing like I'd expected. The woman, who had the reputation for being tough and to the point, was kind, understanding and entertaining. We had an old saying in the critic world, "You can't judge a magazine by its readers."

Patrick once told me he saw a nun on the New York subway reading, *Chicks with Dicks*. He later realized it was a transvestite on his way to a Halloween party; nonetheless, it made for a funny sidebar. The vibration of my cell phone brought me back to reality. It was Morgan reminding me to eat lunch. I told him I'd just finished, and thanked him for caring.

"Dad would kick my ass if I let you get any thinner than you already are. He used to tell me a woman needs a little cushion. Jannine would beg to differ but I kind of like gals with a little meat on their bones. Fragile women scare me."

"I swear, Morgan; it's uncanny how much you sound like your dad. He was so proud of you. Now get off the damn phone and come get something to eat."

"Okay, okay, I'm hanging up now, Mom."

It still made me smile hearing him refer to me as Mom. Marrying Joe gave me a new lease on life. Two beautiful kids, a father-in-law, an instant best friend in Raymond and a piece of God's country that got more spectacular by the day. I heard Morgan and Keough walking toward the kitchen with Lou bringing up the rear.

"Whoa, before you all take another step . . . washroom, NOW!"

Morgan playfully kissed me on the cheek.

"Oh, I see. Now, I'm too dirty and smelly to sit at your table Mrs. Montana."

"Yes, you both smell of barn dust and horseshit!"

Keough laughed, "Yeah, I guess we do smell a bit ripe. But that's what you get when you live with cowboys, Darlin'."

"Don't give me that bullshit Old Man, you smelt bad the first day I met you. And it had nothing to do with you being a cowboy!"

Morgan gave me a high-five. "Wow, nice one, Mom. Hah, she called you a stinkin' old man – too funny!"

Keough gave us the finger, "Shame on y'all for being mean to a sweet and genteel fella like me. Ya' both need to be horsewhipped."

I raised my eyebrow, "You, sweet and genteel? I've met rattlesnakes with better temperament."

Keough winked at me, "Lady, if I didn't have to piss so bad I'd stay here and argue with you, but nature is callin' and I'd like to go now if that's okay with you Missy."

I waved him on, "Then go on and piss ya' old bastard."

He waved back, "Better to take a piss than to be pissed on, right Lou?"

He gave Lou the piss-whistle.

Lou looked at him, then at me and trotted outside.

"Hah, even the dog knows better than to piss me off!"

Keough huffed and slammed the bathroom door shut. He hollered he was going to take a shower and that the toilet roll was empty. I hollered back for him to use his sleeve. I could hear him mumbling something under his breath. All I could make out were the words ornery and mean.

"There's a full roll beside the tub and if you weren't as blind as a bat you would have seen it. And, you smell terrible so don't be skimpy with the soap!"

He hollered, "Oh, so now I'm stinkin', old and blind. "

I hollered back, "Yeah – sucks to be you don't it?"

He came out of the bathroom smelling fresh and clean. "Now, come over here and give an old man a hug."

Charlotte thought he was talking to her and ran over and hugged his legs. He scooped her up in his arms and kissed her.

"Well at least someone loves me. How's my favorite cowgirl. Roped any wild mustangs today?"

Charlotte giggled and pointed outside to Lou.

"Lou is large enough to be a horse. All that's missing is a bridle and saddle," Keough joked.

Charlotte took Keough's cowboy hat off and put it on her head. It covered her entire face. All I could see were hat and shoulders.

"All joking aside, I'm so glad you decided to stay on with us Keough. That little girl loves you so much. And as quiet as it's kept, I love you too."

I hugged him sandwiching Charlotte between us. "Your son would be proud of you."

His eyes started to water. I could tell it saddened him to talk about Lash. They'd only reconciled with each other a few weeks before Joe died.

"Okay enough of this mushy stuff. It ain't good for the baby to see me bawlin'."

They finished lunch and helped wash the dishes. Afterwards, Keough put on his jacket and work hat.

"Now, how about we go out to the barn and brush Daisy. Would you like that, Charlotte?"

A big smile stretched across her face, "YES Pap-Pap brush Daisy!"

I put her barn overhauls over her play clothes. She strolled over to Keough with her hands tucked in her back pockets just like her daddy.

"Come on Darlin' lets go brush the horsey."

Charlotte motioned for Lou. He got up and walked beside them all the way to the barn. *Sometimes I think that dog is half human, he's so smart and sensitive.*

Morgan came into the kitchen fresh from the shower and wearing clean clothes. He needed to go to town for horse wormer, barbed wire pliers and sweet feed. All this stuff was foreign to me until I met Joe.

He asked if I would like some cheesecake from the bakery. I'd never turn down cheesecake.

"Yes, bring enough for dessert. I'm cooking a special dinner tonight. I'm getting a sizable advance for an article I'm writing, so let's splurge!"

Truthfully, I was happy to be writing again. It wasn't about the money. We had more than enough from Joe's royalties, but it was important for my own self-esteem. Call it pride, but it felt good contributing to the Montana Legacy. I'd recently purchased a new laptop with all the newly improved bells and whistles. It was time to give it a workout.

Before I started writing, I checked my email. There were ten waiting in the queue. One was from Mrs. Wellesley thanking me for agreeing to write the article and for the lovely conversation. Her elegance and sophistication had me longing for New York. I missed Soho, Greenwich Village, the art galleries, and the night life; however, I've grown to love Montana. Fifth Avenue had nothing on Big Sky country. Montana is now my home; it's our home, and I couldn't imagine leaving it.

I scanned through the other emails deleting most of them, except one from a gentleman with the same last name as Meryl – Mr. Jameson M. Wellesley.

To: Mrs. Amelia Montana
Fr: Jameson M. Wellesley, Montford-Wellesley, CEO
Cc: Meryl Montford-Wellesley
*Subject: **Thank You***

I wanted to personally thank you for your phone meeting with my mother and your willingness to write the Remington article for our company. You came highly recommended, and it will be a pleasure working with you. I will be in Montana this month overseeing the construction of The Green Play Garden Project. Briefly, our corporation has invested in the building of environmentally safe playgrounds with green gardens for elementary schools in Montana, specifically Dodson and Malta. It will be a good time to discuss the details of the article. My personal assistant will be in touch with you regarding times and dates.

On behalf of my mother and the Montford Wellesley Corporation, thank you for accepting this assignment and please accept our deepest condolences on the loss of your husband.

Sincerely,

Jameson M. Wellesley

I removed my glasses and leaned back in my chair thinking, *His mother? She didn't mention she had a son. Maybe she did; I don't remember – oh, well it's not important. I've got to start writing this article.*

I sent a quick reply thanking him and looked forward to meeting him soon. Perhaps meeting with him will give me more insight into his family. It would help build reader interest and perhaps lead to another article. *If you're listening Joe, wish me luck.*

Chapter 6

"NO! No Mama!"

Charlotte squirmed and pulled away as I tried to comb her hair. It was her first day at the daycare center, and I didn't want her looking as though a barn rat had built a nest on her head. *Now would be a good time to refresh me on how to tie that half-hooey Joe.* After wrestling with her for 20-minutes, I finally got her pigtails looking tidy. I asked her if she wanted bows. She crossed her arms and pouted.

"NO. I want Daddy's hat . . . DADDY'S HAT!"

There is no way in hell I'm letting her wear Joe's prize gray Stetson to daycare! She broke loose from my grip and ran into the office. Grabbing it from the desk, she plopped it on her head. As annoyed as I was, I had to turn away. I didn't want her to see me laughing. Strutting out with his large cowboy hat atop her head with only her chin and the ends of her pigtails showing was too cute for words. I snapped a photo with my cell phone to commemorate her stylish choice of attire and her first official temper tantrum. *Is this what I have to look forward to?* Taking a deep breath, I instructed her to put the hat back in the office.

"NO, I want DADDY'S HAT!"

Her rant continued, "I want my Daddy, I want Daddy!"

She started to cry. As angry as I was witnessing her unexpected act of defiance, it broke my heart to watch and hear her cry for her daddy. *What do I do now Joe, please help me reason with your daughter.*

I tried to pick her up. She continued to squirm and cry. Lou came running in from the living room to comfort her. Charlotte wasn't having any of that. She was determined to continue her tantrum and keep the hat.

Keough came running from the barn.

"What in the name of b'jesus is goin' on? What's the matter, Baby Girl? Is your mama tryin' to sing to you again? Her singin' so bad it'd make a deaf man shoot his own ears off!"

She ran into Keough arms still wearing the hat. "Mighty fine hat you got there. Don't you think it's too big for ya'? How about you try this one on for size?" He handed her a little pink sun hat with yellow ponies on it.

"Now, that's a lot prettier than that big old cowboy hat."

For a moment she resisted, and then she consented to swap the cowboy hat for the sun hat. She was about to put it on her head when Lou snatched it out of her hand and ran into the bedroom.

"No, no! Bad Lou! That's my hat!" Lou kept her occupied while Keough put Joe's hat back in the office.

"Nice move old man. Thanks so much."

Keough grinned, "You're welcome. Not that it wouldn't be side-splittin' entertainment watchin' two Montana women fight, but her bawlin' for her daddy . . . well, it just hurt me to my heart."

"Just when I think I can't stand you anymore than I already do, you go and do something sweet."

Keough smirked, "So you think I'm sweet, huh? Well I'll be damned, Amelia Rose Mathews Montana likes me after all. Hold on, I'm feelin' a warm and fuzzy moment comin' on."

"Don't get cheeky with me ya' old saddlebum, it's just one tender moment. Let's not go overboard."

"Cheeky? When did you start talkin' like that British fella? Speakin' of which how is ol' Nottingham doin'?"

"You know his name is Paul, and he's doing well I suppose. I haven't heard from him since we spread Joe's ashes."

It dawned on me I hadn't heard from Paul in months.

"Maybe he was on one of his OTR trips or maybe he was hurt and had to stop driving or moved back to England."

Keough added, "Or maybe he's got himself a girlfriend, hmm?"

"A girlfriend, what makes you think that?" Keough noticed a tinge of jealousy in my voice.

"I'm just sayin' he may have a gal is all. And why would you care Miss Amelia? A man like Paul must meet dozens of gals on the road."

I never thought of Paul having a life outside of driving. I didn't think he would have the time for romantic relationships – being on the go so much. Funny, I never thought to ask about his personal life. I guess I was too wrapped up in my own life drama to inquire about his. *Some friend I am.* I told Keough next time he's in Montana, I'll be more considerate and ask.

"You mean you'll snoop into his private business, right?" His statement took me by surprise. I became defensive and lashed out at

Keough's belief that I was snooping into his personal life, especially his romantic affairs.

"I'm not a snoop! It would be more like . . . well, more like research. You know, just to get to know him better."

Keough chuckled, "I swear you are too easy to rattle. Speaking of rattle . . . where is Charlotte?"

I was so distracted by our conversation, I'd lost track of the time. She was waiting outside with Lou wearing her new hat.

Morgan took a photo of us to acknowledge her first day of daycare and my first temper tantrum victory. It was a short 20-minute ride from the ranch to the daycare center. The local college organized the daycare as part of their Childhood Education program. There were lots of pre-school children living in the towns which made the center a great place for the college students to learn first-hand early childhood development skills. I parked directly in the front of the center retrieving Charlotte and her daycare gear, which included Little Lou. Morgan and Keough tagged along to wish her well on her first day. *I think they wanted to watch me lose it when she started crying.*

The director of the center met us at the door. A lovely woman named Dr. Sara Henry ran the center. She reassured me that Charlotte would be fine and there was nothing for me to worry about.

"It's a pleasure to meet you Mrs. Montana. Everyone at the center was saddened to hear about your loss. Mr. Montana was an amazing writer and a major contributor to the center. His annual donation helped us achieve last year's fundraising goal and is helping to support our new Green Play Garden. We couldn't have done it without his assistance and the Montford-Wellesley Corporation."

For a moment her statement took me aback. I knew my husband was a generous man; however, I didn't know about his philanthropic side. I was even more surprised to hear about his collaboration with the Montford-Wellesley Corporation. *I wonder if that's the reason she chose ME to write her article.*

I tucked that piece of information away for later and continued into the daycare center. Dr. Henry introduced us to Charlotte's group leader, a sweet young lady named, Grace who didn't look a day over fifteen. The kids called her Miss Gracie. When she told me she was a semester away from receiving her Master's Degree I was floored. She was twenty-seven and had a daughter the same age as Charlotte.

"Mrs. Montana, welcome to the Orange Leaf room. Each room is color coded with an object from nature. It helps our classes learn about the environment and makes it much more fun. Next door is the Purple Owl room and across the hall is the Yellow Fish room."

"What an amazing idea and please call me Rose. It was my husband's nickname for me, and to be honest Mrs. Montana is way too formal."

Gracie later admitted to being a huge Montana Joe fan and read just about every novel he'd ever written. She said Joe's characters were true-to-life, down-to-earth and humorous. I said I would be happy to give her his latest book. He had autographed a few before he died. She graciously accepted. I also asked her if she had any information about the Play Garden, hinting that it might be something I'd be interested in for Charlotte. She didn't know much about it except there was going to be an opening ceremony and ribbon cutting sometime this spring.

"Mr. Montford-Wellesley will be here and of course, Mr. Montana would have attended."

Dr. Henry asked if I'd be interested in attending.

"It would be an honor to have you represent Mr. Montana. There's no pressure, but think about it and let us know."

Charlotte became impatient and ran off to join the class.

Dr. Henry laughed, "Well, she is quite the independent one, isn't she?"

"Yes, she's just like her father in that respect – never wanting to miss a thing."

"She'll be fine. If there's any problem, we'll contact you but by the look of things, she's fitting in nicely."

Charlotte had already staked out her territory by the building blocks with a little ginger-haired boy. Gracie suggested this would be a good time for me to leave. I slipped out the door looking back to see if she had noticed I was gone. It seems my daughter is more interested in the little ginger-haired boy than me. I was about to leave when she turned around and saw me leaving. I heard her crying for her mama. It took everything ounce of my self control not to run back and comfort her. Instead, I continued to the car sobbing more than my baby girl. Morgan and Keough saw that I was hurting and let me sob.

Morgan hugged me and assured me she'd be okay.

"Don't worry, Mom, remember she's a Montana. She'll be bossing the other kids a round by high-noon. And her class is only three hours. By the time we get home, it'll be time to pick her up. How about we treat you to breakfast?"

Keough agreed. I knew both of them were hungry. They're always hungry. I never knew a Montana man who wasn't hungry. I could hear Joe asking if there would be coffee. Breakfast wasn't breakfast without his famous cowboy coffee. It was then that I realized I hadn't had much coffee since his death. I missed his coffee – I missed him.

We arrived at the café just in time. They were about to serve lunch, but they were nice enough to make an exception for us. The manager recognized me from Joe's online biography.

"Oh my goodness, you are Rose, Joe's Rose. It's so good to meet you!"

I was shocked that they considered me a Montana Joe celebrity.

She continued to gush over him and expressed her condolences.

"Mr. Montana always came in for coffee. He would joke with me about how weak it was and ask if he could brew his own pot. He would grind the beans twice and use twice as many beans saying, 'If a spoon couldn't stand up in it then it wasn't strong enough.' And of course who was going to argue with him."

I laughed thinking about the first time I tried his special blend. It took me a few minutes to swallow it. But over time, I learned to love it as much as he did. Maybe it was because he loved it so much that I loved it – I'll never know. Morgan and Keough ordered the Double-Montana Deluxe. I wasn't very hungry, but once I smelled the pancakes, I couldn't resist. They had a light scent of nutmeg. *I wonder if Joe gave them his recipe.* I zoned out for a second when I realized everything reminded me of Joe. I wanted to cry, but I had to let go and try to move on. Joe wasn't coming back, and I had to be strong for Charlotte. She and Morgan were the only piece of Joe I had left.

Ten minutes later, the server came over with our food. For some reason she looked very familiar. As she walked up to our table, I realized it was Joe's super fan, Mona Moon-Rae who we had the pleasure of "running into" at the airport not long before Joe's death. I tried covering my face with the menu hoping she didn't recognize me, but she tilted the menu down and screamed.

"OH MY GOD, if it isn't Rose, Rose Montana, Montana Joe's Rose! Imagine meeting you again. Oh Honey, I'm so sorry to hear about Joe. I cried for months. I still can't believe he's gone. I ordered his last two books and read them at least five times. I even went to a psychic and tried to communicate with him so I could tell him how much I loved them."

Keough and Morgan couldn't keep a straight face. I could see them laughing from the corner of my eye and continued laughing at my reaction to this lunatic. Nevertheless, she was so sincere I couldn't shine her on. Before I knew it, she sat down beside me. *Okay this is getting too weird.*

She continued to babble. "Rose, please tell me what his last words were so I can memorize them. I know he said something awe-inspiring and memorable like . . . it's time for me to meet my maker or adios mi' amigos or I'll be rollin' along with the tumblin' tumbleweeds!"

I was so flabbergasted, it took me a minute to respond. *What the hell is this woman babbling about? She's gotta be on drugs!* I was becoming increasingly uncomfortable. To be honest, she was beginning to frighten me. Thankfully Keough couldn't take it any longer and intervened.

"Miss Moon or can I call you Mona?" She nodded yes. "Rose and I were there when *'Montana Joe'* met his maker and he told us to let you know he considered you his biggest fan. He also said for us to tell you thank you and happy trails."

Morgan mumbled, "And for you to move far, far away from Montana."

I kicked him under the table. I didn't want to upset this woman. She was truly saddened by Joe's death, and I thanked her for her concern. A moment later her boss hollered for her to stop chatting and to serve her other tables. She gave him a snarky glare and excused herself.

"I'm sorry, but my boss isn't much of a Montana Joe fan. He's more like I'm-a-jerk-with-a-small-penis fan! I really need to leave this place. I cook very well – do you need a cook, Rose?"

In unison we all said "NO" and then explained that we had to leave soon.

Morgan smirked, "Maybe we should have ordered our breakfast to go."

I added, "Yes, maybe from another restaurant-- better yet another county."

Keough glanced over at me. "Does she know that *Montana Joe* isn't a real person? And, that Montana Joe was Lash's pen name?"

I shook my head, "I don't know what she knows. I think she lives in a world where no one else lives except her, and thank God for that or we'd all be in big trouble. Sometimes I think if I didn't have all of you supporting me I'd be as loony as Mona. And to be honest, she's a great reminder of how much Lash's fans loved and still love him."

Keough agreed. "She ain't half bad except for her . . . you know . . . being completely loco."

"Perhaps we should invite her over for coffee and get to know her better."

Keough and Morgan hollered, "NO WAY!"

I couldn't stop laughing. When I was able to speak, I told them I was only joking.

Keough frowned, "That wasn't funny Rose! Ya' almost gave me a damn heart attack!"

We left a huge cash tip to keep her from following us and to help finance her timely relocation. On the way back to the car, I looked at my watch – it was time to pick up Charlotte.

We drove back to the daycare just in time to see her playing in the playground still attached to the little ginger-haired boy. Gracie came out with Little Lou and her hat.

"I think your daughter has found a best friend. He's such a sweet little boy. His name is Corey, and his father is a big Montana Joe fan."

"By chance, he isn't married to a woman named Mona?"

Gracie looked puzzled by my question. "No he's a single dad now. His wife passed away last year. He said Joe's novels helped him through his grieving. If I may ask, who is Mona?"

I told Gracie about her and she said she would keep Charlotte's identity confidential. I thanked her for her professionalism.

"There are a lot of crazy people out there, and we never let anyone who isn't on our check list near our kids . . . EVER."

Her statement put me at ease. I'd lost Joe, and I didn't want to lose Charlotte to a deranged fan. Charlotte finally realized we were there and came running over with Corey in tow.

"Mama, say hi to Corey. He's my new friend." She pushed him toward me. I knelt down and shook his hand.

"Hello Corey, thank you for being Charlotte's first new friend."

I could tell he was bashful, but Charlotte wasn't having it. She urged him to speak up saying that Montanas talk loud.

"Say HI LOUDER Corey!"

He screamed "HELLO!" and Charlotte hollered, "THAT'S BETTER!"

Keough walked over and took her by the hand. "That's right Baby Girl, Montanas are a rowdy bunch. If you wanna be heard, you gotta speak up. Or in Lou's case, bark loud. I bet you'd like me to introduce Corey to Little Lou."

Corey took the stuff dog from Keough and handed it to Charlotte. She told him that he was Lucky Lou's little brother and that big Lou was waiting for him back at the house.

I thanked Gracie and Dr. Henry for their thoughtfulness and making Charlotte's first day stress free for both of us. Dr. Henry reminded me to consider attending the Montford-Wellesley event.

"It is next month, and we would love you to come if you're available."

I told her I would seriously consider her invitation. Then I remembered I was meeting with Jameson Wellesley next month about the Remington collection. *I wonder if he'll be attending.*

Chapter 7

Jameson's personal assistant informed him that his driver was ready and waiting for him outside. He needed to sign a few papers before heading to the airport. He slung his carry-on over his shoulder and grabbed *The New York Times* from his desk tucking it neatly under his arm. His mother came out of her office and wished him well.

"Take care, Darling and please give my best to Amelia. Tell her I'll be in touch next week."

He nodded and kissed her on her cheek.

"I will Mother, and I'll call you as soon as I land in Billings."

She let out a long sigh.

"I wish I could come with you. I do miss Montana; however, someone has to keep the company runnin' – so get goin'!"

Jameson laughed at his mother's attempt to revert back to her western roots.

"Okay Ma'am. I'll get goin' before I miss my flight."

She knew he was mocking her for dropping the G's off her words.

James mocked, "You can take the lady out of Dodson but you can't take the Dodson out of the lady."

Meryl pinched his arm and walked back into her office.

He arrived at the airport with an hour to spare. His flight was delayed due to a severe thunderstorm in Chicago. He hated waiting in airports. The people and noise annoyed him. He headed to the Executives Lounge for a drink. It was like a watering hole for VIP's. The bartender knew Jameson. Jameson was a frequent flyer – way too frequent. He asked him where he was headed.

"I'm going to Montana . . ." Before he could finish his sentence the bartender sang, ". . . *Gonna* be a Dental Floss Tycoon."

Both he and Jameson were Frank Zappa fans. They laughed at the impromptu reference to Frank's song.

"But seriously, Mr. J, why and for what reason would you be heading to Montana? And if I may add, you look way too formal to be traveling to Big Sky country."

The bartender reached behind the bar and plopped an old cowboy hat on Jameson's head.

"Now you look like an honest-to-goodness cowboy – except for the Armani suit and tie."

Jameson took it off and tossed it back to the bartender.

"It's for my mother. She was born in Montana and has contracted some woman to do an article on my father's Remington collection. I truly believe my mother is a cowgirl at heart. Take away all the jewelry and makeup and she'd happily ride shotgun on a stagecoach. I think she was born too late. To be honest, I could see her running a saloon, and please don't tell her I said that – she'd disown me."

The bartender was about to say something when they announced the flight to Billings had landed and would be boarding in twenty minutes. Jameson paid his tab and left a twenty-dollar tip.

"Why such a large tip Mr. J?"

He looked at him shaking his head, "For not trying to talk me out of going. God knows I would rather be on the golf course."

He tilted the glass up catching the last few drops of his drink. *The things I do for my mother.*

He'd just arrived at the gate when the call for first class passengers was announced. There were dozens of families traveling with litters of children. They reminded him of the new Green Play Garden they were constructing. He didn't like kids. He was single and had neither the time nor the patience for them. Being an only child, he never learned to share or to experience what it was like to be part of a large family.

When he asked his mother why she never had any more children, her answer would always be, "Why have more when I have perfection with you."

As much as he loved being an only child there were times he thought about what it would be like to have a brother—someone to share his love of sports, cars and women. There were plenty of eligible ladies in his life but not one he would consider worthy of the Montford-Wellesley name. Most saw him as a handsome ATM.

Looking over his notes and his mother's notes, he realized he was the same age as Amelia's husband. He knew of Lash's death from the media coverage. For a moment it made him think about his own mortality. The flight attendant showed him to his seat and asked if he needed anything.

"Yes, I'd like to depart and return to New York as soon as possible."

"I'm guessing you don't want to go to Montana do you, Sir?"

"Nope, but business is business and sometimes you just have to cowboy up."

The attendant smiled at his lame attempt at western lingo. *This is going to be one rough ride.* He fastened his seat belt and stared out of the window. The attendant sat a drink on his tray and said,

"It's not policy but you look as though you could use one before we take off."

He took a deep breath and said, "You read my mind."

He didn't remember falling asleep. The flight attendant nudged Jameson to inform him they would be landing soon and to fasten his seat belt. Jameson slept through the entire flight. *Must have been the pre and in flight drinks.* Perhaps it was the alcohol or the fact that he hadn't had a good night's rest in more than a month. His hectic work schedule, endless meetings and Manhattan restaurant dinners kept him on a steady diet of sleeping pills, energy drinks and high blood pressure medicines.

As the plane taxied to the gate, he checked his cell phone for voice messages – there were three missed calls. Two were from his mother checking to see how his flight went and reminding him to call her as soon as he arrived. The other was his assistant reminding him to call his mother. *I could use another drink!*

As the plane came to a halt, he grabbed his carry-on from the overhead compartment and headed to the exit. The attendant asked if there was anything else she could get him before he departed.

"I could really use another drink."

She slipped a mini-bottle of Scotch in his jacket pocket along with a piece of paper.

She winked, "Call me when you return from Montana."

He smiled saying he would try but couldn't make any promises.

"But hey, thanks for the drink, Babe."

It wasn't the answer she was looking for. She rolled her eyes and gave him a very subtle screw you gesture.

He made his way to the rental kiosk to pick up his car. There was a crowd of people waiting. Some were arguing with the representatives and others were walking off in a huff. *Uh oh, what's going on?*

A very nervous representative announced that due to the overwhelming flight delays they ran out of mid-range luxury cars.

"We have small compacts, vans and a few trucks – sorry folks."

Jameson made his way through the crowd and said he'd be okay with a truck. The representative sent him over to a rental host to switch the paperwork.

"Here are your keys, and again we apologize. Of course the difference in your downgrade will be reimbursed. Again, sorry for the inconvenience and thank you for your patience – it's been a real nightmare!"

"No problem." *Like I'm in a big rush to get to Malta and Dodson!*

He made his way through the crowd, to the parking area and saw a red Chevy Silverado – *hmm not bad, not bad at all.* He took off his jacket and threw his carry-on in the passenger's seat.

I haven't driven a truck in years, but anything is better than waiting in a long line with pissed off people.

About an hour into his drive, he turned on the radio. There was nothing but country music and bible stations. *Thank goodness I packed my CD's.* He reached back into his carry-on and pulled out a hand full of jewel cases. He popped out the disk and inserted it into the player. *Now we're rockin'! There's nothing like a little retro Frank Zappa to keep me awake.*

Over Nite Sensation was his favorite album. If the board members knew he liked Zappa, they would think he'd lost his mind. Most of them were over 65-years old and thought Marilyn Manson was a girl.

He found it amusing that the song *Montana* was playing.

I'm in Montana and I'm listening to Montana. Okay, now I know I'm losing it. It's not funny, yet I'm laughing at the stupid comparison. Must be the altitude? He called ahead to check on his lodging reservation. *I hope it's not as screwed up as the airport rental car fiasco.*

The reservation desk assured him that his room was ready and waiting. He reached over and shoved his cell phone back in his jacket pocket. It clinked against the complimentary bottle of scotch the flight attendant gave him. He cracked it open and emptied the contents in one swallow thinking, *Yes, mother I know it's illegal to drink and drive but I really need to relax.*

He tossed the bottle and the slip of paper with the flight attendant's phone number out the window. *Sorry, Brittany but I barely have time to think let alone date – just not in my life schedule.* He cranked up Zappa and set the cruise control to sixty. Two hours had passed when he saw the sign for Malta and Dodson. *I can't believe mother grew up in these sleepy-little-towns.* A few minutes later he saw the sign pointing to The White Buffalo Road Inn. *I hope it's got running water.*

It was after 7:00 PM when he checked in. He parked the truck and walked inside to the reservation desk. An old gentleman greeted him asking if he was lost.

"No, I'm not lost; I'm here for three days to meet a young lady from Malta."

He smiled. "Son, you came a long way just to meet up with some gal. I hope she's worth it! And if she is . . . does she have an older sister?"

"Eh, let me rephrase that. I'm here to meet an art columnist who is doing an article for our company. She was hired to write about our Remington collection."

The old man nodded, "Oh okay, but you still haven't answer my question. Does she have an older sister?"

A voice from the back room hollered, "I heard that!"

He must have noticed the blank expression on my face.

"Hah, it's just the wife. Why don't you come out and get this young fella checked in."

A petite woman came from the back room. "Welcome to the White Buffalo Road Inn, Mr. Wellesley, I'm Ruthie and this older-than-dirt fellow is Roy, my soon-to-be-ex-husband if he doesn't behave himself!"

He winked then kissed her on the cheek. "She wouldn't know what to do if I wasn't around."

Ruthie whacked him on his arm with reservation paperwork. "Sorry about that Mr. Wellesley. He can be a royal pain in my derriere but somebody has to love him, and I guess he's my life-long responsibility."

Jameson chuckled, "Not a problem and please, call me Jameson; Mr. Wellesley is my dad. It's very nice to meet you Ruthie and you too, Roy. However, I'm completely exhausted from my trip. If you would show me to my room, I'd truly appreciate it."

"Of course Jameson, Roy will bring your luggage in for you."

Jameson shrugged, "There's no luggage, just my carry-on – but thanks anyway."

Ruthie pointed up, "Your room is on the second floor at the top of the stairs. Nothing fancy, but it's clean and cozy. If you need anything just holler. Oh, and breakfast is at 7:00 AM and dinner at 6:00 PM. Hope you like blueberry pancakes? Roast beef's for dinner."

Forget the pancakes. I hope a Bloody Mary is part of the breakfast menu. He smiled and thanked them for their hospitality.

The room was larger than he expected. It had a king-size bed, with a private bathroom. *Hmm, no television or mini-bar? This trip just keeps getting better and better. I wonder what this art columnist is like. Probably some retired librarian who knew Remington personally! Jeez, how did I let my mother talk me into this?*

Jameson heard a knock on his door. *What time is it?* He glanced over at his watch – 7:15 AM. There was a second knock and a bellowing voice.

"If you want breakfast I'd suggest you come down before it gets cold or Roy goes back for thirds."

It was Ruthie. His urge to holler back, 'Okay Mother' would be inappropriate. In fact, he bet she would call him a New York smart-ass and then order him to get his butt downstairs right now. Jameson replied that he was getting dressed and would be down as quickly as possible. She said there was a cup of coffee sitting on the table outside the room. *Bless you Ruthie!*

The aroma of blueberry pancakes hit him the moment he opened the door. His mother never had time to cook. Her career always came first, but she always had time for her son. Their cook would have their breakfast ready and waiting; however, his mother insisted on taking him to school. *I miss those kisses on my forehead and her smile wishing me a pleasant day.* He took a sip of the coffee. *This is good. Much better than the coffee in Manhattan - must be the Montana water.*

He crept down the stairs and waited for Ruthie to give him hell for not being on time, but to his surprise she came from the kitchen with a hot plate of freshly made pancakes along with syrup and soft butter on the side.

"I don't know what kind of breakfast they serve you in New York City, but around here we believe in eating food while it's hot – ain't that right Roy? "

"Yep, that's right Ruthie. Now, if I could grab a couple more of them hotcakes from ya' that would just make my day."

Jameson sat down opposite Roy and placed a napkin over his lap. Ruthie ignored his request and put the plate in front of her guest.

"Here you go Jameson – eat up. And, don't take your eyes off your plate or you'll be missing one or two of them pancakes."

Roy huffed and rubbed his belly, "Ruthie Darlin', if you weren't such a wonderful cook we wouldn't have this problem."

"Oh, now your fat gut is MY fault?" She walked behind him and kissed his head.

Roy tilted his head up and kissed her on her cheek. "Damn you woman, even when I try to piss you off you still find a way to make me love ya' even more than I already do."

Jameson watched them taunt and tease each other wondering if he would ever find a woman who drove him nuts but loved him like Ruthie loved Roy.

Ruthie refilled her guest's coffee cup and explained that Roy was her high school sweetheart and they've been together for 42 years. They decided to retire in Montana and open a small hotel or like they say on the east coast, a Bed and Breakfast. Jameson was glad they did because their place was so cozy and comfortable—not like the large hotel chains that treated you like your room number.

Jameson pushed back his chair and wiped his mouth with the cloth napkin. "Ruthie that was the best breakfast I've had in years! You wouldn't want to come back to New York with me and be my private chef?"

Before she could answer, Roy got up from the table and put his arm around her shoulder.

"Son, you try to steal my Ruthie away from me and you'll be missin' two arms and a lot of fingers!"

Jameson laughed and threw his hands in the air. "Okay Roy, you win as if she would ever leave you for some east coast workaholic guy like me."

The office phone rang. Roy said it was a good thing because he was ready to take Jameson outside and fist-fight him for his gal. Jameson smiled and whispered, "I bet you'd kick my ass too."

He nodded and took our plates into the kitchen. The phone ringing reminded Jameson that he had left his cell phone in the truck. *I bet the battery is dead.* He could only imagine how many phone calls he'd missed. For some reason, it didn't seem to matter. The New York hustle and bustle was hundreds of miles away. Montana didn't have the same sense of urgency as the city – *must be the altitude.*

As he suspected, the phone was dead. *Thank goodness I remembered to pack my charger.* He walked upstairs to his room and plugged it in. There were ten missed calls. *Oh shit, I'd better call Mother.* He didn't remember the phone ringing when she answered.

"Well, it's about time you phoned. I thought your plane had gone down or you were high jacked to some underdeveloped country and held prisoner, but when I didn't receive a ransom note, I assumed you were okay and had fallen asleep. How are you Jameson? Did you meet Amelia Montana yet? Is she as good a columnist as they say she is? Have you been to Dodson yet?"

Jameson took a deep breath, "Hello Mother, sorry I didn't call and yes I was exhausted and no, I haven't met Mrs. Montana or been to Dodson yet. Have I answered your litany of questions in the order received or should I wait a few minutes in case you'd like to ask me more?"

"Yes you have, Dear and your sarcasm is not appreciated! I was worried sick that something terrible might have happened to you!"

"Really Mother, I'm in Montana heading to a map dot town called Dodson. What's the worst that could happen? The general store runs out of Twinkies or there's a sudden shortage of Juicy Fruit gum? Oh, the horror . . . the humanity!"

There was total silence on the other end.

"Now, if you're finish being a rude S.O.B., I just wanted to say how much I love and miss you. Please take lots of photographs of Dodson for me. To be honest, I wish I could have gone with you, but someone needs to run this company. Please give my best regards to Amelia and remember to call me – I love you Jameson."

"I promise I will give her your warm and fuzzy regards, and I also promise to call you the moment I get to Dodson. I love you too Mother, ciao."

Chapter 8

I had just started making Charlotte's afternoon snack when the phone rang. It was Raymond calling to find out how I was holding up. It had been almost a month since we spread Joe's ashes and for the first time since his death, I had a good night's sleep. I'd purchased a new bed – a queen size as I didn't see the need to keep that huge king-sized bed. I felt like I was sleeping on an indoor island. I could lay corner-to-corner, side-to-side and not touch the edges.

Joe used to say, "I never understood why on earth couples would want a big ol' bed when they were going to spoon together anyway. If you ask me it's just seems a waste of space."

He was right. We always slept tangled in each other's arms. I was always cold and Joe was always hot. He'd say, "My Lord, Girl you feel like a popsicle. You know the kind with a wooden stick you break apart? I guess it's on account of them boney legs."

Raymond wanted to invite me to a drum circle. He remembered how much I loved them and thought that now would be a good time to get reacquainted with my Cherokee spiritual side. I told him I'd think about it. I also told him about the article I was hired to write and would it be possible for me to stay at his cabins – the one Joe used when he wanted to write.

"Of course Rose, by all means you can stay in that one or any one you want. The season is coming to a close and most of them are empty. However, if you want to stay in Joe's old cabin, there are a few things I'll need to do before you arrive."

I told him not to do anything fancy, I'm just coming to write; it's not a vacation.

"I totally understand Rose. Nevertheless, I'll need to air the room out. No one has rented it since Joe died. In a way I'm happy. It's just like Joe left it. And, I'd like to smudge it with sage. It will help your creativity, and it will help rid it of any trail lice Joe left behind – the flea-bitten mongrel bastard."

I realized that Raymond had me laughing out loud, and Charlotte came running into the room clapping and smiling.

In a sing-song voice she said, "Mama is laughing; Mama is happy!"

I bent down and kissed her cheek. "Yes, Mama is happy and she hasn't been happy for a long, long time."

She pointed outside, "Mama, is Daddy happy too?"

Raymond heard her and asked me to put her on the phone. He told her that her daddy is very happy because she and Mama are happy. Raymond also told her he had something for her and would bring it the next time he dropped by.

That put a big grin on her face. She told Little Lou that Uncle Raymond had a gift for her. She asked Raymond if he had a gift for Big Lou. He told her he would bring him a big bone for chewin'.

"And, I'll even put a big red bow around it. Do you think he would like that Charlotte? She let out a loud YES and ran back outside to tell Lou.

"You know she adores you Raymond. It's like you two have known each other for years."

"Yes, Nadie is such a beautiful little spirit just like her mama."

Raymond had to stop talking for a second because he became emotionally overwhelmed reminiscing about Joe. He swore to Joe he would be there for me and Charlotte, and he would love us as he would his own family. I knew he was once married, and his wife also died of cancer. I think that's why he became so upset when Joe announced his diagnosis.

"Rose you know you can come to the cabin anytime you want. And yes I think Joe would be happy to see his cabin being used by his lovely wife especially since you've started writing again. He's very proud of you."

I asked him how he knew.

"If you listen carefully, you can hear the spirits speaking to you. They are always with us Rose and when we need to speak to them they tell us things we need to know. Talking to loved ones who've crossed over isn't any different than you watching old videos of those who have passed on – is it?"

"Touché, Raymond. I have been immersing myself in the past way too much. And you're right. I need to start moving forward.

"Yes, I thought that statement would make you sit up and take notice. Now then, let me know if you'd like to come to the drum circle. It's this weekend, and I'll even come pick you up. Take care Rose, and I'll see you soon."

Charlotte was sitting outside with Lou. I tip-toed to the door and watched her while she played. I overheard her talking to Lou telling him that her daddy lived in heaven now, and she missed him. She held her hands up to the sky asking her daddy to kiss them. It broke my heart. I had to go back inside. I cried for her, I cried for me and I cried for Joe. Then I got angry.

"Okay Rose, NO MORE CRYING damn it! Joe is dead and he isn't coming back!"

He would be so annoyed with me for bawling every time his name was mentioned.

"That's it – I'm going into town and buy something special just for me. Not something Joe would like but something I like." *Baby steps Rose, baby steps.*

Charlotte was ready to leave. With Lou and Little Lou in tow we got into the truck. I put her in her car seat and headed for town. Joe's truck was a good ride. It was a much smoother than my small compact and lots of room for a kid and a dog. Lou was like a four-legged babysitter. He would keep an eye on Charlotte while I was driving. He would also sit in the bed of the truck while we shopped. I never needed to lock it up when Lou came with me. Nothing keeps a would-be car thief away from a vehicle like a huge black lab with sharp white teeth. Of course everyone who knows Lou knows he's as gentle as a lamb but his massive head, body and paws provoked fear in the bravest of men.

We drove around looking for a parking space; the shopping center was packed. After three go-rounds I finally found one that could fit the truck. It annoyed me when people driving small compact cars took up two spaces. I flashed back to Paul parking his 18-wheeler. *He would be so proud of me.* I noticed a truck that looked just like Keough's old rust bucket parked a few spaces away from me. We started walking toward it when I saw Keough come out of the men's store.

"Hey you old buzzard what are you doing in town?"

He tilted his hat back to see who was giving him grief.

"Well if it ain't my two best buds – Lou and Charlotte! Oh and howdy to you too Rose? Slug anybody lately? I saw ya' staring at that jerk who took up two parking spaces. It would be a hoot to watch you punch his lights out."

I flashed him a sarcastic smile. "Nope, but the day is just getting started, and I would be happy to throw a few punches your way, Old Man."

We gave each other our customary side hug then a proper hug.

"So, what brings you into town Keough? New seat covers for that old piece of crap you call a truck or perhaps you've taken up knitting and you're here buying more yarn."

He knelt down next to Charlotte and whispered,

"Your mama thinks she's funny. We don't think she's funny – do we   Darlin'?"

Charlotte hugged Keough and said, "No Mama's not funny, but I am." She made a silly face then asked Keough if he would buy her some candy.

"Of course, Baby Girl—as long as it's okay with your mama." I nodded.

"And Rose if you must know, I'm here because I needed some new drawls. The one's I got are wearin' thin so I thought I'd treat myself to some of them fancy ones with the designer initials stamped in 'em. I don't even know who Ralph Lauren is but they looked fancy, so I bought 'em. Would ya' like to see 'em?"

"God, NO! I don't want to see your new underwear. I can barely tolerate seeing you clothed, so you can only imagine how much I DON'T want to see or think about you in your underwear."

He laughed and grabbed Charlotte's hand. "Come on Baby, let's go get some candy. I think I've upset your mama enough today."

"Yes, and for that matter the rest of the century! I don't want to imagine you wearing designer underwear. I think I've fallen into some sort of parallel universe where old geezers wear designer drawls."

"Don't pay any attention to her Charlotte. She's just jealous of my manly physique." He looked at his reflection in the shop window and ran his finger through his hair. "Hah, I must say I'm still good looking, just older, slower and forgetful – remind me . . . where are we going, Darlin'?"

Charlotte giggled, "For CANDY Pap-Pap, candy!"

"That's right Baby Girl. Let's go get some candy. And if your mama behaves herself we'll get her some too."

Charlotte gave Keough the okay sign with her fingers, and they disappeared into candy shop.

I was about to enter the shoe store when I noticed a red Silverado parked two cars away from me. It was newer than Joe's. I was so distracted with Keough, I didn't realize I left my purse in the truck. I headed back to retrieve it and decided to make a detour past the red truck. Looking around to see if anyone was watching, I peeked in to take a look. *Nice, very nice interior.* I also noticed that it was a rental. There were file folders and CD's covering the passenger seat – hmm, Frank Zappa. *Must be some kid heading to Montana thinking they can grow dental floss.*

I grabbed my purse and headed on my shopping spree. I made a mental map of what I wanted to buy. *First stop shoe store, then new jeans and bras—I needed new bras because my boobs got larger after I had Charlotte.* I could hear Joe saying, "And damn it, buy the kind that unhook from the front!"

I was about to go into the shop when a gentleman in a dress shirt and tie brushed by me. He turned, mouthed an *excuse me* then headed towards the parking lot. It was odd seeing someone in an Armani shirt and tie in a small Montana town. I knew it was Armani because my New York boss had the same one. *He's probably a buyer for one of the upscale department stores.* Still, he looked too professional for this shopping center. I made a mental note of him and continued into the store. Something told me to turn around and check on the truck. That's when I noticed him getting into the Red Silverado. I reprimanded myself for judging a person by the clutter in his vehicle. *God only knows why he's in this small town. Maybe he's lost. He's definitely not one of the locals.* I watched him drive away then went into the shoe store.

I thought back to the time I stopped in a small town for lunch. *I wonder how Randy and that waitress are doing; if she finally got the courage to leave her situation and make a better life for her and her kids. Oh well, I'd better get going or Keough will start whining about how long it took me to buy new bras. Plus it's getting late and Charlotte hadn't had her nap. She'll be cranky the rest of the day if she doesn't. I saw Charlotte first then Keough dragging behind her.*

It was the first time I'd actually felt sorry for the poor old fellow. He looked as though he'd been through a tornado. His hair was sticking up in all directions and he had lipstick, or what looked like lipstick, on his cheeks.

"So, Charlotte did you enjoy your day with Pap-Pap?"

She ran over to me with a huge bag of candy in one hand and a straw hat in the other.

"Hi Mama, look at my hat!" It was a pink cowgirl's hat with a flowered hat band. "Pap-Pap let me pick it out."

I told her how lovely she looked in her new hat and thanked Keough for watching her while I shopped. Keough said, "She tried on every dang hat in the store and when she got tired, she made me try them on. Whew, I swear that kid has an excessive amount of energy!"

Charlotte handed me the open bag of candy so she could put on her hat. She looked at her reflection in the store window and twirled around. *This kid is on a sugar high. There's no way she'll be able to take a nap.*

"Okay Keough I've got to ask . . . what's with the red lipstick? Did she take you to the cosmetic department for a makeover?"

"No she didn't. She kept kissing me for buying her the hat. It's that dang red candy she's been eating. Why didn't the gal at the candy counter warn me that kids shouldn't have that much sugar?"

I snickered, "Serves you right ya' dumb-ass! And since this situation is your fault, I'm going to let you try to put her down for her nap."

"You are cruel Rose, plain old cruel! You knew this would happen, didn't you?"

"Yup."

"And you didn't think to tell me not to feed her that much candy?"

"Nope."

"You wouldn't happen to have any of them wet wipes would ya'? I'd like to get this sticky stuff off my face before I start attracting flies."

I handed him a wet wipe and opened one for Charlotte. She was covered head to toe in red taffy.

"Come on Sweetie, time to go home and straight to the tub."

Keough walked us to the truck. I told him about the fellow in the red Silverado. He said he saw him earlier in the men's shop.

"He didn't look like he was from around here especially dressed in them fancy duds. I reckon he's from California or New York City and probably lost."

"That's exactly what I thought. No one around this part of town wears Armani accept Patrick and Daniel."

Keough agreed and headed over to his truck. He noticed Lou was sleeping in the truck bed.

"Oh, so now you want to ride with me, huh Lou?" He stood up and wagged his tail.

"Well, then get in the passenger's side, and I'll take you home. To be honest Lou, I've miss your company. For almost a decade, you've been my only true friend." He gave his ears a scratch, started the truck and headed to the shopping center exit.

He rolled down his window and hollered, "I'll see you gals later. Lou and I have one more stop to make."

What other stop could he be making? He doesn't have any friends that I know of nor does he know anyone else in town except me? I wonder what he's up to.

Keough drove a few miles down the road and parked in front of the floral and garden shop. The bells on the door alerted the clerk.

"Well, howdy Keough! Has it been a year already? Golly, I tell ya' time sure does fly."

"Yeah it does Harlan. It's been a busy two years for me out at the Montana ranch since my son died."

"Yes, I read about his death in the paper – sad, very sad! And I hear tell he recently married and they had a daughter. How are they doin'?"

"They're hanging in there. It's been a rough couple of years for the Montana family. Still can't believe my son is gone. "

Harlan shook his head, "It's gotta be awfully hard on them. Her being a new bride and now a widow with a child, it's just sad I tell ya'.

Keough wiped his eyes with his bandana.

Harlan apologized for bringing up Lash's death. "I'm sorry Keough; I didn't mean to upset you. I just wanted you to know that I understand. My boy Andy was killed in the line of duty this year. The wife and I are still mourning."

Keough noticed an American flag encased on the top shelf of the store.

"Sorry to hear about your boy Harlan. A parent ain't supposed to outlive their kids." Both men nodded in agreement.

Harlan walked in the back and returned with Keough's order.

"Two potted Prairie Roses correct?"

Keough nodded, "Yep, they were her favorite. It would have been her seventy-third birthday tomorrow. I know that flowers won't make up for all the pain and grief I gave her, but I hope she knows how much I loved her. I just didn't have the courage to stop drinking in time to show her."

"I think she'll love them Keough, and I believe she's proud of you helpin' out your kin folk."

"I hope she is Harlan because I gave my son my word that I would dry out and never drink like that again and this time I'm gonna keep my promise. I got folks who need me now – like my granddaughter Charlotte and my daughter-in-law Rose."

Keough pulled out a photograph of Rose and Charlotte and showed to Harlan.

"I do declare they are the most beautiful gals I've ever seen. Lash sure knew how to pick 'em!"

"Yep, he sure did Harlan. Lash and Rose named her Charlotte in honor of my wife. She's just as feisty, and she has me wrapped around her finger just like my wife did."

Harlan grinned, "Next time y'all are in town bring them by the shop. I'd love to meet the gals who stole Lash's heart."

"I will Harlan and again, my condolences to you and your family in regards to your son. He was a good man, a brave man. I was proud to know him."

Harlan thanked him and went to help another customer.

Charlotte and I arrived home to an empty house. Keough wasn't home yet and neither was Morgan. Cecilia had supper ready and had gone out for the evening.

"Well, Kiddo it looks like it's just me and you for now." I took my shopping bags into the bedroom. When I came back into the living room to get her ready for her bath, Charlotte was stretched out on the rug fast asleep. *Joe, I hope you can see this. She'd definitely your kid.* I covered her with her favorite blanket and let her nap. It was rare that she'd fall asleep without a fight, but the ride home in the cool afternoon breeze did the trick. I walked into the kitchen to take a peek at what Cecilia made for supper. I giggled to myself thinking, *I remember when I used to call it dinner. I am turning into a real country bumpkin.*

"Mmmm, roast beef with potatoes, my favorite dish. There's nothing better than slow-cooked beef with all the fixings."

I picked off a piece of beef and wrapped it in a slice of bread. "That should hold me until everyone gets home."

I snooped in the refrigerator and discovered a freshly baked apple pie. *I do love you Cecilia. I've always wondered why I never gained weight when I ate her cooking, but one night of eating out and I'll gain five pounds. I guess it's the difference between old fashion home cooking and fancy restaurant food.*

Charlotte's late nap meant I'd have a fight on my hands at bed time. But what else was new. *It would be the same fight if I woke her up now.* I decided to let her sleep until supper time. *Where the heck could Keough be? I hope he's okay. It's not that I dislike Keough it's just more fun letting him believe I dislike him. I miss the daily banter Joe and I used to have. Teasing me about my snoring and drooling. Honestly, I don't know what I'd do without Keough. He fills a void that Joe left.*

I decided to make a pot of Joe's coffee. I'd committed it to memory and knew exactly how much to use for a full pot. Joe thought brewing a half pot was a waste of time and coffee. The evening sunset was brilliant, and I wanted to sit on the deck to enjoy a brief moment of quiet before the guys came home. It wasn't long ago that I couldn't stand a quiet house. I needed the noise to dull the pain of grieving. But as time passed, quiet became my friend and we learned to respect each other. I waited for the final gurgle and the last drops. The aroma filled the kitchen. There were times I found myself reaching for two cups. However this time was different. This time I reached for my cup and my cup only. *Okay so it's one baby step for Amelia, one giant step towards Amelia's grieving process.*

I sat out on deck and watched the last of the sunset. *Joe, if you can hear me I'm pretty sure you had something to do with it.* He use to call them lipstick sunsets just like the sunset in the John Hiatt song

His CD was still in my car's CD player. *I must remember to bring it inside. It helps me to relax when I can't sleep.* Besides Creedence Clearwater Revival, John Hiatt was one of Joe's favorite singers. If he was having a terrible writing day, he'd play *Have a Little Faith in Me.* That was my cue to come in and give him one of my wifely pep talks. However, I must have faith that I can move past all of this and live my life the way he would want me to—raising our daughter Charlotte and continuing to write and keep the Montana Legacy going for the next generation of Montanas.

The familiar sound of Keough's old truck coming up the driveway snapped me out of my daydream. I poured another cup of coffee and met him at the door.

"Here you go, Keough. I thought you could use a cup after the day you had with your granddaughter."

Keough looked at me in disbelief.

"Why, Rose I do believe this is the first time since we've known each other you've addressed me as Keough and not some disparaging nickname. Hah, I need to babysit more often."

"Don't get used to it. I always feel good after I've purchased new shoes. Not like I can wear them around here. Ranch life and Prada don't get along too well."

Keough laughed, "Still it's nice to know that you do like me, even if it's residual kindness from buyin' them fancy name branded shoes."

The sound of Keough's voice brought Charlotte to her feet. She rubbed her eyes and walked over to Keough.

"Pap-Pap where's my prize?" Keough looked over at me for translation.

"She wants to know what you brought for her – her surprise."

"Oh, okay. Well, you'll have to come outside to see it."

Charlotte followed Keough out to the truck. Keough reached inside and hand her the potted prairie roses.

She looked at the plant then at Keough asking, "This is my prize?" Keough nodded.

"I don't like it. I want candy. I don't want this flower!"

Keough stooped down in front of her.

"This plant is a special plant. It was your grandma's favorite plant. And, I bet you can't guess what your grandma's name was?"

Charlotte shrugged.

"Her name was Charlotte too. You were named after your grandma. She was a very special lady and I'm going to take you to visit her."

"Will she have candy?"

Keough looked over at Rose.

"Honey, your grandma is in heaven with your daddy. She was your daddy's mama."

Charlotte squinted, "Do they have candy in heaven?" Rose and Keough smiled.

Keough nodded yes. Rose added that she was sure her daddy had candy in heaven, but needed a special favor from her.

"Your daddy wants you to go with Pap-Pap and help him plant the flowers. That would make him very happy – can you do that?"

"Okay, Mama I'll go with Pap-Pap and then can I have candy?"

"Yes, you can have two pieces, one piece for you and one for Pap-Pap."

Charlotte seemed to be okay with the arrangement. Then she asked if she could have one for Grandma and one for Daddy. I told her yes, and she could put them next to the flowers. That seemed to put a smile on her face.

Keough said, "Okay that settled. Tomorrow we'll go visit your grandma. And then we'll go where your daddy's ashes were spread and leave a piece of candy for him. Is that's okay with you Missy?"

She smiled and toddled off to her bedroom.

Keough and I walked back into the kitchen.

"Do you think it's a good idea to take her to the cemetery? She's just getting used to her daddy being in heaven. Should we expose her to a gravesite? And, do you think she'll understand?"

I really needed Keough's feedback on this.

He scratched his head. "I think she'll be okay. She's a smart little gal, and she's a Montana. I think she'll be fine."

"I hope so Keough because I'm barely holding on myself."

He whispered, *me too Darlin', me too.*

Chapter 9

"Where the hell am I? All these small Montana towns look alike. Nothing but prairies, prairies and more prairies. And not a damn bar in sight." Jameson looked at his map. He pulled over at a gas station for directions. The clerk greeted him at the door.

"Howdy, can I help you? And I bet you're lost. Am I right?"

Jameson nodded. "As a matter of fact I am. I'm trying to find a place called Malta."

The clerk smiled and said that he was in Malta, and if he'd gone another two miles he'd be out of Malta.

"We're not a big town, but we've got a big heart."

Jameson agreed. "Everyone here is so friendly and helpful. I was in the shopping center's department store and some fellow with his little granddaughter helped me find the men's department. The little girl even gave me a piece of her candy. I tell you it's nothing like New York."

The clerk smiled in agreement then looked out at Jameson's truck.

"If I may ask, who are you looking for?"

Jameson pulled the information out from his inside pocket of his suit jacket.

"I'm looking for the Montana ranch, a Mrs. Amelia Montana to be precise."

The clerk laughed. "Oh, you mean Rose Montana. Everyone around these parts calls her Rose. She is the widow of Lash Montana, you know the western novelist who wrote under the name Montana Joe. He passed away almost two years ago, God rest his soul. They were only married a year when he died. Now she's the heir of the Montana fortune. She'd give it all up in a heartbeat to have Lash back. Theirs was a love story to match all love stories. I tell ya' something else . . . she's one beautiful gal! But I'm sure you didn't come here to hear me rattle on."

"Not a problem. In fact, I really don't know much about her so thanks for the information. It'll give me a better understanding of who she is and how to approach her."

He remembered his mother saying she'd just lost her husband – so no flirting! *Hmm, Mother must know how gorgeous she is or she wouldn't have given me the 'no flirting' warning.*

The clerk pointed him to the mile marker and told him the exit for the ranch was roughly a mile-and-a- half up the road.

"You turn onto the road marked RT 68, and it'll take you to their ranch. Heck, the ranch is as big as our town! You can't miss it."

Jameson thought to himself, *Who are these people and why don't I know about them? If Lash Montana was that rich and famous, I'm sure he would have been in Forbes magazines.*

Jameson reached in the cooler for a bottle of water and asked if there was a liquor store nearby.

"Yup, you passed it a few miles back, but it's not open – it's Sunday ya' know."

Of course it is. I must remember to bring a flask with me when I travel to theses Podunk towns.

Jameson thanked the clerk and walked back to the truck. He fumbled for the keys in his pants pocket. As he went to unlock the door, he noticed his hand shaking. Steadying his grasp, the key slipped into the lock.

Looking up at the sky he said, "Please let this interview go smoothly. I don't think I could take it if I have to do this sober. And NO Mother I don't have a drinking problem. The problem is I have nothing to drink!" His statement gave him a much needed chuckle. He started the engine and buckled his seatbelt. "Okay, let's get this interview over with and then back to New York."

The tires spun a bit as he pulled away. *Steady Jameson. Don't need a reprimand from the local sheriff.* About a quarter mile from the gas station was the sign for RT-68. Beneath it was an arrow pointing to the right with Montana Ranch 2-miles posted on it. Jameson didn't remember driving the two miles. His mind wandered to his New York friends who were probably out partying. *I wonder what they do out at the Montana Ranch for entertainment? I bet they play horseshoes or count the tumbleweeds, hah! And if this woman is as gorgeous as they say, why is she hiding out here?*

In the distance, he saw a large ranch gate straddled across the road. As he drove closer, he could see *L J Montana Ranch.* He continued driving through the thickets for what seemed like an eternity. Finally there was an opening, and he spotted a large ranch-style house. It had to be at least another mile to the house. *Why would anyone live out here!* He looked at his watch. It was after 10:00 PM.

"I think I'll just pull over and sleep. I'm sure they're in bed. And to be honest, I need to some shut-eye before I meet her. He rummaged through his overnight bag for his electric razor, eye drops and mouth wash. "Good thing I took a shower and trimmed my beard and mustache; I wouldn't want to make a ghastly first impression." Five minutes later he was fast asleep.

A loud banging on the truck window jolted him awake. His eyes shot open to find a large Native American fellow with a shotgun pointed at the driver's side window.

Panic-stricken, he started the engine to flee but the man moved around and stood directly in front of the truck.

"Turn your engine off White Man and come out with your hands up!"

Jameson obeyed his order.

"Don't shoot me! I don't have any cash! Take the truck – it's a rental so I don't give a shit. But for God's sake, please don't shoot me!

Jameson opened the door, swung his legs out and stood up with his hands still in the air.

"What are you doing out here and speak quickly or I'll shoot you?" asked the man with the shotgun.

Jameson stuttered his reason for being on the Montana Ranch and how he got lost and by the time he found it, he was so sleepy he fell asleep in the truck."

By this time the man with the shotgun started laughing which scared Jameson even more.

The man sat on the tailgate bumper and said, "You can put your hands down now. I've always wanted to say that to someone. You should have seen your face. White men get whiter when they're scared. It always amuses me."

He held out his hand, "Hello, I'm Raymond Winterbee and you must be Jameson Montford-Wellesley."

Jameson slowly put his hands down. "How do you know me, and why were you going to shoot me?"

At this point Raymond couldn't stop laughing. He told Jameson that Jimmy from the gas station called and said that a man was on his way to the ranch, and he suggested I might want to come out and meet him so he didn't end up in Idaho.

Jameson put on his glasses and glanced at his watch – it was 6:00 AM. *I'm glad I remembered to take my contacts out before I nodded off. Where did I put them?*

Raymond explained that Rose was already up but had to drop her daughter off at the day school then run some errands.

"If you'd like to freshen up, you can take a shower at the bunkhouse before she returns. You smell like a menstruating goat."

Jameson sniffed his armpits. "Yeah, I could do with a hot shower, thanks Big Guy!"

Raymond frowned. "Okay, you can call me Raymond or Mr. Winterbee but no silly nicknames-- understood?"

"Okay Raymond and no more pointing guns as me—understood?"

Raymond nodded and the two men shook hands. Jameson followed Raymond for about 10-minutes. He was driving slowly – very slowly. Probably because Jimmy had already told him the stranger had been lost once, and it probably wasn't good for him to get lost again. Jameson had to admit the drive and scenery were beautiful. It looked a lot different in the daylight. Raymond turned into a driveway and continued for another quarter mile.

Wow, what a beautiful place. It's got a pond and barns. Raymond drove beside the small barn and parked. Jameson parked behind him.

"Welcome to Montana Ranch. This is the bunkhouse. You can take your things up to the loft and settle in. I'll let Rose know you're here."

"And how will you do that – send her smoke signals?"

Raymond squinted, "You know I still have the shotgun in my truck. I could take you out to the prairie, shoot you and bury you before she gets home. And she'll be none the wiser."

For a moment Jameson stopped breathing. Raymond laughed. "For goodness sakes, lighten up Jameson. I was joking. I'll call her on her cell phone." He took his phone out of his pocket and waved it in his face.

"But you promised – no more shotgun threats!"

Raymond reached for the gun. Jameson's eyes widened.

"For the love of everything that's sacred to my people Jameson, I'm not going to shoot you." Raymond laughed and showed him the gun wasn't loaded. "If I wanted to get rid of you, I would have used my knife and taken what little hair you have left. Again, I'm joking. Good grief, you've got the sense of humor of a turnip. I'll see you later. I've got to feed the horses."

Raymond slung the shotgun over his shoulder and headed toward the stables.

Jameson grabbed his gear and headed up the bunkhouse steps turning around to make sure Raymond wasn't following him. He opened the door and was amazed. It was so spacious. Nothing like the old bunkhouses you see in the western movies. It came equipped with an eat-in kitchen, a large bathroom with a shower and ceiling fans. *This place has more room than my condo! Get rid of all the western crap, and it would be a sweet place to live.*

Jameson stripped off his clothes and stepped into the shower. *Nice, very nice.* An unopened bottle of shampoo sat in the soap dish. *Hmm, lavender, not very masculine but it's better than nothing.* He washed and towel dried his hair and felt refreshed and relaxed. *Where is my damn contacts case? I really hate wearing these glasses but there's nothing much I can do about that for now until I find them.*

He stretched out on the bed, reviewing his notes for the meeting. The next thing he knew he was being shaken awake – it was Raymond.

"Jameson wake up, it's one o'clock and I'm about to have lunch. Would you like something to eat or would you prefer to sleep until winter?"

He'd fallen asleep still wrapped in his towel.

"Okay, big g . . . I mean, Raymond. I'm up. Now may I get dressed or would you prefer I eat lunch with you in the nude."

Raymond shook his head, flipped him the bird and headed back into the kitchen.

Whatever Raymond was cooking smelled delicious. He also brewed fresh coffee.

"Raymond, you are officially my best friend. I really need some coffee!"

Jameson slipped on a pair of sweat pants and tee shirt and sat down at the kitchen table. Raymond handed him a cup.

"Here you go. I don't know how you take it, but there's sugar on the table and cream in the refrigerator."

"Thanks, but I drink it black. No sense adding stuff to a perfectly good cup of coffee."

Raymond agreed. Raymond brought in two plates loaded with pancakes and sage sausages. Jameson asked him where he learned to cook so well.

"I'm self-taught. When you live alone and don't want to starve to death, you learn to cook – it's that simple."

Jameson inhaled the meal. Raymond asked if he'd like seconds.

"No thanks, but I would love another cup of coffee. I've never had this blend before. What kind is it?"

Raymond took a deep breath, "I can't say. It's Rose's husband's concoction. Writers live on coffee and Joe was no different."

"I thought his name was Lash? You called him Joe – what's the story behind that?"

Raymond put his fork down and told Jameson that Lash, also known as Montana Joe, fell in love with a woman named Amelia who, when they first met, wouldn't tell him her name, so he called her Rose. Rose, being the quick-witted person that she is started calling him Joe – like the coffee which was his obsession.

"I never met two people who drank as much coffee as they did. I told her she should go to Brazil and buy a coffee plantation—you know-- to cut out the middleman."

Jameson laughed. *Raymond's a funny fellow – I like him.* Jameson also asked if Rose had any ideas about the article.

"Mother asked me to interview her, but to tell you the truth I have no experience with all this cowboy stuff. All I know is Mother loves Remington artwork and sculpture and wants the world to know how amazing they are. She also loves Lash's books. So, I guess it made sense to kill two birds with one stone. You may or may not know this, but my mother was born and raised in Dodson."

Raymond shrugged his shoulders. "I must be honest, Jameson I've never heard of you or your family. I'm sort of a simple fellow. If you haven't noticed I try to stay out of the fast lane. It's better that way."

They continued to talk about the Montana family – Rose in particular. How a born and raised New Yorker could continue to live out here in Montana.

"I guess you'll have to ask her, Jameson. But I must warn you. If you do or say anything to upset her, I will personally scalp you in your sleep."

Jameson didn't know whether or not Raymond was kidding. To lighten the mood he asked, "Will you use a tomahawk or a knife?"

Raymond chuckled, "That's old-school Hollywood movies stuff. I use electric clippers."

Both men laughed, but Raymond was very serious. "I don't want to see her suffer anymore than she already has. Joe was her soul mate. In fact, I married them and I also ministered Joe's passing. So you can understand how close and protective I am of his family."

Jameson swallowed the last of his coffee and nodded. "I promise on my well-rooted hair that I will not upset her or anyone else in her family during my visit. I'll meet with her about the details of the article, have her sign her freelance contract, give her the advance check and then I'm out of here."

"Good. Because I'd hate to scalp you after we've shared such a wonderful meal. Anyway, you'd better get dressed – Rose is home."

Jameson stood up from the table, "Okay, how the hell do you know she's home? I didn't hear any car pull up? Are you psychic? Are you from a tribe of psychics?"

Raymond held his head, "No, you buffalo turd . . . my cell phone vibrated! My God, you are the second most annoying man I've ever met – Joe being the first!"

The more Jameson got to know Raymond, the more he liked him. He wasn't pretentious or phony like most city people he pretended to like. He was honest. If he didn't like you, he didn't apologize. *Maybe I could write an article about him instead? He's probably a lot more interesting than this Rose woman.*

Jameson got dressed in his suit and tie. It was almost 9:00 AM. Unable to find his contacts case, he donned his designer horn rims and followed Raymond to the house. Raymond noticed he was wearing his designer shoes. Oblivious to where he was walking, Jameson stepped in a fresh pile of horseshit.

Raymond chuckled, "Oops, I should have warned you before we left the bunkhouse to put on a pair of barn boots, huh."

"Ya' think Raymond! And here I thought we were slowly becoming the best of friends."

They continued to walk to the house when Keough came out from the barn in boots covered in more horseshit.

"Mornin' Raymond, looks like you found you a stray. Did you brand him yet?"

Jameson took a deep breath and introduced himself. "I'm here to help Amelia Montana with the Remington article for our Montford-Wellesley Corporation."

Keough wiped his hands on his jeans, "Nice to meet you, Jameson. Sorry about the horseshit. If you stay long enough you'll learn to like it."

He wiped his hand on his pants. *Not if I can help it.* Raymond and Keough gave each other their usual masculine-sanctioned hug and continued toward the house. Before they reached the door, Keough stopped. He turned around and looked at Jameson,

"You look awfully familiar."

Jameson said he doubted that they'd ever met as he just arrived in town.

"The only other place I've been is here and Malta. I was in a rush to leave left New York and I'd forgotten to pack socks, so I had to make a quick stop at the department store."

Then it clicked, "Oh, now I remember. You're that fella I gave directions to at the mall. Well I'll be . . . small world ain't it!"

Jameson remembered the encounter. "YES, that was you! And if I might add, you had a beautiful little girl with you. She gave me some of her candy."

"Yep, that would be my granddaughter, Rose's little girl Charlotte. She is the love of this old coot's life. Maybe you can stay until she gets home. She had a half of a bag of candy left if I'm not mistaken."

Jameson smiled. "I'd love to thank her if that's okay."

As they entered the house, a woman's voice bellowed from the kitchen.

"You sons-of-bitches had better remove your boots or I'll pepper your asses with my shotgun!"

Jameson cringed. *Does everyone in Montana own a shotgun?*

Raymond and Keough hollered, "Don't shoot Rose, we have company."

"I don't care. Unless you're God or George Strait . . . take off your boots!" All three men removed their boots and shoes leaving them outside by the front door.

Rose came from the kitchen with a pot of coffee asking, "Who's the stray, and if he ain't carrying a brand, fire up the irons so we can keep 'em."

She put the pot on the table and walked over to Jameson, "Hello I'm Amelia Montana. You must be Meryl's son Jameson, nice to meet you and sorry about the shotgun threat. I never know what these two will drag in. And trust me, most of the time it ain't pretty."

Now understand why mother gave me the no flirting warning . . . she is fucking gorgeous! Jameson smiled and told her it was a pleasure to finally meet her and that Raymond was very helpful guiding him to the ranch.

"In fact, he only threatened to shoot me twice. From what I understand that is a record for him."

Raymond poured a cup of coffee and handed it to Jameson. "Here take this and sit down before I change my mind." He winked at Rose and poured two more; one for him and one for Keough. He motioned for him to come out on the deck.

"Come on you old buzzard. Let's give these two some privacy so he can get back to New York City. I'd hate to see him get lost on his way to the airport. We wouldn't find him until next spring and that's if the coyotes don't eat him first."

Keough laughed, "Aw, come on Raymond, he ain't that bad. Heck, I helped him find the men's department when he was looking for socks. By the way what kind did you get? Hold on . . . I bet he got the kind with them little diamonds on 'em. What are they called Rose?"

"They're called argyles. And you would know that if you ever bought new ones you decrepit heathen. And, don't you both have ranch work to do? "

Raymond put his empty cup in the sink as Keough took a final sip of his coffee. "Okay you don't have to tell me twice. I know when I'm not wanted. Treating me like this will not get you one of them fancy Mother's Day cards next year."

I pointed to the door, "GET OUT . . . NOW!"

"Okay, I'm leaving. Take care that she don't bite you Jameson. Her rabies shots ain't up-to-date."

Both men walked out onto the deck but not before mouthing *Love you Rose* and a friendly wink."

"Sorry about that Mr. Wellesley. Now, how about we start over . . . I'm Rose and welcome to the Montana Ranch."

"Thank you, and please call me Jameson. After being threatened by Raymond and almost shot twice I beginning to feel like family. Of course, it would be the Capone family but hey, like they say you can't pick your family."

We chatted for more than two hours about how his family became one of the largest corporate entities in the United States and abroad.

"We have offices in France and England."

I excused myself and took our cups into the kitchen and poured another cup of coffee.

"Thank you Rose. I love this blend. Raymond told me it was your husband's special brew."

"Yep, Joe did love his coffee. There are times I thought he loved it more than me. But I learned that fiction writers are night dwellers and survive on caffeine and very little sleep."

I started to look over the contract when I noticed it was almost noon and time to pick up Charlotte.

"Oh shit, I've got to go pick up my daughter! She'll think I've abandoned her. Sorry Jameson I've got to run. You can wait here until I come back but I've got to leave now."

Jameson said that would be fine, and if it was okay he'd like to sit, relax and have more coffee.

"Please be my guest and help yourself to the banana nut muffins. Cecelia baked them this morning."

I ran out the door with car keys. A few seconds later I ran back into the house.

Jameson had a mouth full of muffin when I explained in a near panic tone that Raymond had my car blocked in and he was out in the large pasture fixing fences and I needed a ride to Charlotte's school.

"Hey, not a problem, let me clean up the truck a little bit." Jameson ran out to the rented vehicle and started throwing stuff in the back seat. *Thank goodness it has an extended cab!*

I grabbed Charlotte's car seat and ran to the truck.

"Sorry, but it's the law she's gotta be in her car seat or they won't let us leave with her – safety first."

She lifted it in the back with barely enough room to spare. She was pushing empty fast food containers onto the floor when she noticed a Frank Zappa CD lying on the floor mat.   *This is the guy from the shopping center parking lot!*

Jameson ran over to the passenger's side and helped her with the seat. They jumped in the truck and sped off to the daycare arriving with three minutes to spare.

Charlotte was waiting patiently outside the front door holding onto Grace's hand. Jameson parked the truck directly in front of the door. Grace didn't recognize the truck so she stepped back inside the center's door. When she saw me running toward the door, she came back outside with Charlotte.

"I'm so sorry Gracie. I was caught up in an interview and before I realized it was time to pick up Charlotte." I picked up Charlotte and kissed her cheek. "Hey Baby Girl, did you have a good time with Gracie?"

She said yes, then pointed and asked, "Mama, who it that man?"

"That's a very nice man named Mr. Wellesley. Mama is writing a story for him."

Charlotte stared then smiled, "I remember him; I gave him candy!"

I was puzzled by her statement and looked back at Jameson. "When did you give him candy Charlotte?"

She ran over to Jameson, "Hi, my name is Charlotte! This is my doggy lil' Lou." She held up the stuffed toy for Jameson to pet. "He doesn't like candy."

Jameson stooped down, "Well hello, Charlotte. It's nice to meet you again. And thank you for helping me at the shopping center."

She smiled and said, "You're welcome. Can we go home now Mama? I want him to meet Lou."

"Yes Baby, we can go home, and again Grace I'm so sorry for being late. It won't happen again."

"No worries. She is a delight! And it was very nice to meet you Mr. Wellesley. We hope we'll see you at the ribbon cutting of the new playground you and Mr. Montana helped to fund. It's absolutely beautiful and made from recycled, environmentally safe materials."

"Thank you, I would be honored to attend," Jameson explained to Grace. "To be honest, I had completely forgotten about the event, but yes you can count on me to be there. I'm sure Mrs. Montana would be happy to accompany me – wouldn't you Amelia."

"Ah, sure that would be great. I'm looking forward to it." *Pushy son of a bitch!*

They were about to leave when Dr. Henry came outside. "Hello, you must be Mr. Wellesley. I'm Dr. Sara Henry. I guess you could say I run this place. But, truth be told, it's the kids and these amazing graduate students that keep it going. I hope we can count on you being at the opening of our new playground?"

Jameson nodded, "Absolutely! As a matter of fact, both Mrs. Montana and I will be attending."

"Brilliant. The children will be very happy to meet the people who made this playground possible."

I gathered Charlotte's daycare gear and headed over to the truck. After strapping Charlotte into her car seat, I walked over to the driver's side to confront Jameson.

"I don't know you very well but let me say this and I'm only going to say it once. Nobody, I mean NOBODY speaks for me. I'm quite capable of speaking for myself and before you offer me up as a date, I'd appreciate it if you at least ask me!"

Jameson leaned back on the truck and grinned. I was about to walk back to the passenger's side but I did a double-take. *I know that grin. It's the same shit-eating grin Joe would flash when he was trying to put on over on me.* I climbed into the truck and asked him if he were going to get in or stand there looking like a dumb ass.

Charlotte giggled, "Ooh, Mama called you a bad name."

For a moment, I forgot Charlotte was in the back seat. "I'm sorry Baby. Mama said a bad word and thank you for reminding me."

"It's okay Mama. Pap-Pap says bad words too."

I reminded myself to have a word with Keough!

During the drive home, I thought back to her reaction to Jameson's behavior. *It's the sort of thing Joe would do. Come to think of it, there are quite a few similarities about him that remind me of Joe – his grin, his mannerisms when he's joking and his love of coffee. Thank God he looks nothing like Joe. With that mustache, beard and glasses I can't tell what he looks like. He might be good-looking or look like the Elephant Man! Plus Joe had blue-green eyes and his are brown.*

We were about a mile from home when Charlotte needed a restroom break. I'd been trying to potty-train for weeks. We made quick stop at the local gas station and it was just in a nick of time. I praised her for her good work and we washed our hands. I gave her a high-five and headed back to the truck. Jameson was chatting with the station owner when I overheard him asking about where the local bar was. *I haven't known this guy long enough to drive him to drink.* I let it go and put Charlotte back into her car seat.

He walked over toward Charlotte and asked her if she was okay.

"Yes, I made number one and washed my hands all by myself!"

"And clean hands they are." Jameson took hold of her hands and kissed her palms. It caught me off-guard. *Something else Joe would do. This is getting very strange. Maybe he knows more about my family than he's letting on.*

Fifteen minutes later, they pulled up to the house. Raymond and Keough were standing by the barn.

"Sorry we blocked you in. We lost track of the time. Thank you Jameson for helpin' out our gals."

"I was happy to help. I think I'll take a quick nap and go into town to check out the local night life."

Raymond laughed, "Night life? The town had one bar and one movie theater. Not much night life. However, if you stray into the prairie after dark you'll encounter plenty of wildlife. Wouldn't want you to get eaten by lions, tiger and bears – oh my!"

Jameson thanked Raymond for his sarcastic concern and went back to the bunkhouse.

I asked Raymond and Keough to come inside for a second, and I told them about his urgent need to find a bar.

"I'm worried about this. I noticed three small airline bottles of alcohol under the back seat of his truck. He may or may not have been drinking while driving, but it still concerns me."

Raymond agreed with me saying he had the same apprehension. "When I saw him this morning he did seem a bit hung over. Maybe it was travel or jet lag – I don't know."

We all promised to keep an eye on him. I also told Raymond that Cecilia had made lunch and they should come inside and eat. I didn't have to tell Raymond twice. He made a bee-line toward the kitchen. Keough was already eating.

"Hey, save some for me. I need to check my email and there had better be some food left over." I could barely make out their answer through their stuffed mouths.

Twenty-four messages in the queue. Two were from Theo and one was from Joe's email account. Although I knew it was from the prewritten emails Joe left for his lawyer to periodically send me, my heart still skipped a beat when I saw his name. I clicked that one first.

To: Rose
Fr: Montana Joe

Subject: **Convergence by Jackson Pollock & other jokes of art, Part 3 of 5**

Hello Darlin'. Having a terminal illness is as bad as it gets! Some days are lousy and some days are tolerable. Today is a good day, so I'm writing a few more emails to you so that my lawyer can send them after I'm gone. I'm not in too much pain today and dadgumit Girl, I almost feel like my old self. Good enough to take you up into the hay loft for some passionate, cowboy style love makin'! And since the pain medicine is affecting my hung-like-a-horse ability I guess it's a moot point.

With that being said, I hope you and Charlotte are moving on with your lives and tryin' to get back to some sense of normalcy. Is Cecilia still cooking too much food? Being as sick as I am, I couldn't appreciate it as much as I used to. But I did enjoy her enchilada casseroles. Always ate too much but it was worth it.

I'm sorry for leaving you so soon. It ain't fair Darlin' – life ain't fair. But I'm glad it's me who went first. I don't know what I would have done without you. You made this old boy's life worth livin'. Something no one else in the world could ever do. And the anticipation of being a new dad again kept me holdin' on as long as I did. I know I'll possibly be gone before she's born. But I'm happy we found out we were having a girl and decided on her name before my illness worsened. Did I get to see and hold her Rose? I hope I did. I guess I'll never know. Yes, I know I'm writing in past and present tense but I wanted to cover all of my bases, just in case by some miracle I survive this crap!

Baby, I'm startin' to get a bit weary. These dang drugs I'm taking don't help either. I can feel myself driftin' in and out of consciousness, so I'll leave you with a poem I wrote:

The Drifter

Beneath a starry western sky a drifter drifted into town

His face and neck all red and raw
A hat with tattered brim turned down, he says,
"I jist come here to sit a spell and rest my horse a while
to wet my whistle with some drink
to see them purty ladies smile
I ain't been long from east to west
My life is like the wind I guess
But like my name I've come to know
I've got no better place to go
Driftin' along with the tumbleweeds
my painted horse is all I need"
At morning's light, without a sound,

the drifter leaves the western town.

Adios Cuppy. Give our little girl a kiss from her daddy. And always know I love you both more than my coffee, whoa . . . now that's some serious lovin'!

Always,

Your Montana cowboy, Joe

I took off my glasses and wiped my eyes. I was too emotional to open the other emails. *Just when I think I'm okay, I get another email from him. I know his intentions were good; however, I don't think he realized how hard it would be to read his emails after his death. However, as much as they hurt I don't know what I would do if they ended.*

Of course, Jannine would probably scold me. "Rose, I know he meant well, but is this healthy for you?"

In my heart-of-hearts, I knew she was right – it wasn't healthy. *I miss him so much.* I took a deep breath and headed outside for some fresh air. Jameson was sitting on the railing of the bunkhouse on his cell phone, drinking a beer. *We don't drink beer. Where did he get it? God, I hope Keough hasn't started drinking again.*

He waved and tipped the beer bottle acknowledging my glance. I gave a timid wave back and went back inside. Raymond came from the hay barn with Keough behind him. Both men seemed sober. I motioned for them to come over.

"Did either of you purchase beer today?"

They looked at each other and answered no. Keough asked why, and I pointed at Jameson.

"I came outside for some air and saw Jameson sitting outside the bunkhouse, on his cell phone, with a beer. It concerned me because I thought . . ."

Keough took off his hat and looked me in the eye. "You were worried that I'd started drinkin' again, weren't you?"

"To be honest, yes I was worried. I was very worried. But I knew you would never go back on the promise you made to your son."

He held my shoulders. "And I'd never break a promise to YOU! I love you and that baby girl too much to go back to being a worthless drunk."

Raymond said, "Perhaps I should have a word with him. He's already scared of me. And frankly . . . it would be fun to shake him up again."

"I appreciate your offer Raymond. Let's just keep an eye on him – okay?"

"Rose, for you I'll back off. But if he starts acting like a loco prairie rat, all bets are off."

Raymond went back into the hay barn. Keough excused himself and headed toward the bunkhouse. Jameson was still on his cell phone when he noticed Keough coming up the stairs. He turned his back and whispered into the phone, "...*and a fifth of Dewars. I'll be there in thirty minutes* then walked back inside.

Keough walked in closing the door behind him.

"Hey Keough, sorry I had to take that – business call. What's up?"

Keough picked up the empty beer bottle. "Business huh, what kind of business involves ordering scotch? You've been drinkin' since you've arrived in Montana. Now you may or may not know it, but I'm a recovering alcoholic, and I'd appreciate it if you didn't bring that shit into our bunkhouse! I ain't sayin' you can't drink, I'm just sayin' you can't drink here. Ain't a crucible about it – just don't want it around me."

Keough handed the bottle to Jameson who promptly threw it in the trash.

"Sorry Keough, I didn't know about your drinking issues. I should have been more respectful of the Montana household rules. I promise as long as I'm here I will not consume large quantities of the evil brew."

Keough became increasingly irritated with his sarcastic comments. "So you think this is funny, do ya'? Well, it ain't! My daughter-in-law and that beautiful little girl are the most important people in my life. I don't know you, and to be honest I don't like you very much. But you're a guest here, and I expect you to act like you have a horse-hair of decency and stay sober."

"Okay Keough. Now if you don't mind I've got an errand to run." He headed down the steps to his truck.

He brushed by Raymond coming up the stairs. Keough stood in the doorway fuming. Raymond watched as Jameson peeled out of the driveway. "What's wrong with him?"

Keough confessed that he had confronted Jameson about his drinking. "I swear that boy really pisses me the hell off! He's an arrogant, son-of-a-bitch with a drinking problem the size of his ego!"

Raymond shook his head and grinned.

"What the hell are you laughin' at? I'm tellin' you this fella's got a drinkin' problem and you're laughin' like I just told you the dirty joke of the day!"

Raymond said, "I'm laughing because he reminds me of someone else I know. Oh, and in case you haven't figured out who it is – it's YOU!"

Keough's face turned beet red. "What the hell are you on Raymond? That snot-nosed rich kid is nothin' like me! He's obnoxious, and he doesn't respect his elders."

Raymond motioned for Keough to sit down. "Keough, there is an ancient Indian proverb, 'before you judge a man, walk a mile in his shoes. After that, who cares? You're a mile away and you've got his shoes.' "

"That ain't no old Indian proverb ya' dang fool. That's a quote from comedian, Billy Connolly!"

Raymond shrugged, "Billy Connelly, old Indian proverb, same-same. My point is you are judging him the same way you judge yourself. You remember the pain that drinking caused your family and in some selfless way you want to keep him from making the same mistakes."

"ME . . . helpin' him? I ain't doin' nothin' of the sort. I could care less if he drinks himself into a coma. He annoys me beyond belief!"

Raymond stood up and placed his hand on Keough's shoulder. "Yes, he is annoying. And I hate to say he reminds me of another annoying white man – your son, Joe."

Chapter 10

Morgan stared at the gate waiting to catch a glimpse of Jannine. Her flight was running late. He fiddled with the case in his pocket which held her engagement ring. *What if she says no? Come on Morgan, enough of the negative self-talk.* He flashed back to the first time he picked her up from the same airport. It seems like years ago. *She was intolerable, and now she's the love of my life.* A few minutes later, he saw her dressed in jeans, a tee shirt and a suede jacket holding on to a small carry-on. *How time and love changes a person.*

Morgan tucked the ring case deeper into his jean pocket. He wanted to surprise her – but not yet. He wanted to wait until they arrived at the ranch just in case she said no. *Relax, I can't imagine her refusing expensive jewelry.*

She saw Morgan and let out a screech. "Well hello Handsome! You look good enough to eat. How've you been holding up without me? And you had better say horrible. I've missed you Sweetie."

"You know I've missed you and so has Rose. You're her best friend in the world, and I can see why."

He lifted her off her feet and gave her a long kiss. "Why don't we continue this back at the ranch? I hear tell there's a secluded hay loft just waiting for two people to roll in."

Jannine smiled in agreement. On the drive back, Jannine caught Morgan up with all the New York gossip—how their condo neighbors were getting a divorce, how they finally fired their Executive Director, Bernard Pollintino for the handling of Rose's termination and how the magazine promoted his female executive assistant to take his place. She then promoted Rick for defending her and Rose.

"And here I thought Rick was a wimp. When he told me he stood up to old Bernie and told him to go fuck himself for trying to fire me, I cried. It turns out Rick is one hell-of-a-decent guy. I guess it's true. You can't judge a book by its cover, huh."

Morgan agreed. "That right Darlin', if I'd judged you by your cover, I would have hauled ass the moment we met. And look at us now. We're madly in love and living together. And I'm about to ask you to . . ."

He stopped his sentence in a nick of time. He almost blew her surprise. Thank goodness Jannine wasn't paying attention and was reaming him out over the haul-ass comment.

Morgan caught her up-to-date on the goings on at the ranch which included how Keough stayed sober and has become such a good grandfather to Charlotte, how Raymond hired someone to look after the cabins so he could stay on helping Rose and how Paul, the British trucker has become a frequent visitor.

"He's really a nice fellow. I really enjoy talking with him when I can understand him."

Jannine thought that was very interesting. "How's Rose with that? Does she, eh, enjoy his visits?"

Morgan knew what she was asking in a roundabout way.

"If you're asking if she's interested in Paul, well yeah, she likes him; but, I don't think she's ready for that kind of relationship. However, I bet if anyone could get her out of her funk – it would be Paul. He's a great guy and cares about her more than he lets on."

Jannine thought the ride to the ranch seemed shorter than the last time she visited. Perhaps it was the fact that they talked the entire way and this time she knew where they were going. An hour later, they pulled into the driveway.

Jannine stepped out of the truck. "Hola Casa Montana, you look and smell just like I remember!"

I heard the truck and hurried out to greet them. "Oh my God, how the heck are ya' Girl. I've missed you so much!"

Morgan came out of the truck with her carry-on, and I did a double take.

"Okay, I see Morgan has your makeup bag – where's the rest of your luggage?"

Jannine stuck her tongue at me. "Hah, very funny Rose, for your information, this is all I have. And yes, I'm wearing Wranglers and a tee shirt. I'm horrified to admit your western style has rubbed off on me. But I draw the line at Carhartt."

I hugged her and told her I didn't care if she came to Montana in Bill Blass overhauls and Jimmy Choo work boots; it was good to see her. Charlotte and Keough came from the kitchen. "Well, if it ain't the most beautiful gal in New York City come to visit us. How are ya' Darlin'?" Charlotte ran over and hugged Jannine's legs.

"Aunt Jan-Jan, you look pretty, just like Mama!" Jannine knelt down and hugged her. "And how's my little cowgirl princess! I can't believe how much you've grown. You must be at least 5-years-old, right?"

Charlotte yelled, "NO, I'm two-and-a-half, almost three – right Mama?"

"Yes, you are Baby Girl and just as ornery as you're Aunt Jannine!"

Morgan picked up Charlotte saying, "You're not ornery, Charlotte; you're just extremely opinionated."

Charlotte giggled and kissed Morgan on his cheek.

I grabbed Jannine by the hand and led her into the kitchen. "You two must be starved. I was about to fix dinner, but if you'd like a snack, Cecilia has a bunch of leftover barbecued chicken. Nothing fancy so grab a couple of pieces and chow down."

Jannine and Charlotte didn't wait for us. They had already started rummaging through the refrigerator and found the plate of chicken. Morgan motioned for me to come back into the living room. He took a small blue velvet box from his pocket.

"Is that what I think it is?"

"Yep, after dinner I'm going to ask Jannine to marry me. And please don't start crying or it'll ruin my surprise."

"Oh Morgan, she is going to be so happy! You know she really loves you. And to be honest, I never thought she would ever settle down. She's such a free spirit; however, if anyone could lasso her, I'm glad it's you. I'm so excited for you both!"

"I'm really excited too, so let's try to stay calm until I slip it on her finger, okay."

I promised not to say a word. He'd tucked it back into his jean pocket when she came out the kitchen looking for us with a chicken leg in her hand.

"Morgan, if you're not going to eat, I'm having seconds. I swear I can't seem to stop eating when I'm in Montana – must be the altitude."

I smiled at Morgan and whispered, "We'd better go and eat or she'll think something is up. Your fiancée is very intuitive."

We hugged and headed into the kitchen.

Later that evening, Charlotte and I decided to go visit Raymond. I wanted to let Morgan and Jannine have the house to themselves so Morgan could pop the question without a rambunctious toddler interrupting the moment. I decided to take Joe's truck. Charlotte loved riding in Joe's truck instead of my compact car. I think it was because it belonged to her daddy. She said she wished Daddy could come with us. I told her that Daddy was always with us, and if she closed her eyes, she could feel him hugging her. That made her smile. I must admit there were times I could feel his presence telling me not to gun the engine and ease up off the clutch sooner. Before we left, I told Morgan not to wait up for us. If it got too late, we'd stay overnight at Raymond's place. Jannine asked why we were going out when they'd just arrived.

I had to think quickly, so I told her I had to pick up a blanket Raymond had made for Charlotte. I was telling the truth; he did make a beautiful Indian blanket for her, but there was no rush to be picked up.

I winked at Morgan and mouthed, *good luck!*

Jannine brought two glasses and the rest of the dinner wine into the living room. They sat and chatted about how big Charlotte was getting and how I looked just as radiant as ever. Morgan moved over toward Jannine and kissed her.

"That was nice, but what was that for?"

"Nothing, do I need a reason to kiss one of the most beautiful girls in Montana. Well, not counting Charlotte and Mom of course."

Jannine laughed and kissed him back.

"You know Morgan, as much as I hate to admit it, I'm beginning to love Montana. Who'd have thought that I, Jannine Westone, an incorrigible New York diva would enjoy living in the wilderness – crazy huh?"

"Yep, that's you, an incorrigible diva, with closets and a heart as big as the state of Montana."

Morgan asked her to close her eyes and to visualize Rose and Joe on their wedding day.

"Can you see how happy they were and how unbelievable their love was and still is?"

"Yes, I can. I remember every minute of that wedding. I also remember how handsome you were."

Morgan stood up telling her to keep her eyes closed.

"Hurry up Morgan. I can't stand the suspense! What's going on?" Morgan slipped the ring on Jannine's finger. "Okay, you can open your eyes now." She stared at him then at her hand.

"OH MY GOD Morgan! I can't believe it, and I can't believe you picked this out all by yourself. And more importantly, why the hell didn't you let me go with you? Oh who cares! I love it . . . love, love it!"

Morgan laughed, "You know you would have tried on every ring in New York City before you made up your mind. We'd end up saying our ' Do's with two pieces of twisted bailing wire."

Jannine held out her hand and kept looking at her ring.

"I wish I could honestly say that it didn't matter what kind of ring you gave me, but this huge diamond ring is so me – it's perfect.

Morgan held her hand and kissed her palm. "Do you think Dad would like it?"

Jannine nodded, "Yes, I know Joe would love it." They sat back down on the couch. "I wish he were here. I'd hoped your dad would be our best man and Rose my matron of honor. It's not fair Morgan! Joe was more like a father to me than my own father. He was the only man who took me seriously."

Jannine wiped her eyes on Morgan's sleeve. He was going to tease her but realized she was genuinely upset. He offered her a napkin.

"It's okay to cry Jannine. I miss him too. No one ever expects to find a long-lost parent only to lose them."

Jannine said, "I'll tell you a secret Morgan. When I first met your father I thought he was the strangest man on the face of the earth. To be honest, I thought he was some whacko stalker obsessed with Amelia. But after seeing them together and watching them fall deeper and deeper in love, I knew it was genuine – a unique and once-in-a-lifetime love. It's the kind of love I hope we'll have after we're married."

Morgan reached out for Jannine's hand. He looked at the ring, then at Jannine.

"If we have half the love Rose and Dad had, we'll have an amazing marriage."

A moment later, Charlotte and I walked into the kitchen to find Jannine and Morgan misty-eyed in each other's arms. I cleared my throat and asked if it were okay to come in. They motioned for me to come in and have a seat. Jannine's cheeks were covered with tears and smeared mascara. I handed her a wad of paper towels. When she reached for it I noticed the large rock on her finger.

"Whoa, old on Missy! When did this happen?"

Jannine said, "Morgan slipped it on my finger a few minutes ago, and then we started thinking about how Joe wouldn't be here to see us get hitched. The next thing we knew we were sobbing , and my eye makeup was ruined and oh, Amelia, we miss Joe so much."

It took a few seconds to follow Jannine's train of thought. But it was Charlotte who snapped me back into reality.

"Mama, will Jannine be my other mama because she's marrying Morgan?"

Jannine laughed. Morgan said, "No but she will be your big sister-in-law, isn't that exciting?"

"YES, I love Jannine!"

Jannine picked up Charlotte up and said how happy she was to be her big sister and how much fun they would have playing with all of her dolls. "How about your soon-to-be big sister gives her soon-to-be little sister a bubble bath? And you get to pick whatever bubble bath you like – how's that?"

"I would love that! Goodnight Mama and Morg."

"Goodnight Sweetie, I love you."

She blew us a kiss and disappeared with Jannine down the hallway.

Jannine offered to bathe her so that Morgan and I could chat about the evening's event. I was eager to find out how everything went. Did he get down on one knee or did he hide the ring in the dessert or a glass of wine? Morgan was obviously different from Joe who carried my ring around in his saddle bag for weeks. I thought he was pulling out a piece of jerky when he pulled out the ring—not that jerky isn't romantic, but the perfect two-carat diamond ring made me weak in the knees. Everything Joe and I did seemed romantic – it was just his way. Whether it was mucking out the horse stalls or changing the oil in his truck, we enjoyed doing it as a couple.

Morgan asked if I'd like a cup of tea. It was late, and we didn't want to be up because of caffeine. I said I'd love a cuppa. Morgan looked at me and laughed, "A Cuppa? Hmm, sounds quite British if you ask me. I think Paul's lingo is rubbing off on you."

I was embarrassed but had to agree. Listening to Paul talk was soothing. I guess it's because his accent is so different from everyone else's in Montana. *I wonder how he's doing. We haven't heard from him in weeks.*

Morgan sat down and told me how much he loved Jannine. He thought back to the first time they'd met saying how different they were.

"How someone like her could ever be interested in a Montana cowboy like me," he reminisced. "Then I thought about you and Dad and how the universe brought together two people from completely different walks of life through countless insane twists of fate until you fell in love and married. How amazing is that!"

"Yes Morgan, it was a remarkable journey of random occurrences; a remarkable union that brought you and Jannine together. And people say there's no such thing as miracles?"

The whistling of the kettle reminded us the water for our tea was ready. It was a blend Paul brought me during one of his visits. He said that the tea in America wasn't strong enough, so his brother Tom would send him British care packages consisting of tea, biscuits and English sweets. I had to admit it was nice having tea in the evening instead of Joe's potent blend of coffee. Not that I would give up coffee, but tea was a pleasant change of pace. We finished our conversation and tea at the same time Jannine finished bathing and reading to Charlotte. I asked her if she was getting practice for the future.

She laughed, "No not yet, but maybe, someday Morgan and I will have kids. I never thought those words would ever come out of my highly-lip-glossed mouth, but I never thought I'd find someone like Morgan."

We all agreed it was a topic for future conversation as it was getting late. Morgan gave me a hug and said goodnight. He and Jannine headed off to the guest room. I grabbed a blanket off of the couch, wrapped it around my shoulders and walked outside. Gazing at the stars made me feel closer to Joe. I searched for the stars he'd dedicated to me and Charlotte, but the moon was so bright, I couldn't locate them. I could still see the horses grazing in the small pasture. *I must remember to order more sweet feed.* I'm sure if I asked Morgan and Keough, they would pick it up for me tomorrow. Maybe Jannine might like to go with them to get a taste of what it's like to work a ranch. *I still can't picture her in barn boots and work gloves.* The visual made me chuckle although it wasn't long ago I laughed at that same image of me in the exact get-up.

As I was about to head inside, the clouds dipped in front of the moon and I was able to see our stars. It was as if Joe moved them aside just for me.

"Thank you, Baby and remember no matter how our lives change, we'll always be Montanas." I blew him a kiss, and I swore I felt Joe's lips kiss me back. "Goodnight Joe."

The smell of freshly brewed coffee woke me up. Keough must have made a pot before he fed the horses. *God bless that man!* Then I remembered it was Saturday. I didn't need to get Charlotte ready for day school. The only thing I needed to do was to edit the article for the Montford-Wellesley Corporation. Hopefully, I'll have it done today so that her pain-in-the-ass son can go back to New York. *I can't believe how annoying and arrogant he is! But to be honest I said the same thing about Joe when I first met him. And look at how that turned out. Come to think of it, there's something about him that reminds me of Joe. I wonder what he looks like under all of that facial hair and without those designer glasses; probably just a clean shaven asshole.*

I laughed to myself and poured some coffee. I bet he thinks the same thing about me; just another haughty, pontificating art critic who just happened to marry well and inherit a ranch the size of Manhattan. Then again, what the hell do I care what he thinks? He'll be gone soon, and I'll get a big fat check in the mail courtesy of the Montford-

Wellesley Corporation. I took another sip of my coffee and noticed a note on the kitchen table.

Rose,

Jameson said he'd be by the house at 1:00 PM and wanted to know if you'd like to finalize the article over lunch – his treat. Keough . . . PS I added the 'his treat' part; let the son of a bitch pay for it, ha-ha-ha!

I agreed with Keough. We'd put up with him for almost a week, so let him shell out some cash for a change.

I'd just picked up my notes when I noticed Morgan was up and heading towards the shower.

"Hey Mr. I'm-engaged-to-be-married, how did you sleep?" I handed him a cup of coffee. He thanked me saying he slept well except for Jannine's cold feet.

"Good Lord, I've never met a woman with such cold feet. They're like icebergs!"

His tone of voice and statement sounded so much like his dad. It made me smile. Joe always complained about my cold feet and pointy elbows.

"That's okay, after you're married you can be her love quilt and keep her warm."

"Why wait until we're married?"

I gave him a motherly look and pointed to the bathroom. He laughed all the way down the hall and closed the bathroom door.

Morgan had stepped into the shower, and I saw Jannine came stumbling down the hall. I recognized that look. It was her I'm-in-dire-need-of-coffee look. I guided her over to the kitchen table and poured her a cup. I asked her if she slept well. She nodded. "So you were warm enough?" She nodded again then took a long swig of coffee.

"Okay, now I'm awake . . . what where you saying?"

I told her that her fiancé was in the shower and mentioned something about her iceberg feet.

"Oh, REALLY! He's saying MY feet are cold? His could be used as a method of cryogenics! After we're married I'm going to make him wear socks to bed."

"I know I'm going to regret asking but . . . why after you're married, why not now?"

"That would be weird Rose. He's my fiancé for goodness sakes. I don't want to see him butt naked wearing only socks! Once we're married it won't matter what he sleeps in."

No one else in the world made me laugh like Jannine. Her outlook on life was priceless, and the funny thing was that most of the time she was being dead serious. I asked Jannine if she'd thought about where and when they would tie the knot. She said they hadn't planned anything yet, but she assured me it would be in Montana.

"Rose, I've become very fond of this state and to tell you the truth I wouldn't mind living here. But please don't mention anything to Morgan. He'll have me wearing overalls, cowboy boots and saying words like y'all, reckon and fixin'.""

Glancing down at my own barn boots, "Y'all say that like it's a bad thing, Miss Jannine."

She gave me a huge hug. "I love you, Amelia." I hugged her back and whispered, "You'd better check on her fiancé or you'll be taking a cold shower for the wrong reasons. He's been in there for over 30-minutes."

"Oh really?" She walked over to the kitchen sink and turned on both facets. Morgan let out a yell.

"What the hell just happened? The water went icy cold!"

Jannine walked down the hall and opened the door. "I just wanted to make sure you saved some hot water for your fiancée . . . now get out!"

She tossed Morgan out with only a towel wrapped around his bottom half. He asked if he could have another towel to dry his hair. Another towel flew out the door barely missing his face.

He looked over at me and said, "I swear that gal's as loony as a bedbug. But oh how I love her so."

He is definitely Joe's son. I wish he was here to see how happy he and Jannine are together. *Joe if you're listening, give me a sign.* I waited a few seconds truly expecting him to send me some kind of response. But nothing happened. *Maybe he's on a coffee break.* I chuckled to myself and headed to the barn. I met up with Keough on the way and asked him if he'd seen Jameson.

"I ain't seen hide or hair of him. And it'll be too soon before I want to see him again. He really rubs my whiskers the wrong way!"

I thought it was an odd thing for him to say that seeing they were so much alike in their demeanor. There were times he acted more like Keough than Joe. *I wonder if he notices the similarities. Maybe that's why Jameson gets under his skin.*

"If you see him before I do, tell him I'm finished editing the article, and I'll email a copy to his mother. If they need me to tweak it, I'd be happy to do so."

Keough begrudgingly said he would deliver the message and reminded me to take him up on his lunch. I told him if we did have lunch, I would bring him back a doggy bag. He flashed me the *okay* sign and headed back to work in the small pasture.

I could see Raymond's truck coming up the driveway. It had been very dry lately, and the truck's rear wheels kicked up a cloud of dust behind them. He parked in his usual spot beside the barn. Before getting out, he reached in the back seat and grabbed a small bag then walked over to the door to meet me.

Raymond bent down and grabbed a handful of dirt. "We could really use some rain. It's not good for the pasture grass or the horses."

"Hey could you teach us a rain dance? Maybe if we all did it together, we'd create a good soaking, huh?"

Raymond shook his head, "Now, you sound just like that flea-bitten-mangy-desert vermin husband of yours. And here I thought you were better than that Rose."

He winked and me and tossed the dirt back onto the ground. "Nonetheless, I would teach you all the rain dances I know, if it would bring some rain our way."

"Oh before I forget, I have a present for you. Well, it's a present for you and Nadie. Speaking of Charlotte, where is she? There is a present in the bag for her too."

I told Raymond that she was still sleeping, and I'd like to keep her sleeping for at least another hour. "Lord knows I love that little gal, but she is a handful."

"Yes, just like her father," Raymond agreed. "It still puzzles me what you saw in that loco old saddlebum. I swear he still annoys me just thinking about him. And, I loved him like a brother."

"And he loved you too. I thought there were times he loved you more than me. I've never had a true friendship with anyone like you and Joe had. The closest friend I have is Jannine and she's more like a sister-daughter than a peer."

Raymond looked at me and smile. "Trust me, Amelia, Joe loved you more than life. He still does – look over there."

Three hummingbirds gathered around a patch of wildflowers growing near the barn. They hovered for more than a minute while we watched them jockey for nectar. One of them darted over towards us and hovered between us. Raymond told me to hold out my hand. I didn't want to move because I knew it would fly off.

"Trust me Amelia, hold out your hand and watch what happens."

I slowly stretched out my hand and was completely shocked that it hovered directly over it – then perched on my palm. I stared at it for a full minute; afterward, it shot off and joined the others. Such a moving and mystical experience I'll never forget. Raymond said that the hummingbird was a good sign and a gift.

"Oh, I almost forgot to tell you, there's a drum circle happening next week if you'd like to go. I'd be happy to escort you. It'll be fun."

"I'd love to Raymond. Remember the last time we went, and I thought I heard Joe's voice. Who knows—maybe he'll send a message to us. Do you believe in that kind of stuff?"

"Of course I do, I'm Blackfoot. We are very spiritual people. I believe that energy never dies. It travels through eternity reminding us that we are all one – well, except for Joe. He was a one-of-a-kind. Sometimes I wonder how the universe would react if there were two of him. It would probably cause an apocalypse. I shiver to think about two Joes. One of him in my life time was more than enough!"

Both of us had a good laugh at Joe's expense. He wouldn't want us mourning him. That wasn't the kind of man he was or as he would say, "It ain't my style."

Raymond asked if he could borrow one of our saddles. He was rehearsing a pre-wedding ceremony and the couple wanted him to ride in dressed in his full Blackfoot regalia.

"Of course you can. I didn't know you owned a horse."

"I don't. May I also borrow a horse too? It would be rather silly riding a saddle with nothing under it. How about Daisy, she's gentle and slow just like me?"

I had to laugh because I always assumed he was an accomplished rider. I knew he'd be okay riding Daisy. She was such a sweet and well-trained horse. Joe did a great job with her and Keough was getting Daisy Duce to follow in her hoof steps. Raymond put the saddle into the back of his truck. I helped him hook up the trailer and load Daisy.

He was half way down the road when Charlotte came running out of the house screaming. "Mama, why is Daisy going with Raymond?" Her screaming turned into weeping. I assured her that Raymond would bring her back and she was helping him with a special event.

"Daisy is going to be in a wedding. Isn't that exciting! She's going to have flowers and ceremonial feathers in her bridle. I bet if you ask Raymond, he'll take a photo for you of her all dressed up. Would you like that?"

Charlotte nodded. "I hope she behaves at the wedding and doesn't fart. That would be funny wouldn't it Mama?" We giggled imagining Daisy passing gas while the couple was saying their vows.

Laughing about Daisy kept her from crying. I remembered the gifts Raymond brought us. I handed the bag to Charlotte. "Oh, Raymond brought us a prize. Let's see what's inside shall we?"

She reached into the bag and gave me two beautifully carved animal spirit guide totems. One was in the shape of a bear the other a hummingbird. There was a note attached to each one explaining what each animal meant. My name was attached to the bear and Charlotte's to the hummingbird. The hummingbird experience prior to him giving me the totems freaked me out. *How did he know?* *Did he summon the birds?* *Is he a hummingbird whisperer?* Charlotte was running around with the totem pretending that it was flying. I clutched mine and put it into my pocket. I'll read what the bear totem means after lunch. Keough grabbed Charlotte flinging her onto his shoulder.

"Let's see how high your bird can fly. I bet if you hold it up, your daddy will see it. Can you do that?"

She held it up in one hand and waved with the other. "Daddy, say hi to my bird." She blew him a kiss then kissed Keough on the top of his head.

"Well, thank you, Darlin'. What did I do to deserve such a sweet kiss?"

"I didn't kiss you, Daddy did."

Keough reached around and hugged her. "Tell your daddy I said thank you and I love him too."

"He can hear you Pap-Pap." Keough felt another kiss on his head.

"Is that another one from your daddy?" She giggled, "No, Pap-Pap that was from ME!" Keough lifted her off of his shoulders and she ran back into the house.

He looked up at the beautiful Montana sky and whispered, "Son, I promise that I'll always be there for that little girl. She and Morgan are the only pieces of you I have left."

Chapter 11

Paul threw the tarp over the large flat-bed load and latched it down. It was his last delivery before heading to Montana to visit Rose. She'd been on his mind a lot since their last visit. *I hope she's okay. I haven't heard from her in weeks.* He climbed into the cab of his truck and headed north. It would take him a little over 18-hours to reach Billings from San Diego. Tucked in his sun visor was a photograph of Rose, Charlotte, Raymond, Morgan, Jannine and Keough. *I really love this lot. They are the closest thing I have to a family in America.* He checked the passenger seat to make sure he had their gifts secured. He'd picked up a beautiful piece of pottery in Taos for Rose and a little handmade poncho for Charlotte. Visiting them empty handed was never an option. And honestly he enjoyed it. Watching Charlotte's eyes light up when he'd give her what she called "a prize" made his heart melt. *What a sweet bab'bee she is – just like her mum.*

Paul liked Rose. He liked her from the first awkward moment they met. And he was always respectful of Rose's love for Joe. But his feelings for her were becoming harder and harder to deny. He respected Joe as a man and accomplished author. Rose had given him a few of his novels to read on the road. Paul fancied himself a mountain man who was born too late and in the wrong country. *I must remember to ask Raymond about the history of Montana.*

Paul tried to think of something else, but his thoughts always drifted back to Rose. *What a bloody bad roll of the dice she's had. She's such a brilliant woman; finding her soul mate only to have him taken away so soon. A bloody shame it is!*

He lowered the rig's window to clear his thoughts. The evening air swirled around the cab. The scent of wet sagebrush refreshed him. He thought about how much he missed England and wondered if Rose had ever been there. Again his thoughts turned to Rose. *STOP IT Paul! Keep your mind on the road or you'll end up in a bleeding ditch.*

He'd been on the road for more than eight hours. His back was aching, and his hands had started to cramp. A sign alerted him to the next truck stop which was 30-miles further. He needed a bathroom break and coffee or as the truck drivers called it internal petro. Paul also noticed that he was running out of hours. He shifted gears to the rig's highest regulated speed. Getting pulled over for out-of-hours driving would delay his visit, not to mention award him a hefty ticket. His exit off ramp came up quickly. He could see the rest area. It was loaded with truckers and there were only a few spots left. He put his rig into reverse and backed into one and shut down his truck for the night. After taking a long restroom break and drinking down some much needed coffee, he went back to his cab and climbed into the bunk. His thoughts drifted once more to Rose. He thought about how lovely she was and her beautiful smile. She always smelled of lavender just like the lavender in his mother's gardens in England. The fragrance was intoxicating and soothing. With a faint smile lingering on his face, he tried to sleep. He thought to himself *Forget it Paul; she's not yet ready for another romance* and drifted off to sleep.

The infernal rumbling of a refrigerator unit's engine and a throbbing erection woke him out of a sound sleep. He'd slept through his alarm. *Paul, what the bloody hell is wrong with you! Stop thinking about Rose and get your arse in gear and back on the road.* He poured some of his bottled water in his hands and splashed his face. Drinking the last of his now cold coffee, he hit the road.

A message came over his Qualcomm unit notifying him of an unexpected pick-up in Utah that needed to be delivered to a warehouse in Montana. They knew he had a partial load and was heading in that general vicinity. He read the location and realized it was less than 20-minutes from Rose's place. He accepted the job thinking he could use the extra money. The town seemed very familiar. *Where have I heard the name Dodson before? I don't believe I've been there. Then again all these bloody small towns in America look the same to me.*

Paul loved to drive. It gave him a sense of freedom rolling from state to state. Being a career CDL driver, He lived in his truck. It was decked out with all the luxuries including a micro-shower, television-video combo and web access. Not being married also helped him enjoy the road. He didn't have anyone relying on him and that's how he liked it. Being tied down was to him a form of torture. How anyone would want to be married and live in one place was a mystery to him. Those were his feelings until he met Rose. He could see how even the dedicated of drivers would happily give it up for a woman like her. Nonetheless, her heart will forever belong to Joe. Paul snapped back to reality when he noticed his rig was drifting. *Keep your mind on the bloody road Paul.*

His exit for the Montana load was ten minutes away. They notified him that it was ready and waiting. *Thank goodness because I really didn't fancy helping them load this bleeder.*

The warehouse was not too far from the exit. He noticed the sign on the side of the building – Wellesley Corporation Outdoor Manufacturing. *That name sounds familiar too.* Paul felt as though he was experiencing déjà vu. He'd seen the name before, but he couldn't remember where or when. The guard at the gate flagged him in and pointed to bay SB-66. He drove over to the loading dock and backed into the cargo bay. Four forklift drivers loaded what looked like playground equipment onto his flatbed. It was wrapped tight which made it easy to strap down. One of the dock workers handed him the clip board for his signature and in less than thirty minutes he was back on the road.

The playground equipment reminded him of Charlotte. *I hope she likes her poncho.* Paul was less than forty minutes from the ranch but sadly had run out of driving time. He'd have to stop driving and shut down for ten hours. *So close yet so far. Maybe I should call her? She might offer to pick me up and bring me to the ranch. But then I still need to drop off these two loads, so it would be a waste of time having her come all the way out here– oh well. It was a nice thought. But I could email her.*

He grabbed his computer and started to compose an email.

To: Amelia Montana

Fr: Paul Saxton

Subject: **Greetings**

Greetings . . . Is that the best you can come up with Paul!

He tried to think of something more original but nothing popped into his mind. Oh well, greetings will have to do.

Greetings Amelia, this is Paul. Well you already know that from the "from" section. I'm about 40-minutes from the ranch but had to shut down for the night. I have two deliveries near you and would like to drop by if that's okay. Hope you and the bab-bee are doing well. It'll be good to see you both. See you soon.

Cheers,

Paul

He hit the send button then thought how lame his email would sound after her brilliant emails from Joe.

"I must sound a right chuffed, more like a pillock!"

A few minutes later he heard the ping of his email notifications it was Amelia replying to his email.

Fr: Amelia Montana

To: Paul Saxton
*Re: **Subject: Greetings***
Well hello Paul. I was just thinking about how I haven't heard from you. So, imagine my surprise when I received your email. You are less than 30 minutes from the ranch? Would you like me to pick you up? It would be wonderful to see you, and I've got dinner started. You know how I always make too much and I know you haven't had a home-cooked meal in quite a while. Being on the road as much as you are, you must be a thin as a rail (smile).
"Rose"

Paul panicked. *What do I do now!* He sent a quick reply.
Fr: Paul Saxton
To: Amelia Montana
*Re: **re: Subject: Greetings***
Would love too but have two more deliveries to make. However, I would appreciate a rain check afterwards, if that's to your liking. I'll even bring wine or milk or whatever . . . now I'm rambling. See you later perhaps?
Paul

Five seconds later she replies: *"YES, we would love to see you later! Love, Rose"*

He was taken aback. *Love Rose? Paul, don't read too much into it. Maybe she ends all of her emails that way.*

Still the *Love, Rose* closing left him optimistic. *Perhaps she feels something more than friendship for me.*

He banished the thought from his mind. "Alright then Paul, stop pratting about; it's time to get some rest and refrain from daydreaming about her!" He took a deep breath, "Gordon Bennett, now I'm talking to myself."

Paul was up before his alarm went off as he was anxious to get his loads delivered. He wanted to get a jump on his day, so he'd have time to visit Rose. *This five-day-old beard is getting rough. I'd better call ahead to the truck stop barber to schedule a haircut.*

His first load was a quick and easy delivery – less than twenty minutes. The second was to be delivered to an Early Childhood Development Center near Malta. It took him two tries to find the delivery area. It was in the rear of the center and still had workers working on the playground's construction. *I wonder if this is the same daycare Charlotte attends.*

A large group of workers with cranes and forklifts stood ready to unload. A gentleman in a suit and tie walked over to greet Paul.

"Good Morning—if it's still morning. Thanks for getting here so quickly. We need to have this project finished by the end of the week."

Paul jumped down from truck's cab, wiped his hands on his pants and shook the gentleman's hand.

"The name's Paul, nice to meet you Mr. . . . ?

"The name's Wellesley, Jameson Monford-Wellesley to be exact. And I do believe you picked up all of this equipment from our warehouse and not a moment too soon. Again, thanks for the impromptu detour."

Jameson reached in his pocket and handed Paul a hundred dollar bill. "Again, thanks so much Pete!"

"Paul, the name's Paul. No need for the tip mate. I do quite nicely in salary, thank you very much." Consider it a donation to your project. I believe my friend's daughter attends this daycare. Her name is Charlotte Montana. Her mum's name is R . . ."

Jameson cut him off. "Amelia Montana, the art columnist who also goes by Rose Montana? You know her?"

Paul wasn't sure how to answer his question. He didn't know this fellow and didn't want to give out any more information than he already had.

"Yes, I know Amelia or as she prefers to be called Rose. From time-to-time I deliver hay to her ranch. We've become friends of sorts. And how do you know Mrs. Montana, if I may ask?"

Jameson went on to explain that he was staying in town until the project was completed and that his mother had sent him to help Rose write an article about their Remington collection.

"If you haven't noticed Paul, I'm not a western kind of a guy. I can't wait to get out of this shit hole and get back to New York. I miss the nightlife – especially the bars.

Paul could smell the faint scent of alcohol on his breath. He tried to cover it with mints but it wasn't working. His family owned a pub in Coventry and knew all the ways patrons tried to mask their drinking. He thought it best to end their conversation.

Jameson excused himself thanking Paul again for his speedy delivery. He handed him his card. "If you are ever in New York, look me up. Hey, I'll even buy you a pint, that's the right phrase isn't it? Well, cheerio Mate."

Paul nodded. "Cheers to you Mate." Walking back to his truck he thought, *what a bloody wanker! Be that as it may I'm in such a good mood not even a pompous tosser can dampen my spirit.*

He could see the sign for the truck stop in the distance. *It'll be good to get a proper haircut and shave.* His hair had grown so long he could pull it back into a ponytail. He glanced in his rear-view mirror and ran his fingers through his hair. "I look like a bleeding hippie!"

There was a long line at the entrance of the truck stop. It would be at least fifteen minutes before he could get a parking spot. An attendant went from truck to truck giving the drivers a numbered ticket.

"Sorry about the back up. There's been an accident blocking a portion of the highway. It should be cleared soon but keep your CB radio on and we'll shout out your number when a spot becomes available."

Paul thanked him and turned his radio on station-19. He very rarely used it because most of the American drivers couldn't understand his accent. Most of them had a thick southern accent which he found very crass. There were times he questioned his moving to the United States. However, his love of the American cowboy culture spurred his move. He loved driving though Utah specifically Monument Valley. For Paul, it was how he envisioned the American Wild West would have been. One of his favorite films was John Ford's *Stagecoach*. It was one of the first movies to bring Monument Valley to the attention to filmmakers and tourists.

It wasn't long before they called Paul's number. He parked his rig and headed into the driver's area where his shower was also ready. *These clothes need to be burned; I could clear a room from the stench of this shirt.* Sniffing his underarms and shaking his head, he peeled the dirty shirt and pants off, kicking them to the side of the shower room. Truck stop showers were always clean and tidy. Drivers relied on clean places to bathe and eat, and if the word got around that a place operated unsanitary conditions, it would be the kiss of death for that truck stop. He stepped into the shower holding his head underneath the shower head. The hot water felt good on his face and neck and the steam warmed his body as he lathered his hair. His thoughts again turned to Rose. Scrubbing his legs, the cloth brushed against his inner thighs which lead to an involuntary erection. *Paul, stop it. This is not the time or place for a wank.* Embarrassed by his uncontrollable hard on, he turned the hot water off causing the shower to go ice cold. The sudden shock ended his erection. Glancing at what was once a lengthy penis, he chuckled. *Looks like an acorn in a bird's nest!*

He toweled off and rummaged through his bag for clean clothes. Tee shirts and work pants were all he had left to wear. *I seriously need new clothes.* Clean and refreshed, he walked next door to the barber's place. The barber remembered Paul. Not many British drivers come through Montana, let alone drop in for a haircut.

"Well if isn't my favorite driver. How are you? From the looks of your hair and beard, it's been quite a while."

Paul smiled and said he was doing well and ready for a bit of R and R. "I've been on the bloody road for four weeks and need to be sheared. Make me look handsome, Mate."

"Handsome? I don't have the time or the tools to make that happen."

Paul laughed and gave him the British version of the bird. "Naff off and get to work cutting."

Thirty minutes later, a pile of hair and beard circled the chair. The barber gave Paul a hand mirror.

"Not too bad. I look a bit more human now."

He brushed the loose hairs from Paul's shirt. "Human? That's a stretch. When you walked in, I thought you were Bigfoot!"

Another round of playful abuse ensued. He tipped the barber and said he's see him in a few weeks.

"Okay Paul, you take care and drive safe. Oh and by the way, who's the lucky gal who gets to see my expert work?"

Paul looked surprised. "And what gives you the idea I'm seeing a woman? Isn't it possible I want to look good for myself?"

"Nope, because it's been my professional experience when a trucker gets all cleaned up, it's always for a gal, and this gal must be very special for you to get a cut and clean shave."

"Well, if you must know you nosey Gus, I'm having dinner with an old friend and I thought it proper not to show up smelling of road and looking a right chuff!"

"Sure. Old friend you say. Now I know she's special because you are trying too hard to downplay it."

Paul smiled, gave him another flip of the British bird and left the shop.

On his way back to his rig, he saw a red Silverado pulling up to the car fuel pumps. *Oh bugger, it's that pillock Jameson!* He was so busy pumping gas that he didn't notice Paul coming around the far side of his truck. Paul looked inside and noticed a bag that looked to be a fifth of scotch on his passenger seat. *This guy is a bloody pisser.* Driving drunk or after drinking was something Paul abhorred. Driving was his livelihood, and he would never risk it for alcohol. He watched too many of his family's pub patrons jailed for drinking and driving. It didn't appear to be opened but still Paul made a mental note. *I don't want this guy anywhere near Rose and Charlotte.*

He continued walking toward his rig. Before Jameson finished filling up, Paul climbed into his rig and drove off heading north to Rose's place.

I sure hope Paul is hungry because I cooked way too much food for me and Charlotte. I dropped the spoon on the floor. When I bent down to pick it up, I accidentally knocked my head on the corner of the table. Charlotte giggled at my clumsiness in the kitchen. Most of the time, Cecilia cooked their meals, but I wanted Paul to sample my culinary skills. It was a matter of pride for me to be able to prepare a meal on my own. Joe did a lot of the cooking on Cecilia's days off. He was a very good cook, but never let Cecilia know how talented he was. Her meals were always hot and ready unlike mine. My skill was reheating anything she cooked. Even her leftovers were better than my freshly cooked dinners.

"Mama, I'm hungry can we eat now?"

"It won't be long, Baby Girl; the lasagna is almost done. Would you like a breadstick? You can dip it in some of the sauce I made."

"YES, I love 'mater sauce!" She grabbed a breadstick and started nibbling on it before I could dip out a cup of sauce for her. I placed the cup on the table then walked over to the stove with a breadstick and dipped it into the pot. I daydreamed about the first time Paul and I met. How infuriated he was when I commandeered his rig to use his internet. I also thought how incredibly fortunate I was to have such remarkable men in my life. In two years I'd gone from dating obnoxious narcissistic jerks to being cared for by men like Paul, Keough and Raymond—not to mention our loving son, Morgan and, of course, Patrick and Daniel.

Patrick and Daniel have their own life and are happily married. They'd been my rock for so long they deserve time off from the Amelia Co-Dependency Network. Anyway, their lives were about to change. At the age of 52, their best friend Jonathan died of a massive heart attack leaving behind his 8-year old daughter, Chelsea. They were already her godparents; therefore, the logical decision for them was to adopt her. Jonathan's partner died five year prior from a prolonged viral infection.

I thought to myself if any two people have the skill and ability to raise a young girl it would be Patrick and Daniel. With their sense of style and common sense, they'd have her running companies like Channel or Prada by the time she was thirteen. I chuckled at the thought of Daniel teaching her to walk in high heels. In his younger years, he was part of a drag show called, *Ladies or Gentlemen.* He dressed as Celine Dion and lip synced *"It's All Coming Back To Me Now."*

The thought of Daniel dancing around dressed like a female torch singer made me laugh and snapped me out of my daydream. Charlotte had already eaten two bread sticks. I'm sure her appetite was already spoiled, but I needed her to eat a well balanced meal. She'd become quite a picky eater since day school. Their lunches were much more fun than mine. Eating healthy sandwiches shaped like hearts and stars was much more exciting than a white bread bologna sandwich with no crusts. But Cecilia was able to get her to eat broccoli by telling her it was a baby tree and how exciting it was to eat an entire tree for dinner. I would never have thought of such a reason; I guess that's because I'd never been a mother before. Cecilia's kids were grown, but they had decided not to have kids. She never pressured them about it saying it was their choice and they were happy and that's all that mattered. She loved Charlotte like a grandmother. I thanked Joe everyday for having the good sense to hire such an amazing woman. Anyone who could handle him and get my kid to eat vegetables was my hero.

The timer on the oven went off. Dinner was ready. All I needed to do was to get cleaned up before Paul got here. Charlotte needed a bath as well. *I believe she is wearing more sauce than she ate.* I got her clothes off and ran the water for her bath. Jannine gave her some fancy bubble bath from New York, and now Charlotte would not take a bath without it. *Thank you Jannine for getting my daughter addicted to the most expensive bubble bath Neiman Marcus sells.*

I was drying off Charlotte when I heard Morgan come in. He'd gone into town to pick up some barbed wire and horse feed. Although there was plenty of hay in the barns, the horses needed additional sweet feed to keep them full and energetic when cold weather set in. The thought of snow and ice gave me a chill. But Joe's coffee was like antifreeze. I guess that's why he made it so strong. He'd lived in this climate his entire life and knew how to say warm and awake. Ranch work isn't easy on a person. It's hard work and can be very unforgiving. Frozen fuel and water lines, broken car heaters, cracked hoses could stop a man in his tracks when livestock is involved. Keough, Morgan and Raymond made it look easy. They worked well as a team and knew how to get the job done without any muss and fuss. *I don't know what I'd do without them.*

Charlotte insisted on dressing herself. That meant she'd be coming to dinner in her pink tutu, purple and white-striped tee shirt and green cowgirl boots. I stopped fighting with her months ago knowing Joe's child would never listen to reason. I learned to pick my battles, and as long as it was clean I didn't care. As an artist myself, I chalked it up to personal self expression.

Morgan stuck his head in the bedroom. "How are my girls doing? And what is that smell? Is that you stinkin' good Charlotte?"

He stooped down and stuck his nose in her neck. She tried to wiggle out of his hug. "Stop Morgan, that tickles and I don't stink!"

He sniffed the air. "And what is that delicious smell – lasagna, am I right?"

"Yes, you are correct Morgan, and I made it so no wise cracks!"

He looked down at Charlotte, "What do you think? Should we eat it"? She nodded, "Yes, it's yummy for the tummy, isn't it Mama?"

We laughed at her reason. She was developing quite a vocabulary. It was then I realized she wasn't my little baby girl anymore but a sweet and precious little lady. One who had us wrapped around her little finger. *Joe, I wish you were here to see how beautifully she's grown.*

The wind was picking up, and the wind chimes Raymond hung on the deck were flooding the house with a gentle song. I stood outside for a minute and closed my eyes imagining Joe standing behind me with his arms wrapped around my waist and his head resting on my shoulder. I honestly thought for a second I felt his cheek brush against mine. Was it the wind? Or was it his spirit? I don't know.

Off in the distance was Paul's truck. I could tell from the rumbling of the engine, the plumes of dust and the sound of crunching gravel. Sound traveled out here long distances because no tall buildings stood in the way to muffle it. Although he was more than a mile away, I knew he was on his way. I went back inside to freshen up.

"Shit! No time for a shower!"

I splashed some water on my face, put on a bit of lipstick and ran my hands through my hair. That was the best I could in the little time I had before he pulled into the driveway. *Rose what you are doing! It's Paul for Christ sake. He wouldn't care if you came to the door butt naked. Well, he might be shocked but he wouldn't care – or would he?*

His familiar three knocks on the door brought Morgan from the back door mud room. He'd just taken off his barn boots. I could hear their voices from the kitchen. It was the usual manly bullshit and chatter. I heard Paul asking about me. Morgan pointed toward the kitchen.

"Hello, hello, a little budgie told me something about homemade lasagna? Well there just happens to be a terribly hungry Brit here who would eat a piece of shredded tire if it had enough seasoning on it."

I smiled, "Hello Paul it's good to see you, and don't you look clean and tidy. What's the occasion?"

His mouth twisted to one side. "Oy, hang on. I do take the occasional bath when I'm coming to visit special ladies."

"Then I guess I should be honored. And you shaved your beard and cut that wannabe ponytail. I barely recognized you – nice, very nice!"

He gave me a friendly hug and kiss on the cheek. "All kidding aside Amelia, it's good to see you. Where's the bab-bee? I have something for her and a little something for you too. Although I'm not sure you're getting yours. Shame on you for insulting me—wannabe ponytail, you got some bottle girl!"

We laughed. It was good to see Paul. I never realized how charming and witty he was. He always made me laugh even though, more times than not, I never understood what he was talking about. His accent was delightful. He could read instructions on installing a fuse and he could make it funny. I needed to laugh. I needed to remember it was okay to laugh.

Charlotte heard Paul's voice and came running out of her bedroom. She hugged him around his legs then stretched her arms up for him to lift her onto the shoulders.

Charlotte asked, "What did you bring me?"

I interjected, "Excuse me, Young Lady, how about 'Hello, Paul. How are you doing?' and not what did you bring me?"

I gave her my stern look. She knew she'd been reprimanded. I continued, "Now let try that again."

"Okay, I'm sorry, Mama." She started again. "Hi Paul, how are you? What did you bring me?"

He told her to close her eyes then took the poncho out of the bag. "Now, open your eyes." She opened her eyes and stared at the beautiful poncho.

"Mama, it's like the one Daddy's mama had on in the picture! It's pretty!"

I looked closer and sure enough it was identical to the one Joe's mother wore in one of the only photographs he had of her. I whispered, "Say, thank you."

Charlotte motioned for Paul to lean down and whispered, "Thank you Paul."

Paul laughed and gave her a hug, "You're so very welcome, Poppet. I'm glad you like it."

"I LOVE it!" Charlotte kissed him on his cheek and ran back into her bedroom to model it for her dolls.

He walked over to me and handed me a white box. "And this is for you Amelia." I carefully opened the lid removing the tissue paper.

"Oh my God, Paul this is exquisite! This is a Mata Ortiz, I can't accept this! It's way too expensive a gift."

Paul's eyes squinted so much and all I could see were two slits. He shook his head unable to speak. But when he did finally utter words, I wasn't prepared for his tirade of abuse.

"WHAT ARE YOU LIKE? Oh, and in case you don't know what that means in England it means, what the hell is wrong with you! I pick out a brilliant gift for you and all you can say is its too expensive? Hello, my name is Paul Saxton. I drive a bloody huge truck for a living. I do quite well at it, I might add. So don't tell me how much to spend or what to buy for someone I love!"

Love, did he just say love? I don't know if I was more shocked at him hollering at me or the fact that he'd just admitted to loving me. *Say something Rose.*

He sat down drumming his fingers on the table. "Well aren't you going to say something? Come on Amelia you've never been at a loss for words, say something."

I motioned for him to stand up. I leaned into his ear and whispered, *thank you Paul* and gave him a quick kiss on the lips.

He cleared his throat and tried to brush off the kiss as a part of my apology. But the blush creeping across his cheeks told something completely different. I think me kissing him was a total surprise to him and to be totally honest – it surprised me. I changed the subject and asked him if he wanted wine with his dinner.

"Yes, red would be fine if you have it, thank you."

I handed him the cork screw and the bottle of wine he'd brought me on his last visit. He recognized the bottle and smiled.

"Not much of a drinker are you now, Amelia?"

"Not anymore. Now that I have a toddler running around, I barely have time to think let alone enjoy a quiet glass of wine. Those days are long gone."

Paul chuckled. "Well, tonight we'll have a quiet meal, sip some wine, which I might add was also a gift from me and enjoy each other's company – how's that sound?"

"I'd like that Paul. It's been a while since I've had an adult conversation over dinner."

As we started to eat, Paul filled me in on his whereabouts in the United States. He said he took a couple of days off vacationing in Tombstone, Arizona.

"I've always fancied myself an old western cowboy. I love American history especially the Wild West era. I guess Joe rubbed off on me more than I thought. By the way, I'm reading the novels you gave me. I must say they're brilliant. Your husband was quite the fiction writer."

Paul's eyes twinkled when he talked about the old west. I could picture him sitting in a saloon watching some gunslingers fighting over a crooked card deal. I imagined him shooting a single warning shot toward the ceiling to quiet the place down so he could continue to sip his whiskey. Paul wasn't what you would call a strikingly handsome man. However, he had a rugged charm that fit him well. Wearing a white western shirt with jeans and cowboy boots, he could easily pass for a Montana cowboy as long as he didn't speak. The accent instantly gave away his British heritage.

He talked about England and asked if I'd ever been to Europe. I told him the only place I'd visited was Italy and that was on our honeymoon. He described his village, his primary school and then mentioned his ex-wife. I'd never asked him, if he had ever married or was involved with anyone special. But then again I didn't know much about Paul's life in the United States or England. What brought him here? Why did he leave? I wondered why he divorced his wife or why she divorced him. *Maybe I should leave well enough alone.* We ended dinner and continued our conversation outside on the deck. The sky was dark, but the stars and full moon gave us plenty of light. Paul leaned against the deck railing and looked up at the sky.

"It's beautiful in this part of the country. I've been thinking about settling down here. This way I could be close to you and the bab-bee in case you needed me. It would certainly give Keough and Raymond a break. I'm pretty good at repairing farm and ranch equipment."

I was about to answer him, when I noticed Jameson's truck barreling up the driveway. At first I thought he would plow into the side of the barn.

Paul asked, "Who the bloody hell is that?"

"It's the guy who I'm writing the article for. His name is J . . . "
Paul stopped me mid sentence.

"Jameson, Jameson Wellesley to be precise. He's the bleeding idiot I met at the warehouse!"

He headed toward the house with a handful of papers. Before he could knock on the door, I opened it.

"Oh, hey Rose, I have your contract and payment paperwork. All I need is your John Hancock and I'm back to New York and out of your hair. Lovely hair I might add."

Paul came from behind the door and asked me if everything were okay.

"Well, well if it isn't my British buddy. Sorry, I don't remember your name."

Paul squinted, "It's Paul, and you're the pillock from the warehouse. Still drinking?"

Jameson was baffled by Paul's question.

"What? Drinking? Ah, no . . . what's it to you and why would you care?"

I could tell there was about to be an altercation so I asked Jameson if he could come back tomorrow and pick up the paperwork after she had a chance to review them.

"No problem. I need to get a shower and trimmed for the playground dedication tomorrow. You are going right?"

I'd forgotten all about it. Between the article and Morgan and Jannine's engagement my mind was multitasking to the point I didn't know what day it was. I didn't want to go, but I had promised Dr. Henry that I would be there representing Joe.

"Yes, of course I'll be there – good night Jameson."

"Okay, I'll see you in the morning, goodnight Rose." Paul smiled and whispered, *goodnight ya' plonker!*

"I swear that bloke really sends me round the twist!"

I had to laugh. Paul was so worked up, and I didn't have a clue as to what he was talking about. Plonker, round the twist, pillock none of these words were in any way shape or form familiar to me. I couldn't stop laughing. Paul looked at me as if I'd lost my mind.

"Girl, what are you like? You're shrieking like a bleeding budgerigar!"

His statement made me laugh even harder. I couldn't catch my breath. He began laughing and we both had to sit down to compose ourselves.

"Paul, at some point you need to educate me on British slang because I have no idea what you're talking about."

He promised me he would give me a tutorial in British insults and compliments at another time. I knew I needed to get to bed as the dedication was tomorrow morning at 9:00 AM.

"I'd like to accompany you and Charlotte if that's okay."

"Absolutely, I'll need all the moral support I can get. You can stay in one of the guest rooms if you'd like."

"No, that's not necessary I'm perfectly okay sleeping in the rig."

"You'll do no such thing. Get your gear and take it to the room at the end of the hall. If you're going to be my moral support, you'll need a good night's rest in a proper bed."

"A proper bed, well that sounds terribly British. Thank you and goodnight, Amelia."

"Goodnight Paul. See you in the morning."

Chapter 12

"Here's your boarding pass, Mrs. Wellesley. First class will be boarding in five minutes. We'll have someone take your carry on to your seat."

It had been a years since she'd been to Montana. As excited as she was to be going back to Dodson, Meryl was somewhat apprehensive. Would she remember anything about it or would it be frozen in time and exactly the way she left it? The flight attendant escorted her to her seat. Staring out the window, she daydreamed about her life and how she and her husband turned a small shipping business into a worldwide Fortune 500 conglomerate. They were truly a rags-to-riches story. Her husband was out of the country on a business trip and wasn't due back until next week. He always brought her and Jameson something from his travels. She remembered how excited Jameson would get as a child when his dad pulled a special gift for him from his suitcase. *What a wonderful son.* She still carried a baby picture of him in her purse. *Such a beautiful boy; those beautiful eyes! The moment I saw him I fell in love with him.*

The flight attendant made the announcement for all passengers to turn off their electronic devices and to fasten their seatbelts. Meryl tucked the photo back into her purse. He'll be surprised to see me. It's been a while since she visited Dodson, Montana. She had fond memories of growing up there, school, college and meeting Mr. Wellesley. They fell in love and a year later married. After her parents died, they moved into their home and tried their hand at ranching. The Montfords were an old ranching family producing most of the beef for the state. Her mother and father were born in the United States; however, her grandparents came from England. She'd visited their small village on one of their business trips to London, and she brought back home boxes of family photographs and letters. After five years, they realized that ranching wasn't their cup of tea. They decided to sell and move into their own home. The money they made from the sale of the cattle and ranch was their seed capital for their shipping business. They hired a wonderful housekeeper named Charlotte Burnell--a young woman who wasn't much older than Meryl. They became close friends. Meryl spent a lot of time alone while her husband traveled and Charlotte's husband wasn't around much either. When Meryl asked about Charlotte's husband, she would say he had a drifter's heart, and this was the price one paid for falling in love with a wayward rodeo man.

As her flight drew closer to Montana, she reminisced about the ranch and about Charlotte. *She was my saving grace—an angel of mercy. If it were not for her, I wouldn't have Jameson.* The announcement came over the intercom that they'd be landing in Billings in fifteen minutes and to fasten their seatbelts. Meryl opened her purse and took another look at Jameson's baby picture. *Such a beautiful gift.*

Meryl spotted a limousine driver standing by the baggage claim and holding a sign displaying her name. She followed him outside. She held on to a wrapped gift and her purse. Once outside, she took off her sunglasses and looked up at the brilliant blue sky. *Hello Big Sky. You don't know how much I've missed you.* She took a deep breath and stepped into the back of the limo.

The alarm had gone off for a second time before I got out of bed. *Let this ceremony go off without a hitch so that asshole Jameson can leave Montana. He's only been here three days but it seems like a lifetime* I laid out my clothes and jumped in the shower. Cecilia had already bathed and fed Charlotte. I was drying off when I heard a knock on the bathroom door. It was Cecilia with a cup of coffee in hand.

"I thought you needed some extra time this morning, so I fed and bathed Charlotte. And I knew you'd need coffee."

"Cecilia you are an angel of mercy! Yes, I need coffee and two aspirins please. I think I drank too much wine last night. And there's no way I'm dealing with Jameson with a headache."

"If I may be frank Amelia, he's a royal pain in the behind! I don't care how rich he is, nobody piles their plate with MY food, lets it go cold then throws it into the trash! A spoiled brat is what he is!"

"Whoa, Cecilia, you're becoming a true hard-ass – I like it!"

She blushed a bit but stood by her words. "I'm sorry, Amelia, but pardon me if I don't get teary eyed when he leaves." I laughed at her honesty and said ditto!

As I dressed, I thought back to her dinner with Paul. How nice it was having a proper dinner with someone whose food she didn't have to be cut into small pieces. Then I thought of Joe. How wonderful it would have been to attend the dedication with him and having his fans show up to meet him. I smiled thinking how it would have taken the thunder away from Jameson. *What is it about that man that annoys me so much?*

Charlotte came running into the bedroom. "Look, Mama—I look pretty!" Cecilia had her hair pulled up into a ponytail with a little pink ribbon that matched her pink and violet outfit. I looked down at her feet. She was still wearing her bedroom slippers.

"Are you going to wear your My Little Pony slippers? They are quite beautiful, but how about you put on your shoes and socks? Can you do that by yourself or would you like me to help you?"

"I can do it all by myself, Mama. Remember I'm a big girl."

I thought, *Yes you are and looking more like your daddy every day.*

She ran down the hall and almost ran into Paul.

"Oy, and where are you running off too so quickly? You almost knocked me over young lady!"

She giggled telling him she'd forgotten to put on her shoes.

"Okay, then carry on, but the next time you run that quickly I'll have to give you a speeding ticket!"

He walked into the kitchen and started to pour a cup of coffee when I heard Cecilia ask him if he would prefer a cup of tea.

"Oh I would LOVE a cup of tea! Cream with sugar would be lovely."

Cecilia brought him his tea and asked him if he would be staying. "If you are coming back after the dedication ceremony, I'll cook the large roast. We'd love it if would could stay for dinner. Paul took note of the word "we'd". *I wonder what Amelia and Cecilia have been rabbiting about before I walked in?*

"Of course I'd love to. That's if it's okay with Amelia." Cecilia smiled, "Oh I'm pretty sure it will be alright."

Her statement aroused his curiosity. "Cecilia, did Amelia mention anything to you about me staying longer? I would feel dreadful if I gave her that impression. She's been so kind. I wouldn't want her to feel any sort of obligation."

Cecilia smiled. "No she didn't Paul, but even someone with failing eyesight can see she enjoys your company."

Paul felt his face flush red. *She enjoys my company, 'ay? Stop it Paul; she's just being polite.*

I walked in just as his face was bright red. "So what's going on? Did Cecilia flash her breast or offer to wash your back?"

Cecilia laughed so hard she had to take off her glasses and wipe her eyes.

"Oh my God, Amelia, you're beginning to sound just like your husband, God rest his soul. I knew it was just a matter of time before his naughty nature rubbed off on you."

Paul shook his head and offered Cecilia a napkin. "Shame on ya' Amelia! This lovely woman was offering me a place at your dinner table tonight, and I was about to say *yes* when you walked in spouting all sorts of rubbish."

"So you're staying for dinner are you? Well, we'd better get the good china out. We'll be dining with royalty."

Paul winked at Cecilia. I'll accept your invitation only if I get to do the washing up afterwards – if that's okay with you, Rose?

"Yep, I've got no problems with that, how about you Cecilia? Shall we let this British bloke stay as long as he does the dishes?"

Cecilia nodded and asked, "Oh, by the way is that Jameson fellow having dinner with us? If so I need to know where Joe kept the barn's rat poison – only kidding. Well maybe not."

Paul asked if there was anyone who liked this fellow.

"I don't like him that's for sure! He's so obnoxious," I offered. "I also find it very interesting that he's nothing like his mother. She's such an elegant and poised woman. It's like he was found on the side of the road. Maybe he's adopted. Hah, now that would be more believable than him being the son of such a sweet woman. But in the true spirit of being a gracious host, I think we should give him one last meal before he leaves."

A knock on the door brought them back to reality – it was Jameson.

Paul laughed. "Well speaking of the devil himself."

Charlotte answered the door. "Hey there, Squirt, is your mom ready to leave?"

Charlotte frowned then shouted, "Mama, it's that man you don't like! And he called me Squirt, that's not nice is it?"

"No, it's not, Baby. Jameson come in and please try not to piss anyone off today? Or I'll have Raymond take you for a one-way-trip ride into the prairielands."

"Geez, I was just trying to be funny – sorry. Anyway, is everyone ready?"

"Yes, we're ready and Paul will be driving. Is that okay with you Paul?"

Jameson looked puzzled. "What's the problem with me driving?" We looked at his truck and back at him.

"Paul will be driving my truck. It's got much more room and less...eh...trash."

Jameson shrugged, "Hey, no skin off my nose. Then let's go Jeeves, and the sooner we get there, the sooner we can get this dedication over with. No disrespect, Amelia, but I'd like to take off directly afterwards. There's a bartender in Manhattan whose family is starving because I've been away so long – that's a joke."

"A dreadful one at that I might add. And again . . . the name's PAUL ya' blooding plonker!" *I really hate this bloke!*

"Whew, tough crowd," Jameson mumbled.

I handed Paul the keys. "And Paul, please call me Rose. My good friends call me Rose. Amelia is way too formal. You're family."

Paul could feel his face flushing again and tried to concentrate on his driving. Jameson nodded off throughout the ride. The faint whiff of scotch lingered above his breath mints. *And this bloke wanted to drive! No way . . . no way in hell would I ever let him drive Rose and her daughter!*

A hotel staff member brought Meryl's luggage into her room. She gave him a very generous tip. "Thank you ma'am, thank you very much. Enjoy your stay!"

Meryl knew she'd given him way too much, but she remembered how things were when she and her husband were struggling to make ends meet. They were two young people living on love and determination. *It seemed only yesterday we gave up Montana for Manhattan. Where has the time gone?*

She called the front desk. "Hello, would you please have my driver meet me out front. Thank you so much."

I hope Jameson will be so excited to see me. I know how much he hates surprises but it's a mother's right to surprise her children.

Meryl asked her driver to stop by the florist. She wanted to present Rose with a bouquet of flowers to thank her for her well-written article. It wasn't too far out of their way and would be a lovely gesture. *I wonder if Harlan still owns the shop. It would be good to see an old friend.*

About twenty minutes into their ride, Meryl lowered the windows and took a deep breath. *I miss the smell of Montana. It's nothing like Manhattan.* The air was fresh, clean and familiar. The city was filled with fumes and subway stench. The only smell that made her happy was the roasted chestnuts and the Christmas tree in Rockefeller Center. She thought back to the first time she took Jameson ice skating. He was a clumsy child, and she hoped ice skating would help his balance. Over time it did improve his coordination and he became quite good at it, winning a trophy for best figure eights. It was only a plastic cup, but to him it was solid gold. *I was so proud of him.* Sadly, his father wasn't there to see him. Business before pleasure was his motto. He rarely saw any of Jameson's achievements. *At times I think his absence was intentional.* His lack of interest in him only strengthened their mother-son relationship. She didn't know what she would do without him.

Meryl's driver lowered the partition and informed her that they would be arriving at the center in five minutes. She took out her compact and powered her nose and chin. Applying a quick bit of lipstick, she checked the mirror then clamped it shut.

I checked my hair in the side mirror fluffing the back flattened by the head rest. Charlotte had dosed off and was drooling. I could hear Joe's mocking-toned voice *Just like your mama.* Paul was heading towards the visitor's parking lot when he noticed Dr. Henry motioning for him to park in the employees parking area. He acknowledged her request. His parking was flawless. I smiled and remembered watching him park his rig back at the truck stop. Three backups and like magic his rig was secured. Jameson couldn't wait to jump out of the vehicle.

"Well, that was an uneventful ride. I guess that driver training education does pay off, huh?"

Paul glared at him. "Another bloody joke I presume?"

"It was supposed to be an admiring comment, but if you thought it was funny, then it was a joke."

Paul shook his head and helped Charlotte from her car seat. She immediately ran over to Dr. Henry and gave her a hug.

"I'm so glad to see you Charlotte, and I see you brought your mama and two handsome gentlemen. I know this gentleman." She extended her hand to Jameson. "But I don't know this one." She walked over to Paul and shook his hand. "Hello, I'm Sara Henry, Dr. Sara Henry and from what I hear I run this place. It's nice to meet you and you are . . .?"

"Paul, the name is Paul Saxton – how do you do, Ma'am? I've heard nothing but wonderful things about you and your children's center. In fact, I was the driver who delivered the playground equipment for the Play Garden."

"Well, I'd like to be the first to thank you so much for getting everything here in one piece. The driver who brought the new cafeteria tables was not as conscientious. Most of the tables were damaged. If it weren't for Mr. Montana insisting the company reship new ones, the kids would be eating off scratched and wobbly lunch room equipment. Did you know Mr. Montana?"

"Yes I did. However, it was a brief acquaintance, God rest his soul. He was taken from us much too soon. Why is it that the good blokes always go before the wankers? "

Doctor Henry looked puzzled. Paul quickly apologized for his inappropriate language.

"I don't believe I'm familiar with the term wanker, but from your tone of voice I don't think it's a term of endearment."

Paul laughed and glanced over at Jameson, "Indeed, it's not a term of affection, but trust me, it fits!"

Jameson became irritated at the developing bond between Paul and Dr. Henry. He walked into the center leaving them to continue their conversation. Charlotte and I were about to go inside when Charlotte broke loose from her grasp and ran over to Paul.

"Come on Paul, let's go. I see cupcakes."

He excused himself and said he was being summoned by the youngest member of the Montana clan.

Dr. Henry laughed. "I believe it's time to go and begin the program – shall we?"

Paul linked arms with the director and escorted her inside. A few minutes later, Meryl's limousine pulled up. She stared at the center then paused for a moment. *What a beautiful building. And to think my son helped develop it.* The chauffeur ran around and helped her out of the car. He then walked her to the building and opened the door.

"I'll call you when I'm ready to leave. I can't wait to surprise my son," she said to her driver who nodded in agreement. Meryl watched as he drove off to the parking area. Checking her hair once more in the door's glass reflection, she entered the center and headed to the auditorium.

The building was spectacular. Large skylights illuminated the main hallways giving the building an airy and open feel. The auditorium doubled as an amphitheater and boasted an incredible roofing system that retracted in good weather. Meryl took a seat in the back of the room and patiently waited for Jameson to give his presentation. Rose and Charlotte were seated next to him. Meryl recognized Amelia from her promotional photographs. *My goodness, she IS stunning. I now understand why Lash Montana fell in love with her so quickly. I wish my Jameson could find a lovely lady like her. Why he insists on dating the superficial wannabe fashion models and actresses is beyond me.*

The program began with a video of Lash talking about his life in Montana and how excited he was about building the new state-of-the-art green play garden. He acknowledged Montford-Wellesley Corporation saying the project would not have been possible without its generous donation. He also credited the center's director, Dr. Sara Henry for her dedication and tenacity and quipped that she would have made a great town sheriff. But most of all he thanked his inspiration – his beautiful wife Amelia and his family's soon-to-be new addition who will probably enjoy this amazing play garden when she is old enough.

The video ended with Lash's usual closing, "Thank you and adios mi amigos."

Lash J. Montana 1951-2001.

The audience gave a standing ovation then turned to me and Charlotte. I took hold of Charlotte's hand, stood up and thanked them for their gracious welcome. Charlotte had no clue why they were clapping. She started clapping then let out an unexpected *Yahoo.* Everyone laughed at the impromptu cowboy cheer from the toddler. It also caught me by surprise.

I picked her up asking, "Was that yahoo for your daddy?"

Charlotte nodded then stared at the stage screen, "I miss my daddy."

I knew not to cry because I had to make my presentation directly after Jameson. Paul was sitting in the front row and knew he needed to distract Charlotte or I would start bawling. He looked at Charlotte, smiled and gave her two thumbs up. She glanced and smiled and returned the gesture. I mouthed a *thank you* to Paul. Before I could sit down, Charlotte bolted off the stage and jumped into Paul's lap.

Jameson laughed saying she must have read the draft of his presentation. The audience chuckled. He continued to talk about the building and how sustainable communities were quickly becoming the norm in Montana. Four minutes into his presentation, he noticed his mother and lost his concentration. He recovered by making her presence known.

"And, I just noticed we have a special guest in the audience. I'd like to introduce one of the most important women in my life . . . my mother, Meryl Montford Wellesley."

Meryl stood up as the audience applauded. She acknowledged her son and the audience then returned to her seat. I was surprised to see her. Meryl was a slender, petite woman – nothing like I had envisioned. Jameson continued and introduced me next.

"It's my pleasure to introduce the inspiration behind this project; the muse of Montana Joe and my little critic's Mama, Amelia Montana or as she prefers to be addressed Rose Montana."

I walked to the podium and began to speak. I thanked everyone for attending the play garden's ribbon cutting ceremony and the Montford-Wellesley for their support. It was then I noticed Keough, Raymond and Morgan in the audience. They were visibly taken aback by the video. Seeing Joe was overwhelming to say the least. Charlotte turned, saw Keough and hollered, "Pap-Pap!" Again, the audience laughed at her innocent outburst. She hopped off Paul's lap and ran down the aisle directly to Keough.

"Well, Baby Girl you sure know how to make an entrance or should I say an exit?" She giggled and pointed to the screen, "Pap-Pap, I see Daddy in heaven!" Keough kissed her on her forehead and hugged her. He asked if she could listen to her mama talk for a few minutes. She gave Keough the thumbs up and snuggled against him. He put his arm around her shoulder and I began my speech.

Knowing Charlotte was in good hands, Paul concentrated on Rose. For the first time, he noticed how beautiful she was, not to mention an eloquent speaker. He could feel himself zoning out. He wasn't paying attention to what she was saying but was focused on the tone of her voice. It was commanding—and sexy. *Lash you were one lucky bloke – she's mesmerizing.* It took him a few seconds to realize she'd finished her presentation. The audience and guests headed to the lobby for a guided tour of the center.

I stepped off of the stage and headed over to Paul. "So how did I do? Tell me the truth, Paul. How boring was it? "

"I don't know because I haven't a clue what you're on about."

"Hah, okay I know what on about means! I'm getting better at this British lingo. But seriously how was I?"

Paul smiled, "You were brilliant, simply brilliant Poppet. But I must ask . . . how are you? Were you aware they were going to show a video of Lash? I must say it took me round-the-twist so I can only imagine how you felt."

"I'm okay Paul. I was more worried about Charlotte but like a true Montana she was great. And thank you for keeping an eye on her. She can be a handful as we all can see since she darted down the aisle."

Keough, Raymond and Morgan came up to hug me and offer congratulations on a job well done. Raymond gave a quick look around and asked,

"Are there refreshments? Listening to people talk it makes me hungry. The more they talk the hungrier I get. So you can imagine listening to Jameson yammer on and on – I starved! Oh, by the way, Rose, great presentation. Joe would be beyond proud."

Keough gave me a gentle chuck on the arm. "I'm proud of ya' too, Darlin'! And I'm honored to call you my daughter."

"You mean daughter-in-law don't you?"

Keough held me by my shoulders, "No, I mean daughter. You gave an old man a chance when no one else would. For that I'm eternally grateful. I love you, Rose Montana. And please don't you go cryin' or I'll be forced to make fun of you; so cowboy up."

I winked at Keough. "Okay, you've got a deal. It'll be our little secret." I leaned into him and whispered, "And by the way I love you too."

Keough blushed a bit then cleared his throat. "Let's stop this mushy stuff and get somethin' to eat. For once I agree with Raymond – I'm starved."

"You go ahead and if you wouldn't mind, could you take Charlotte with you? I need to talk to Jameson and introduce myself to Mrs. Wellesley."

Keough picked up Charlotte and headed to the refreshment area. Jameson was about to bolt out of the front door when I caught him by the arm. "Whoa! Not so fast! Aren't you going to introduce me to your mother? After all she also made this project happen. And I don't know what you've been drinking but before you do any introductions, I suggest you seriously pop a mint. For God's sake, Jameson, it's eleven o'clock in the morning!"

"Okay, so I had a shot to take the edge off. I hate public speaking, and I surely didn't want to screw up in the front of my mother. Anyway . . . what's it to you if I drink?"

I was about to rip into him when his mother walked up.

"Hello, you must be Amelia Montana. My son speaks so highly of you and now I can understand why. It's so good to finally meet you."

"It's so nice to meet you too Mrs. Wellesley. And please call me Rose."

"Then I insist you call me Meryl. I was saddened to hear about your husband's untimely death. Mr. Montana was quite the philanthropist. His generous donation was the catalyst that made this center possible. He was a fine man. As a matter of fact, we had a lot in common."

I must have looked a bit bewildered. "Let me explain," Meryl offered. "Lash and I had a deep appreciation and fascination for all things western. I have read all his novels; most of which are personally autographed. Besides a day at the spa, his books are my guilty pleasure."

I agreed thinking how great it would be to have a full day at the spa. It was something I would do at least twice a week in my pre-Montana life. The days of dirty martinis and late night dinners were now replaced with play dates and cookies and milk. Jameson excused himself saying he was heading back to the ranch to pack his things for his return trip to New York.

Meryl stopped him. "May I ask why the rush? Are you so eager to see those double-jointed, brain surgeon fashion models you've been dating that you can't spend a day or two with your mother?"

I turned away trying not to laugh. Jameson rolled his eyes.

"Of course not, Mother. But seriously, is there any reason you need me to be here. I'd really like to get back to the City. This Montana climate just doesn't agree with me."

"Yes, I need you to stay a bit longer. Pardon me if I'd like to spend some time in my old hometown with my son. Do you have a problem with that? Jameson raised his eyebrows and shook his head in surrender. "I thought not. I'd love to know if any of my old friends are still living there."

Jameson rubbed his temples. "Okay mother, I'll stay a few more days while you take your walk down Montana's extremely dusty memory lane or trails. I don't remember very much about Dodson. To be honest, the only person I remember was that clingy housekeeper who insisted on kissing me every time I left for school. What was her name? Carlotta, Carmelita? There were times she acted more like my mother than you did."

For a moment Meryl's face paled. I could tell the subject upset her. She seemed on edge and nervous, then quickly changed the subject. *Something Jameson said must have struck a nerve. But then again everything Jameson says plucks my nerves.*

They were still bickering when I thought, *Dodson. Why does that place sound so familiar?* Then it dawned on me. Dodson is where Joe's mother is buried. *What a coincidence. Perhaps they knew each other.*

I invited them back to the house for lunch. I'm sure Cecilia prepared plenty of food. It would be interesting to watch the interaction between mother and son. Joe always said that everyone had an intriguing story behind the story they presented to the general public. I bet the Montford-Wellesleys had a hell of a story to tell.

Keough and Raymond pulled into the driveway minutes after we'd arrived. It seems Charlotte wanted ice cream and bullied Keough into buying it for her before lunch. *I swear that little girl has those two grown men wrapped around her finger.* Why they can't say no to her is beyond me – *must be the dimples and her father's shit-eating grin.*

Chapter 13

Joe's publicist Hanna called and left numerous messages on my cell phone. After the presentation, I'd forgotten to take her phone off vibrate and missed Hanna's attempts to call. *Wonder what's going on? Montana Joe royalty checks were deposited and in our account, and the bonus check I had given to her had cleared. She only calls when something is terribly wrong or something fabulous is about to happen. God I hope it's a fabulous call.*

I called her hoping to get her voice mail, but she answered the phone on the first ring.

"Amelia, I've been trying to reach you all day. I've got . . . "

Before she could say another word I blurted, "Please Hanna, tell me its good news. We just returned from the ribbon cutting of the new play garden Joe and the Montford Wellesley Corporation donated to the Childhood Development Center at the university. I'd like to end the morning with more good news.

"Well Darling, you're got your wish. I just got off the phone with filmmaker, Graham Pahmeier. Mr. Pahmeier is the guy who produces and directs all of westerns for the Wild Western Channel on cable. He called because he's interested in making Lash's, *Outlaws of Burnt Canyon Crossing* into a miniseries. I almost pissed my Victoria's Secret panties! And are you sitting down? He's offering an upfront payment with media rights. We're also talking huge book royalties here Amelia. He needs an answer by tomorrow. What do you say? Should I approve and sign the deal?"

My head was spinning. Hanna was good at her job hence her big bonus check. This deal would mean Charlotte would be taken care of for the rest of her life—not to mention her children and her children's children.

"Of course, yes that's fantastic news, amazing news Hanna! Do it. And again, I'm sorry for the delay in returning your call."

"No worries Amelia. I've got to go, but I'll keep in touch with the details as they progress – bye!"

Before I could say goodbye, she'd hung up. *I wonder if she ever sleeps.* I chuckled to myself envisioning Hanna brewing pots of Joe's coffee working through the nights, checking and sending emails to get things done.

Speaking of emails, I realized I hadn't checked them in three days. I dreaded to think how many were waiting in the queue. There was a time I couldn't wait to check them. To see how many were from Joe. I miss them. I still don't know how many he instructed his lawyer to forward to me.

I opened my email, and as I suspected there were 35-emails, all of which were business except one. It was from Joe's account. Why he insisted on having his lawyer send them after his death was a mystery to me. I was excited to see them but always hesitant about opening them. They were like grab bags. I never knew what I was getting. In Joe's case it was definitely entertaining, but always peculiar.

To: Rose

Fr: Montana Joe

Subject: **Convergence by Jackson Pollock & other jokes of art, Part 4 of 5**

My Darlin' Rose,

First, I love you. Always have, always will. This is gonna be a tough email for you to read Rose, so you may want to sit down. It's time I admitted the truth to you. I'm dying of cancer Darlin' and I've known it for a while. It's a lousy condition this throat cancer. It can take a strappin' fella and turn him into an empty shell of a man. It breaks my heart that I won't be there for you; that our daughter will never know her daddy. It tears me to pieces not being able to grow old with you.

Let me tell you a little story, Baby: There was this beautiful gal who walked into a small town rural library. She never expected to be pestered by a handsome but lonely cowboy writer. All she ever wanted was to have an adventure. To travel out west maybe hang out in a cowboy bar or two, dine on bad road food then return back to her career with a few embellished stories to tell her co-workers. Little did she know that she'd be pursued and eventually marry some old, overworked, head-over-heels-in-love-with-her rodeo man turned successful western novelist; who would drink roofing tar if it had enough sugar.

She was unbelievably beautiful, with soft golden skin and the sweetest brown eyes he'd ever seen—not to mention a temper that would stop a Brahma bull in its tracks. Well, this old cowboy fella was smitten. He did everything he could to impress her but she'd have none of that.

This gal was fiercely independent but the old cowboy wouldn't give up. Wasn't in his nature to give up so he left a trail of irresistible challenges that he knew she couldn't pass up. It worked. She softened. She even told the old cowboy he was tolerable, even a tad bit sexy. He melted in his boots. He'd forgotten every other woman he'd been involved with and gave his heart to her.

She began to warm up to the old cowboy then something totally unexpected happened. She fell in love with him. After that the old cowboy and the beautiful lady of his dreams were inseparable. So much so he asked her to be his forever cowgirl. She accepted and they married. But this old cowboy was hiding a dark and terrible secret. Less than a week before he met this lovely lady he found out he had terminal cancer. He cursed God. Then he thought maybe this is just the lousy hand he was dealt, quit squawkin' and enjoy the time he has with her. He knew he should have told her right then and there, before they married. But he thought she would have married him out of pity. Not what the cowboy wanted. He wanted to give her the moon and stars; he wanted to show her the loving side of the old cowboy, not the sickly dying side. He struggled with his decision, but the cowboy was selfish. So he didn't tell her until it was absolutely necessary. The cancer spread quickly, the cowboy grew weak. She stood by his side until the bitter end or that's what I'm assuming.

I'm assuming you were there when I met my maker Darlin'. Please forgive me for the pain and sufferin' I caused you. But Darlin' know that finding you, marrying you, and having a beautiful baby with you was pure joy. My life with you was like a beautiful dance and Baby, you were the dance of my life. Please remember that I love you Amelia Rose Montana, always and forever.

I've gotta stop now Darlin'. I'm in a lot of pain. Pain from this damned cancer, pain from lying to you and the pain never seein' you again.

Your very own (eternally sorry for lying to you) cowboy, Joe

I could feel my blood pressure rising. He knew. He knew he was sick. He KNEW he was dying. I slammed my laptop onto the table.

"SON-OF-A-BITCH --HOW COULD YOU DO THIS TO ME?" I realized I was screaming. My heart was racing. I began pacing the floor with my hands atop my head. It felt as though my brain was going to explode.

Theo must have known. I'm going to strangle him for not telling me; to hell with patient/doctor confidentiality. He was my husband damn it! I should have been told. Joe was the love of my life, and he lied to me! They lied to me.

I was devastated. The man I thought I knew so well had been lying to me all along. Part of me understood his reasoning. He didn't want to upset me or have me doting over him like a pity-happy Florence Nightingale. But whatever he thought I might do or how much I might hurt, it was my right as his wife to be informed.

I ended up outside on the deck. I didn't remember going out. My mind was in a thousand places trying to think of any clues or hints he may have given me about his condition. I remembered back to the throat spray, but his reasons for using it always seemed benign until his fainting in the bathroom of the hotel. I thought that was the start of his illness. But now I realize it was the beginning of the end. He knew all along that his time on earth was short. That's why he was so enthusiastic in the pursuit of our relationship. I thought it was because it was love at first sight – I don't know. I guess I'll never know. Unless, of course his final email, the fifth one that was scheduled, would explain everything. It would be just like Joe to leave me hanging.

"If I wasn't so angry, I would find the humor in this, but I'm extremely livid with you right now Joe! But you did tell me that you were a man of many surprises. I never realized your diagnosis of throat cancer was one of your surprises. Well Mr. Montana I am not surprised or amused! And I can't believe I'm talking to myself!"

Keough walked up onto the deck as I was having the tirade with myself.

"What's the matter Rose? Or should I ask? You're as pale as a gunfighter who showed up to a gunfight without his guns. You look like you've seen a ghost."

I glared at Keough. "I haven't seen a ghost, but I've just heard from one . . . your son!"

Keough took off his hat and scratched his head. "Rose, now please don't take this the wrong way. But what in the hell are you talking about? Are you hearing voices? Has that damn Raymond got you believing in the spirits of the happy hunting grounds?"

"No, I'm not hearing voices. Your son, or should I say his lawyer, just sent me another email-from-the-grave." I opened my computer back to the email and show it to him. "Here, read it."

I sat down on the steps of the deck while Keough read the email. A few minutes later he looked up from the screen and shook his head.

"All this time my son was dying, and I never knew it. My only son was dying of cancer, and I didn't give a shit enough to contact him because of my drunken pride."

Keough came over to sit beside me on the steps.

"Rose, what kind of father does that to his only son!"

He tried to hold back his tears, but the pain was too much for him. He held his hands over his face in disbelief. I was too angry to cry; too angry to console Keough. All I could do was sit there and fume.

"I know he wanted to protect my feelings, Keough but who the hell was he to think I could or could not handle this type of situation?" *The reason you fell in love with me Joe was because I could hold my own – why didn't you trust me enough to handle this.*

I stood up ready to rant and pace but noticed how upset Keough was. I knelt in front of him. He looked up at me, face wet with tears.

"Rose, I didn't know my son very well, but I do know is that he loved you more than anything else in the world." He wiped his eyes with his shirt sleeve. "He probably would have died sooner if it weren't for your love. You gave him a reason to live. In return, he gave you his life, eternal love and a daughter. Now I know you're madder than a rabid prairie dog, but when you think about it, all he wanted was someone to love him through this and that amazing person was you. You also gave me the opportunity to reunite with my son before his demise. For that I'm forever grateful. I love you Amelia Rose. And I promise I'll love you and my granddaughter enough for my son until this wrinkled old carcass bites the dust."

I sat beside him resting my head on his shoulder. "I don't know what I'd do without you Keough. I know we stared off on a craggy road, but along the way I've come to realize how wise and loving a man you really are. Joe knew that you and Lou would stay here to watch over me and Charlotte. And for that I thank you."

"Rose, there are times I believe you know me better than I know myself. I've never been one to express my feelings and to be honest, it worked well for me until I found out I had a family—a family that loved me. Never thought I was worth anyone's love. You and that precious little baby girl changed that, and now I can't imagine not having you both in my life.

"Keough, if you haven't noticed, you and I are more alike than you think. We both have major trust issues. And look at us now. I trust you with not only my life but with my daughter's life. You're a good man Keough Teal Montana."

I kissed him on the cheek and went back into the house. Keough headed inside the tack barn and sat down on a hay bale. *Maybe I'll call my pain-in-the-ass twin brother Kurt and ask him if he'd like to come over for dinner. He's the only one who's ever been square with me besides Amelia, and I think it's about time I've told him how much I miss him. He'll probably think I've lost my mind, but it's time to make amends. Plus he's got a box of my old photographs I stored at his place.*

Rose and Charlotte might get a kick out of them seeing photos of Lash and his sisters when they were little buckaroos with their mama. Not to mention me in my rodeo days.

Keough thumbed through his wallet and pulled out an old faded photograph of him and Charlotte before they were married. She was sitting in front of him on a rodeo horse wearing his chaps.

What a good lookin' couple. I can't believe we were ever this young. The photo was taken before Lash was born. *Hmm, and if my memory serves me well, I believe it was the day after Lash was conceived. That was some night. I'd just won a gold buckle. She said she was so proud of me. And how'd I thank her? I got dead wood drunk. Drunken celebratory sex was the beginning of Lash's life. I never wanted my son to ride the rodeo circuit, but it was in his blood. I was so proud of him when he decided to quit and become a writer.*

He put the photograph back in his wallet and started cleaning the tack and oiling the saddles. Shortly thereafter, Jameson and his mother arrived at the ranch. Cecilia had put out a large buffet lunch. I changed into my work clothes as I never saw fit to wear good clothes all day, especially on a working ranch.

I met them at the door.

"Hello Meryl. I'm happy you talked this guy into coming to lunch. And I'm glad to see you found your way to our ranch, Jameson. I know how lost you get on these Montana roads."

Jameson gave me an awkward smile then asked if he could have a glass of water.

"Is it me or is Montana the dustiest place on earth? Ever since I've been here my throat has been drier than the Sahara desert. And, I've actually been to the Sahara desert, so I know what I'm talking about."

His mother rolled her eyes then walked over towards me with her hand extended.

"I'd like to thank you again for having us over for lunch and for speaking at the grand opening of the center. "

"Meryl, one thing you need to know about the Montana family – we are huggers."

I gave her a hug and thanked her for joining us for the lunch. "Cecilia is one of the finest cooks I've ever met, probably in the entire state of Montana. And I've eaten all over the world, so I know what I'M talking about."

I glared at Jameson and flashed the same fake smile. He took a deep breath and mumbled something incoherent about how long a lunch this was going to be.

Cecilia put out quite a spread. We headed into the dining room with our plates when Keough, Raymond and Charlotte came in. Charlotte ran directly over to the dessert tray. I placed myself as a barricade between her and the sweets.

"Oh not you don't Little Girl; no dessert for you until you've eaten lunch."

She turned toward Keough as if to say, "Hey Pap-Pap, help me out." He looked at me and I shook my head.

"Well, Baby Girl, your mama says *no* so we'll have to honor her request. How about you and I have some strawberries with whipped cream?" He flicked a bit of cream on the edge of her nose. She giggled and wiped it off.

"Pap-Pap, that's not nice! Mama look at what Pap-Pap did. You are being bad. Make him sit in the bad chair, Mama."

We laughed at her disciplinary instructions while Keough wiped the cream off of her nose with his napkin.

"Amelia, she is such a beautiful little girl. There were times I wished I had a little girl to dote over. Be that as it may, I wouldn't trade this handsome son of mine for anything."

Jameson blushed at his mother's admission. "I'm very happy being an only child, thank you very much."

I thought to myself, *I'd trade him for a happy meal. Thank goodness there's only one of you in the world. The world's not ready for two pain-in-the-ass spoiled brats!*

"He'd be much more handsome if he'd get rid of this beard and mustache" Meryl stroked his face before offering her opinion to her son, "It makes you look so much older than you are."

I agreed with her. If he shaved off all that growth, he might look human.

"Okay, okay after lunch I'll shave it all off. If it'll keep you two happy and quiet, it'll be worth it."

I also noticed the roots of his hair were not the same color as the rest of his hair. They were a silvery gray. *Well I'll be damned, he dyes his hair! This guy is such a fucking diva. Thank God Lash wasn't as conceited as this bastard. I would have never let myself get involved with him. No matter how handsome or charming he was, that would have been a deal-breaker.*

Funny, when I think back, Lash was playfully self-absorbed. He always complimented himself before I could compliment him or he would boast how handsome he was whenever he saw his reflection in a window pane or mirror. But it was always tongue-in-cheek, nothing serious. I noticed that Keough does the same thing. *This guy thinks he's God's gift to women. But I'll be cordial as long as his mother is here.*

During lunch, Meryl looked over my Remington article.

"Amelia, you are a superb writer. I'm very happy you took me up on my offer and that you're writing again. I've read some of your magazine articles – very impressive."

"Thank you so much. At first, I wasn't sure whether or not to accept the assignment; however, I must admit I was very excited to write again especially for a company as prestigious as the Montford-Wellesley Corporation."

Meryl smiled, "I appreciate your enthusiasm. And if I may be so bold I would say that you are as an accomplished a writer as your husband."

"Wow, I've never been compared to the great Montana Joe. I'm flattered."

She laughed at my sarcastic reply. I really enjoy Meryl's company. I also love a woman who enjoys a good dose of sarcasm. It's been a while since I've conversed with a business woman of her stature and success. Her son was an entirely different subject. He was self-centered, impressed with his own career, not to mention a budding alcoholic. I've never known anyone with such an obsessive personality. He's the antithesis of Joe or is he Joe's evil doppelganger? He is to alcohol, what Joe was to coffee. The similarities are coincidental at best because there could never be another Lash Montana. Like Joe used to say, "The world isn't ready for another handsome cowboy writer. That title belongs to me and me alone."

After lunch I asked if they'd like coffee. "Now I must warn you that it's my husband's recipe. It's definitely not for the faint of heart. Raymond calls it watered down black top with a dash of sugar. Jameson declined saying he'd had enough caffeine for the day. I interpreted that to mean he needed something stronger and more potent. He excused himself and told his mother he'd catch up with her later. Meryl glared at him asking if he'd be back before dinner.

"Don't worry. I'll be back in a few hours. I just need to make a run into town. I've got to pick something up before the town rolls their sidewalks up for the night."

"Why must you always mock my hometown Jameson? I don't want to hear another snip at Malta or Dodson-- is that understood?"

He nodded and kissed her on her cheek. "I'm sorry, Mother. I'm just not a small town kind of fellow. I need a little more action than these towns can offer. Hey, I'll even stop by the bakery and pick up that strawberry cheesecake you love so much, Amelia. So, are we good?"

Jameson bolted out the door and took off in his truck. Meryl shook her head and apologized to me for his abrupt exit.

"You have nothing to apologize for. He's a grown man and if I want an apology from him I'll grab his collar and choke one out of him!"

Meryl smiled, "I bet you would. Lash Montana married a heck of strong woman. It's good to see women who are able to stand on their own two feet especially after a spouse's death. I honestly don't know what we'd do if Mr. Wellesley died. He's the backbone of our family not to mention the corporation."

I disagreed with Meryl. "I believe you could hold your own in a bar fight. You're one tough lady Mrs. Montford-Wellesley." I heard the coffee pot's final gurgle. "How about we toast to beautiful women being strong over a cup of authentic Montana Joe brew? Are you game?"

Meryl stood up and threw her shoulders back. "Does a coyote howl at the moon?"

I laughed out loud, "I like your style Meryl. Let's let the men folk do whatever it is they do and have coffee outside by the pond. It's a lovely day, and I could use some fresh air."

I offered her a pair of my old boots. She took off her heels, put them by the door and walked outside in her bare feet.

"I do miss Montana. I'd forgotten how good it feels to walk barefoot in the grass. Is it okay if I wade in the pond?"

I was shocked by her request. *Who knew she loved the outdoors.* I grabbed a pair of my jeans and a work shirt. She returned wearing my old plaid work shirt and jeans, with her hair unpinned. She shook it out letting it fall onto her shoulders.

"Now that's much better. It's been a while since I've literally let down my hair."

We walked to the pond and sat in the grass.

"So tell me Rose how did you meet Lash? I'm a sucker for a good love story."

I told her about my need for an adventure which led me to stop at Currysville Library where I ran into Lash. From there, he pursued me like a man possessed. In fact, I thought he was some crazy Midwestern cowboy stalker. I was tempted to buy a can of pepper spray, but after two days of getting to know him, he'd won me over. I fell hopelessly in love with this charming, over caffeinated, sexy cowboy fiction writer who lassoed my heart. Lash was my husband and confidant, but more importantly, he was my best friend.

Meryl could tell it saddened me to reminisce about Joe. She quickly switched the conversation and asked about Lash's latest works. I told her about Hanna's fantastic news regarding his last series being made into a mini-series on the Wild Western Channel.

"That's wonderful news Amelia! He was a superb western novelist. His books truly portray the experience of the old west. It's as if he lived during that era and was writing from memory."

If you ask Raymond he would beg to differ. His incessant need to research everything about that time period made him the bane of Raymond's existence. I chuckled to myself thinking back on their incessant arguments over a trivial historical fact.

The sound of Jameson's truck racing up the driveway stopped us midsentence. I didn't realize we'd been talking so long. Three hours had passed since he'd left. He hopped out of the truck running around to the passenger's side to retrieve a white bakery box. When he turned around, we noticed that his beard and mustache was gone. He looked completely different. Some people call it the Clark Kent/Superman Phenomena when someone can change their appearance by simply removing facial hair or eye glasses. He also had a little bit of a gap between his front teeth like Joe. In fact without all the crap on his face, he was sort of handsome. For a minute, he reminded me of Joe. But his brown shifty eyes and glasses were nothing like Joe. I missed Joe's beautiful blue-green eyes. What I wouldn't give to see one of his winks and a shit-eating grins.

"Here ya' go, Rose, just like I promised – one strawberry cheesecake. I had to wait for them to put the fresh strawberries on so I thought I'd head over to the barber for a quick shave. And that's your gift, Mother – do you like it?

"Oh my goodness, yes I do! You look like my son again."

He smiled, "Great, now if you two ladies wouldn't mind I'll excuse myself. I've got lots of emails and paperwork to finish if I'm going to be stuck out here for a bit. Not that I mind being stuck with you, Mother. And I'm sure Rose will be happy to have her home and life back. I would never want to overstay my welcome."

I thought, *that's the first smart think you've said since you've been here Jameson. And if it wasn't for your mother I would have put a boot up your ass days ago.*

Meryl and I walked back to the house. She was visibly tired. I suggested she take a hot bath and quick nap before dinner. "I think I'll take you up on that Amelia. I must admit I'm somewhat exhausted from the day's event. A little rest would do me good."

We walked down the hallway and passed Joe's office. She peeked in. "You must miss him so much Amelia."

"Yes, I miss him more than anyone can imagine. But everyday it gets a little bit better . . . and please do call me Rose. Nothing bonds two people like Joe's incredibly strong nuclear waste coffee."

"Okay, Rose and you may call me, well . . . Meryl."

We laughed so hard we both snorted. "You are one funny lady, Meryl."

"And I think you are one beautiful and brilliant lady, Rose. But enough of the mutual admiration accolades. I do believe you said something about a hot bath."

"Yes I did and did I forget to mention is also has a whirlpool setting?"

Meryl grinned, "Okay, now you're just trying to butter me up. Thank you for your gracious hospitality. It's truly appreciated."

I brought in extra towels and a terry cloth bath robe and went into the living room.

My lovely afternoon chatting with Meryl took my mind off Joe's email. My logical side totally understood my eccentric husband's rationale for not telling me about his condition. But my emotional side was extremely hurt by his lack of trust in me. I wanted to look into his eyes and tell him it didn't matter if he were sick. But he was right. As a caretaker, I would have smothered his spirit. And that would have killed him long before the cancer.

As angry as I am with you Joe, you were right. You were always right. It was something I loved and hated about you.

A knock on the door broke my concentration. I heard Cecilia formally greeting someone who sounded like Keough. It was his brother Kurt.

"Hello, Miss Amelia it's good to see you again."

"Kurt, it's good to see you again and what's with all this formal stuff – call me Rose."

He chuckled, "Okay, howdy Rose. I swear you look younger and prettier every time I see you. How's the baby?"

"The baby is almost three-years-old and a handful. She'll be getting up soon from her nap. I'm sure she'll be happy to see you although she may mistake you for Keough. I swear you two look so much alike. Did twins run in your family?"

"From what I understand they do. Our grandfather was a twin and so was our pappy. In fact that's why I'm here. Keough left this box of photographs at my place before Joe died. He thought you'd get a kick out of seeing them. They're some of Joe as a kid, his sisters and their mama Charlotte. I think there's one or two of our parents and grandparents."

I couldn't stop staring at Kurt. He was the spitting image of Keough only he was a little thinner in the face. But just like Joe, both of them had the same blue-green eyes.

Meryl, still clad in her bathrobe, came from the guest room into the kitchen. Kurt caught a glimpse of her and did a double take.

"Oh I'm sorry Rose. I should have called before dropping by. I didn't realize you had company. Attractive company I might add. And who may I ask is this lovely lady?"

Before I could answer him, Meryl walked into the living room.

"Oh Meryl, I was just about to introduce you to my father-in-law's brother, Kurt. Kurt, this is Meryl Monford Wellesley, head of the Montford-Wellesley Corporation."

For a brief moment they stared at each other.

Kurt squinted, "Very nice to meet you and pardon my asking, but do I know you? You look very familiar and I pride myself on never forgetting a beautiful woman."

Meryl paused for a moment then replied, "I'm from Dodson. Have you ever lived in or near there?"

Kurt scratched his head. "Well, my brother and sister-in-law lived near Dodson. Maybe that's where we've met. Either way, I'm Kurt Montana and I have a miserable old brother named Keough. If you haven't noticed we're twins – I'm the handsome one."

"Meryl's eye widened. "Yes, now I remember you. You owned a small ranch outside of Dodson. My husband used to buy cattle from you."

Kurt laughed, Yep, that's me. I remember when you first started ranchin', your husband didn't know a bull from a cow. He learned quickly when he tried to milk a bull, hah!"

"We gave up ranching long ago. He's doing quite well; in fact, we just dedicated the green playground to the Early Childhood Development Center at the college."

While they were catching up, I went to check on Charlotte. She was up and about playing with her toys. I motioned for her to come into the living room and meet her pap-pap's brother.

"Charlotte this is Kurt; he's Keough's twin brother – can you say hello?"

She looked at me, then at Kurt then back at me.

"Two pap-paps, Mama, there's two pap-paps! "

We all laughed at her confusion; however, Charlotte was not amused. She couldn't figure out the concept of twins. And to make matters worse, Keough walked in from the deck door.

"What's all this commotion about? Hold on I smell something rotten. What the heck is it? I'd know that foul smell anywhere. Hello, Brother."

"Well if it ain't my miserable baby brother. How are ya' Keough?"

The two men hugged slapping each other on the back. "I found that box of photographs you left at my place and thought you might like them back."

Keough laughed, "I was just thinkin' about them photos the other day; must be a twin thing. Anyway, I see you've met the lovely Miss Meryl. She grew up around these parts too."

"Yes, we're having a pleasant conversation; well it was pleasant until you showed up."

Keough, Meryl and I continued chatting. Kurt still couldn't remember why she seemed so familiar besides living in Dodson and then it dawned on him.

He whispered to Meryl, "Now I remember! Didn't Keough's wife work for you? That's how I know you. She was your housekeeper for a while. My nephew Lash used to play with your son Jamie. I do believe they were the same age. Am I right?"

Meryl looked very uncomfortable. *Please don't let him put two and two together. Jameson would never forgive me!*

Meryl composed her thoughts then excused herself saying she was going for a nap claiming jet lag had finally caught up with her.

Keough and Kurt tipped their hats acknowledging her departure.

Keough readjusted his hat, "Okay, Big Brother since you're here, why don't you give me a hand with the horses. You do remember how to work horses, don't you?"

Kurt bristled, "Yeah I do. Sadly, you don't remember how to take a bath. You stink like you're getting paid by the hour!"

Both men laughed and continued insulting one another until they reached the horse stalls. I noticed the box of photos sitting on the floor beside the coffee table. I took a few photographs out and thumbed through them. There was one when Joe was a kid. He was sitting on a horse in front of a woman. *This must be his mother Charlotte. She's beautiful.* Joe had her smile. *And here I thought he got his shit-eating-smile from Keough!* There were pictures of his sisters playing in the hay with Joe and wading in the cattle ponds. *It must have been fun growing up here as a child.* I noticed one picture of Charlotte sitting on the bed with Joe in her arms as a newborn. But something about it puzzled her. There was another child lying on the bed beside her. *Hmm, maybe she was taking care of someone else's kid?* As best as she could tell they looked to be the same age. Not much bigger than my Charlotte when she was a month old. She put the photo back into the box.

I should ask Meryl about Joe's mother. Maybe she could tell me a little bit more about her. Speaking of Meryl, I'd better check on her. She seemed very pale when she went for her nap. I hope she's okay.

Chapter 14

Raymond was busy preparing his cabins for the summer season. He opened the door to the cabin Joe used to reserve. As he stepped through the doorway, he expected to hear Joe yell at him for ruining his concentration. All would be forgiven when Raymond would hand him a cup of coffee. It felt strange not having him around. He continued to tidy up when he noticed a photograph tucked in the frame of the wall mirror. The photo was of him and Joe sitting on the porch steps. They both held coffee cups in their hand. *I remember when Rose took this photo. It was just before she found out his cancer had spread.*

A handwritten message on the back read, "A true friend is someone who knows every unsavory thing about you and still likes you."

Raymond slipped the photo into his shirt pocket. *I must frame it. It probably is one of the only photos I have of me and Joe not arguing.*

He chuckled to himself and continued his cleaning. An hour had passed, when his stomach reminded him it was lunch time. Gathering his cleaning gear, he headed back to his office. Before he stepped inside, he noticed that a red truck had turned into his road. *I know this truck.* He put his gear down and walked over towards the parking area. It was Jameson. *What the hell is he doing out here? Better yet, how did he find this place on his own? He could get lost in a revolving door.*

Raymond walked up to his truck, "Jameson is that you? What happened to that mangy prairie dog that covered your face? What a surprise to see you out here. Are you lost again?"

Jameson reached into the back seat and took out a small overnight bag. "Hello Raymond, it's good to see you too. And to answer your question, I shaved the prairie dog off today. In case you didn't realize, *that* was sarcasm."

"Yes, I know sarcasm, Jameson. And, it's wonderful to see you again. I've missed you like a fever blister. Now that all the bullshit is over—again—what are you doing out here? Does your mother know you've run away from home?"

Jameson slammed the truck door. "Hah, no she doesn't and let's keep it that way for now. I just needed to get out of that town for a while. She wants to stay for another week or two reminiscing about her childhood. I love my mom, but I don't want to travel with her down memory lane. So, I skipped town. May I stay here for a few nights?"

"Of course, you may stay as long as you like, but you still haven't answered my question? How did you find this place? It's not like the five star hotels you're used to staying in."

Jameson sat on the steps. "To be honest, I felt smothered. Mother is expecting us to have some sort of mother-and-son-bonding week, and I can't stand this place – no offense."

Raymond was surprised by his honesty. *This guy's been cocky since the first day I met him and now he wants to mellow out and have a kumbaya moment.* He pretended to listen to Jameson's attempt to explain why he felt so bored.

"So, can you help me understand this Raymond? Everyone seems to consider you a good listener and having all the answers to the world's problems."

Raymond stood up and scratched his head in confusion. *Should I dazzle him with Blackfoot bullshit or should I tell him I zoned out minutes ago listening to his rich boy problems? Either way, I'll have to listen to it all over again – oh well.*

"Jameson, let me tell you that your problems are small and insignificant compared to the problems of the world. As soon as you realize this, you will have the power to solve all of your issues – does this make sense to you?" *I hope he buys this because this is all I can offer him at the moment.*

Jameson shook his head. "Yes, it makes sense to me Raymond. Thanks for listening to me. I had to vent and I appreciate you lending your ear."

"You are welcome, Jameson. I've always been a great listener; I hope I helped." *Jeez, this guy is so gullible. Maybe I can sell him my special bag of wooden nickels.*

Raymond started to walk away when Jameson stopped him and asked another question. "Since you're in such a great listening mode, can you tell me why this Lash Montana is such a legend in this part of the country? I'm going to be honest with you, I'd never heard of him until Mother told me about him. Is it true he's written over one hundred books? Are people really that interested in that cowboy crap?"

His questions caught Raymond off guard. "What do you mean cowboy crap? His so-called cowboy crap is what built the Montana Joe business empire. It's worth billions—not so crappy, huh?"

"Wow, so this guy was really famous, huh? Maybe I should get some of his novels and read them while Mother is on her Dodson pilgrimage."

"I'm sure if you ask Rose she will give you a few. I would add that you ask her nicely. You haven't made yourself very likeable in her eyes. This will give you the opportunity to redeem yourself. Look at it as a peace offering of sorts."

"I will, Raymond. I'd like to know more about this man, Lash Jackson Montana. And I'd like to know how the hell he scored a hot babe like Amelia."

Raymond's brow furrowed. "First of all, Amelia is not a hot babe she is a lovely, smart and attractive woman, one you will respect – is that clear? And secondly, Lash and I were good friends for years. I can tell you anything you'd like to know about him even though from time-to-time he was a huge pain in my ass."

Jameson chuckled. "I'm glad someone else besides me was a pain in your ass. I feel quite honored to be on the short list of people who annoy you."

Raymond smiled. "Okay now you've made me laugh. That in itself deserves a fresh cup of coffee. Come on – I just made a fresh pot and nobody else will touch Joe's special blend. Are you brave enough to try it?"

Jameson nodded, "I'll give it a try. We all have to die of something. And again Raymond thanks for your time. I'm feeling better."

"Jameson, I'm glad you're feeling better. Now, are you stalling or are you not brave enough to drink this over brewed pot of buffalo shit?"

They talked for hours; Raymond telling him about Lash, their friendship, his marriage to Amelia and his untimely death. Jameson was surprised by the fact that they were the exact same age, born in the same month of August and a day apart.

"My mother and Lash's mother must have been pregnant at the same time. He was born on a Friday and I was born on a Saturday. That's wild!"

Raymond thought it was very interesting as well. He knew of the hospital. It was the only hospital near Dodson and wasn't very large. Raymond tucked the piece of information away in his mind. *I'll ask my old friend Sheila if she remembers anything about the births. She was a nurse back then and might remember the details. Amelia might get a kick out of knowing that Jameson's mother Meryl and Joe's mother Charlotte were giving birth in the same hospital at the same time. As Joe would say it's got the makings of a good story.*

The phone rang in Raymond's office. It was a New York phone number.

"Hello, Winterbee's Seasonal Montana Cabins."

"Hey there Raymond, it's Jannine Westone, or should I say the soon-to-be Jannine Montana; how is it going, you incredibly handsome man?"

"Jannine, you must have the wrong number. There's no handsome man here. You must need glasses."

"Hah, and I love you too Raymond. Morgan says hello and hopes you haven't scalped anyone lately."

"Tell Morgan no not yet, but the day is new and there are so many people out here who I'd like to scalp, but I'm sure you didn't call to talk about scalping. What can I do for you?"

"Well, Morgan and I have been talking and we've decided to hold off on the wedding until next year. It doesn't feel right us getting married when Amelia is still grieving. I love her so much and I wouldn't want to add to her pain by asking her to be a witness to us getting hitched. Morgan agrees with me. So, the question is – can we count on you to perform the ceremony same time next year?"

"Of course Jannine, this is not a problem. You and Morgan are like my kids. Not to worry."

"Thanks so much Raymond. Plus, Morgan and I want to visit my family in Japan. Being part Asian I can only imagine what they will do when I bring over an honest-to-goodness cowboy. I'll have to video their first meeting! Oh my God, it'll be too funny," Jannine prattled on. "My mom is so unbelievably traditional Japanese, and my dad is such a jarhead. I guess that's why I'm a holy terror. Military brats generally are. My dad is a huge western fan. You know the type who's seen every John Wayne movie ever made. Maybe Morgan should grab a couple of Joe's books and give them to him as a welcome-to-the-family gift."

"With or without books, I'm sure they'll be happy to see you both. Thanks for calling me Jannine. I miss you two kids. Keep in touch, okay?"

"We will and keep in an eye on Amelia for us. I'll call her later, but we wanted to make sure you were okay with our change of plans. Bye Raymond."

Raymond went back inside to see Jameson pouring what looked to be bourbon to his coffee.

"Jameson! What the hell are you doing?"

He spilled what was left in the pint bottle onto the table. "Jeez, Raymond you almost gave me a heart attack!"

Raymond walked over and grabbed the empty bottle from his hand and tossed it into the trash.

He sat directly in front of Jameson looking him straight in his eyes.

"I'm only going to tell you this once. So blow whatever mule shit you have out of your ears and listen closely. I'm sick and tired of watching you drink yourself into a stupor day after day. And in case you don't know, EVERYBODY knows about your drinking. My buddy Keough, Joe's father, is a recovering alcoholic. It took his son's death the dry him out. What's it going to take for you to quit? Car wreck, DUI, or the death of someone you love or yourself?"

Jameson's face turned red. No one had ever confronted him about his drinking. Most were too afraid of losing their gravy train bar tab to be this brutally honest with him.

"Raymond, don't you think I've tried to stop drinking. Don't you think I know what this is doing to me and my family? My dad won't even talk to me anymore. He's given up on me. My mother is in denial about it thinking a few extra days in Montana will sober me up. Everybody thinks I'm just a loser rich kid with no will-power, so that's what I aspire to be – high aspirations, huh?"

Raymond took the cup out of his hand and poured the contents down the drain.

"The first step is the hardest. I just took it for you by pouring that stuff down the drain. Now it's up to you to take the second step."

"Okay, so what's the second step? Can you answer me that Raymond? How am I supposed to know what step two is?"

"How the hell should I know, I'm not you, and I'm not an alcoholic. That, my inebriated friend, is your journey. However, I think there is something that might help you – are you game?"

"Will I hate it?

Raymond smiled, "Absolutely, but like I said I'm willing to help if you're willing to take the next step. I've invited Rose to join me at a drumming circle tomorrow. It's a spiritual cleansing of sorts. It helps the mind and body release bad energy and replace it with light, love and wisdom. You're more than welcome to join us."

Jameson hesitated then responded. "Okay, what have I got to lose? Plus it'll give me another reason not to go to Dodson!"

Raymond slapped him in the back of his head.

"OUCH! What the hell was that for?"

"For using the drumming circle as an excuse; the first thing you must learn is to take full responsibility for your life. Either you want to attend the drumming circle or you don't."

Jameson rubbed his head. "Okay, okay. I get it. No excuses. I'll go!"

Raymond handed him his phone. "Call your mother and tell her what's going on. It will be difficult and you will feel frightened, but afterwards your conscience will feel lighter and free – trust me."

He picked up the phone but before he called, he asked Raymond how he knew all of this.

"I'd like to say the spirits of my ancestors come to me at night and bestowed this wisdom in my dreams. But the truth is I get most of this crap from watching Dr. Phil and Oprah."

Jameson laughed out loud. He thought how good it felt to laugh. Raymond laughed with him.

"It's good to see you laughing Jameson. Laughter is also good for the soul."

"Did you get that one from Oprah too?"

"Nope, I think I stole that one was from Milton Berle."

Jameson walked over to Raymond and shook his hand. "As much as I hate to admit it, I appreciate your concern and you taking the time to help me. Thanks Raymond. I understand why Lash and Amelia love you like family. I wish my dad would take the time to talk to me the way you just did. Strange, I'm nothing like my parents. I don't have any of their traits – good or bad."

"I'm sure your father would enjoy talking to you if you asked him nicely and didn't act like an arrogant asshole. And I'm sure you do have their traits but you are too wrapped up in your own thoughts, fears, and self-inflicted weaknesses. When you return to New York, talk to him about your concerns, he might surprise you. Now go take a shower . . . you smell horrible!"

Jameson made a snarky remark under his breath then left for his cabin. He reached in the back of the truck for his toiletry kit. *Whew, I am a bit ripe. A long hot shower will definitely help.*

Raymond called Amelia to remind her of tomorrow evening's drumming circle. He also wanted to give her a heads up that Jameson would be attending.

"Okay Raymond. Hah, very funny. You and I both know he would never attend anything like this. If it doesn't involve beer, gold diggers or cell phones he's not interested."

"I'm not joking Amelia, he's coming with us. He came out to the cabins just to chat with me. In fact he's staying here tonight. I had a long talk with him, and I think some of it sunk in."

I asked Raymond what kind of things they'd talked about. He said, "We talked mostly about you and Lash."

"He wanted to know about the man who stole the heart of such beautiful woman. Did you know that he was born the day after Joe, in the same hospital and the same year?"

"No, I didn't, but let's get back to him thinking I'm beautiful."

Raymond laughed, "He also commented on how modest you are. Anyway, we can talk about this later. I just wanted to remind you of the circle. I'll see you at the cabin at 7:00 PM. We can all go in my truck."

"I don't think so! The last time I rode in your truck the windows wouldn't close and I ended up eating bugs. Not to mention we stalled half way home. I'll drive."

"Okay, Rose if you insist. I swear you are sounding just like Joe."

"Oh really, is that a bad thing?"

"No just an observation, Rose. They say married couples tend to take on each other's characteristics. If you start to badger me about old ancestral Blackfoot customs and history, then I'll know you are channeling Joe's spirit, and I'll be forced to make fun of you. Bye Rose."

The phone rang again – it was Jannine.

"Well hello there stranger! How are things going in the Big Apple?"

"Hey Amelia, Morgan and I are about to head out for dinner, but I wanted to give you the news before Raymond told you."

"Uh oh, what's going on? I was just talking to Raymond, and he didn't mention anything. If it's bad news I don't want to know."

"No, it's not bad news. It's just that Morgan and I are postponing the wedding until next year. And before you go all panicky, I just thought it would be good for him to meet my folks before we tied the knot."

I let out a deep breath, "This is good news Jannine. I think that's a smart idea. It's always nice to meet your future in-laws before they become a permanent fixture on your life. Are you going to Japan or are they coming to the USA?"

"We're going over this summer. I have loads of vacation time from working with you so that won't be a problem. I'm also thinking of leaving the magazine. The woman I'm working for is nice, but she's not you. Even worse, she's wearing last year's Valentino with this year's Dior! Who does this? Anyway, Morgan says it's totally up to me. I enjoy working, but to be honest, Amelia, I really miss you. Sweetie, I've gotta go. Morgan's getting antsy not to mention hungry. Give the baby a big kiss from me and Morgan and I'll call you later, love ya' and miss ya'. . . Bye."

Jannine if you only knew how much I miss you too. I really miss my confidant and partner in crime. We had such a good time working for the magazine, but the times are changing. Internet publishing is supposedly the wave of the future. It will be interesting to see what happens to the magazine.

Hanna had already thought about the advances in book technology coming down the pike and said one day they could turn Joe's books into e-books and audio books. But for now, people will just have to read Montana Joe hardcopy books. I laughed to myself thinking what his books would sound like in Japanese.

The next morning, I realized I was out of shampoo and hair conditioner. I'd been using Joe's lavender products, but even they were now gone. I needed to go into town and pick up a few odds and ends. I also decided to have lunch. It was strange eating alone. I missed sitting across from Joe and talking about Timothy hay verses alfalfa. I noticed Grace from the Early Childhood Center was also having lunch. She saw me and came over to my table. It was good chatting with her about the Play Garden and how much the kids love it.

She glanced down at her watch, "My goodness, it's after four o'clock. I'd better get going. It was such a pleasure having lunch with you, Rose."

Oh shit, it's already passed 4 o'clock! I'd better get back home. I need to get showered and head over to Raymond's place."

Cecilia had dinner ready. Meryl was still sleeping. I told Cecilia to let her sleep. It was obvious she needed to rest. Montana's climate can take a toll on you if you're not use to it. It took me months before I felt comfortable. New York City is at sea level compared to Malta's altitude which is a little over 2,200 feet. Cecilia said not to worry about the Charlotte and the guys.

"I've cooked enough food for an army of soldiers with tapeworms."

"Eww Cecilia, that's disgusting! I'll just trust your judgment on that one."

Cecilia wrapped up a few slices of her homemade sour cream pound cake for Raymond. "I know how much he loves it. Oh and there's a few slices for you. My goodness, Amelia you could stand to gain a few more pounds. People may get the impression I'm a lousy cook!"

I laughed thinking no one would ever believe such a statement. If nothing else, Cecilia was a fabulous cook. Her Tex-Mex dishes were to die for as were her cakes and pies. I was surprised I wasn't as big as a barn eating her meals.

I collected my things and left for Raymond's place. It felt good driving back to a place that meant so much to me and Joe. Along the way, I reminisced about the first time we stayed there. It's also the place where we conceived Charlotte. Joe was over the moon when the pregnancy test turned positive. He refused to throw it away until we saw the doctor. I guess he wanted a memento of his manly fertility.

It was dusk when I arrived at the cabins. I parked beside Jameson's truck taking a quick peek inside the cab. *No beer or whiskey bottles – that's a good sign.*

Raymond came out to greet me. "Hello Rose, glad you made it here okay. And what's that I smell? Is it Cecilia's sour cream pound cake?"

"Yep, it sure is. You can smell it from the porch?"

He laughed. "I'd like to string you along with Blackfoot mumbo-jumbo, but Cecilia just called and told me you were bringing it. She just wanted to make sure you arrived safely."

I chucked Raymond on the arm. "I never know when you're bullshitting me or just being sagely."

"Most of the time, I'm full of it Amelia. It's one of the many things I would do that annoyed Joe to no end. I tell you Rose, what I wouldn't give to hear his irritating, western drawl arguing with me one more time. I miss him too—more than I'm willing to admit."

"What in the tarnation are you two yammering about now?"

We froze in our tracks. *Oh my God . . . Joe?* We turned around only to find a snickering Jameson.

"So, how's that for a Montana drawl? Did it sound authentic?" *He sounded so much like Lash it was frightening!*

After our initial shock, Raymond could tell I was visibly shaken. He tried to play it off saying he didn't sound like a Montana native; however, he might pass for a toothless hillbilly trailer park resident. "Rose, I know you hate riding in my old truck but how about you let me drive us to the drumming circle. I've even fixed the window so you don't have to worry about the bugs in your hair."

"Okay Raymond, I'll sit in the back seat, and Jameson you can ride shotgun." Raymond wasn't too pleased about the seating arrangement but agreed to her request.

We arrived at the circle early. A few people had started gathering wood for the bonfire. Some I recognized from my last visit. They said how sorry they were to hear about Joe's death. One elderly Blackfoot woman said that she would ask the spirits for Joe to attend. I wasn't too thrilled about her offer, but I wasn't about to tell an old lady she was full of proverbial shit and not to bother. Who knows maybe she's got some ethereal connection to the spirit world.

More people started showing up. The fire was growing stronger with every attendee. Each person brought something special to help fortify the bonfire. I didn't remember this part of the ceremony. I guess it was completed by the time Raymond and I arrived. I asked him if he'd brought something.

"Yes, in fact I've brought something for you and Jameson. He handed me and Jameson a small carved animal. Mine was a hummingbird. Jameson's was an owl. We asked him why he chose these two animals.

"The owl brings the energy of hidden knowledge—a knowledge that is silent and unspoken."

Jameson looked puzzled. "Why do you think I have hidden knowledge? People usually say I'm an open book."

Raymond laughed. "Hey, I don't know why my spirit guides chose it for you. If you want to blame anybody, blame them. But I must tell you it's not a good idea to piss off spirit guides."

Jameson shrugged his shoulders and continued to examine the owl.

"Rose, you already know why you received the hummingbird. It has visited you numerous times and each time it brings you closer to inner peace."

Raymond also explained that at a point in the ceremony, we were to toss the carvings into the bonfire.

"If there's anyone or anything you want to connect with, the totems will deliver the message to them or it and will relay the answer to you in the form of a soul whisper. Only you will be able to hear it."

Jameson raised his hand as if in a class room.

"Hold on Raymond. I understand the 'anyone' element, but what the hell do you mean connect with anything? I've connected with a few fists in my day, but that was strictly in self defense."

He shook his head. "You know Jameson, you really know how to suck the joy out of everything – just relax you'll understand in due time."

Raymond thought *Maybe we can ask the spirits to drop kick him into the bonfire.*

After parking the truck, we walked to the drumming area. I felt a sense of calm then anxiety as we walked towards the kindling and logs. *Relax, Rose it's not like you've never been to a drumming circle.* Raymond noticed my tension.

"You will be okay, Rose. I'll be with you and so will Joe. He's always with you if you take the time to listen."

I stopped and looked at Raymond. "How do you know? How do you know there is this afterlife where those who've passed over are watching us?"

Raymond knew I was sincerely curious. I wasn't making fun of the spirit world like Jameson tried to do.

"Rose, I want you to do something for me. When the drumming starts I want you to sit quietly. Listen with your heart and spirit—not your ears. Things will come to you. You will remember these things. I'm feeling that Joe will send you a message. I've felt his presence around me for quite some time. But he's never sent me any messages. I think he's waiting for you to hear him. Are you prepared?"

"I think so, Raymond. I also have a few choice words for him as well. Did you know he KNEW he was sick and dying a few weeks after he met me?"

Raymond sighed. "Yes, Rose I did. He begged me not to mention his illness to you or anyone else. He didn't want people feeling sorry for him. He was a strong willed man who wanted to live and die by his own rules. It was one of the things I loved about him and one of the things I hated about him. So many times I wanted to say something to you, but Joe would intervene."

"But if he loved me Raymond, why did he lie? Why didn't he trust me to support and take care of him?"

"That's exactly why he didn't tell you, Rose. He didn't want your support or sympathy. He wanted your love. He wanted to take care of YOU and not the other way around. Rose, if you haven't realized it yet, you were the one and only love of his life. You were and still are his soul mate. He didn't want anything to interfere with the physical love you two had for each other."

I noticed Jameson was getting anxious too. I asked Raymond if we could continue the conversation later. "Of course, Rose. Let's enjoy the circle tonight. Hey, maybe the fire spirits will give Jameson a hot foot. Now that would make me laugh out loud."

I laughed, "We can only pray and hope."

We found a spot beside a large log to watch the ceremony. Jameson seemed uninterested until people started showing up with the traditional drums.

"Wow, I thought they would have recorded music. You mean people really play the drums?"

Raymond looked at me and shook his head.

"What did I tell you Rose, he's far worse than Joe when it comes to having a humongous empty space between his ears."

Once the drumming began, the elders chanted prayers around the drum circle bon fire. It quickly blazed into a large and steady fire. They asked us to throw our carvings into the fire and to ask any loved ones who've passed over to join us. If we had a question for them now would be the time to do so.

Jameson tossed his in right away. He *probably asked something stupid like who was going to be in the Super Bowl.*

I waited a few minutes then tossed my hummingbird into the fire. Raymond went back to the truck to get his drum.

"I must be losing my mind. How do you forget to bring your drum at a drumming circle – I'll be right back."

Jameson sat directly beside me. "So what did you ask?"

"Well, obvious what I asked for didn't come to fruition because you're still here and breathing. And it's none of your business what I asked or prayed for!"

"Okay, okay sorry. But I just thought since we're getting all spiritual you might want to know what I asked for. Would you like to know?"

"Not really, but I have a feeling you're going to tell me anyway."

He said he wanted to know why he never felt like he belonged to the Montford-Wellesley family.

"I'm not what you would call Fortune 500 material. If I wasn't a Montford-Wellesley, I probably couldn't get a job at a fast food place."

It must be the drumming or the smoke from the fire because Jameson was actually being honest. I asked him if he'd ever discussed his feeling with his parents.

"I tried to talk to Mother, but she would clam up about my childhood insisting how much she wouldn't change having me for a son for anything in the world. I never got a straight answer from her or Father. But hey, what can I do? I guess I'll never know, huh?"

I told him maybe you'll get your answer during the drumming circle.

"Possibly, but I doubt it. I'm not into this woo-woo shit, but I hope you get your answers. I know we've had our differences, Amelia, but I really admire and respect you. Lash Montana was one hell of a lucky man to have you in his life—no matter how short a life it was."

I was touched by his statement. It was easy to dislike Jameson but listening to him voice his concerns made me reassess my opinion of him. Raymond returned with his drum and joined the drumming. Jameson and I sat quietly, closing our eyes letting the drums guide us through our journey. The first few minutes were uneventful. I was more involved with the chanting and drumming than trying to hear my spirit guide. After a while the drumming got softer and the chanting lowered to a whisper. I could hear voices drifting in and out of my mind and glimpses of people and places flashing as well. I saw my old elementary school and my dad picking me up in his new car and the distinct smell of the leather. Visions of college friends, co-workers I hadn't seen or thought about in years emerged too.

I was about to open my eyes when I heard someone whisper, *Baby, I'm sorry . . . I'm so sorry I had to leave you. Please forgive me but don't forget me. Move on Darlin'. Move on. And for goodness sakes quit your droolin'.*

Raymond's hand on my shoulder brought me back to consciousness. He handed me a tissue. "Here Rose. I wasn't sure if you were crying or drooling."

I realized I was sitting with my mouth hanging slightly open in amazement. "Oh my God, Raymond I heard Joe! I'm sure it was him. He told me t . . ."

Before I could finish Raymond said, "Rose, whatever you heard is sacred to you and you alone. Let it sink in before you share it with anyone."

I also noticed people where packing up to leave. "How long have I been out of consciousness?"

"Almost an hour or so, Jameson is still zoned out or sleeping – not sure."

Jameson stood up, shaking his head trying to focus. "What the fuck just happened? One minute I was thinking about nothing if there is such a thing as thinking about nothing. The next thing I know I'm hearing a voice whisper, *I wish I'd known you brother.* I don't even have a brother! This is some screwed up shit. I need a dri . . ."

Before he could finish his sentence Raymond interjected. "You will not drink; you will remember; you will learn."

Raymond's statement didn't bode well with Jameson until I told him that I had something similar happen, but I wasn't ready to talk about it. "Jameson, don't brush off what you heard. It could make sense later on.

The ride home was quiet. Jameson was still bewildered by what he heard, and I was in shock. It was after midnight when we reached the cabins. Raymond invited us to join him for some tea.

"It'll calm you so that you can sleep; my blend of chamomile and apple mint."

Jameson declined and went directly to his cabin. I decided to stay up a while longer with Raymond. I told him what I'd heard. "Joe wants me to move on. How do I do that Raymond? How do I move on?"

We sat outside on the steps barely able to see our cups in the front of our faces. Raymond brought out a lantern and hung it on a hook over the porch. Seconds after he hung the light, something flew beside it.

We thought it was a large moth, but we were surprised to see it was a hummingbird!

Raymond stuttered, "I...I don't think I've ever seen one fly at night. Rose, if you don't believe in signs from the spirit world . . . here's your proof!"

Chapter 15

Paul was running out of things to do. Keough and Kurt had the barn and stall work completed and Cecilia was handling all of Charlotte's needs. He'd cleaned the kitchen, vacuumed the rooms or as the British say—hovered. Lou had stretched out on the floor as if to say, *Hey Paul, why don't you take a cue from me and relax!*

The only thing that was on the table was his cup that he used for tea. *That's an idea. I'll brew myself a nice cup of tea.* He refilled the kettle and sat in the kitchen until it was ready. There were some cups with Montana Joe book covers on them. *Hmm, probably novelty cups made by his fans.* He also noticed a photograph of Rose and Lash kissing in the kitchen on one of the wall shelves. *They must have taken it themselves.* Digital cameras were quickly becoming the new thing – instant memories of the sort I guess. *I still love the old fashioned photographs. They looked so happy. It's pitiful him dying at such a young age. They never had the chance to enjoy life. A shame it is, a bloody shame!*

The kettle's whistle signaled his water was ready. He poured some of the water into his cup to heat it. Proper Brits heat their cups before adding tea. *Bloody Americans wouldn't know how to brew a proper cuppa if their lives depended on it! And why on earth would they ruin it with lemon! Cream with sugar is the only way to have it.*

He took his tea and a hand full of Cecilia's homemade biscuits or cookies as Americans called them and headed outside on the deck with Lou in tow. "What a brilliant day, Lou. Now I understand why they call this Big Sky country. It's so clear for miles. Far superior to the drizzling bloody rain we have in England."

After a few sips, his mind wondered back to Amelia. *Such a young and beautiful person she is. The sort of woman, I'd settle down with if given the chance. But I could never compare to Lash. No one could ever compare to him. He was one-of-a-kind that's for sure. I wonder if she'll ever find love again. Any man in his right mind would kill to have her as a wife. I'm a self-confirmed bachelor, but I'd change in a blink if she'd have me as a husband. Like that would ever happen. Why on earth would she marry a British truck driver? I'm not unattractive. In fact, she once told me I cleaned up rather well. I'm sure she'd laugh in my face if I mentioned marriage. She's my friend. But of late, I've had feelings for her beyond friendship. Feelings I never had for any women here or in England.*

He finished his tea. As he headed back inside, he caught a glimpse of his reflection in the door. He smoothed his tousled, sandy brown hair then looked at the three-day growth of his beard and mustache. *Gordon Bennett, I need to get rid of this facial hair again!*

He rinsed and washed his tea cup then headed to the guest bathroom. An hour later, he emerged clean shaven.

"Ah, that's much better. I actually feel human again." He stared at his face in the bedroom mirror. *I'd forgotten I had dimples. Bloody hell, I look 12-years old. Has it been that long since I had a complete shave? What a sad sod I am.*

He heard Keough and Kurt walking in. Paul met them at the door. Keough pretended to have a gun. "Okay, Kid, who are you and what have you done with Paul?"

Keough laughed and grabbed Paul's face turning it from side-to-side. "I swear you look like a 10-year old without all that fur on your face. Why'd you shave? It wouldn't be to impress my daughter-in-law now, would it?'

"Like it's any business of yours . . . Naff off!"

Kurt chimed in. "So, it does have something to do with the lovely Amelia. Hey Brother, I do believe this English fella is sweet on her. It don't bother me none, but he's so dang British I can't understand most of what he says. What does naff off mean? "

Keough laughed. "Well Big Brother, let's just say it ain't a compliment and leave it at that."

Lou jumped up and ran to the door. He knew the sound of my truck. Jameson was behind me.

Keough walked to the door letting Lou out to greet us. "Well if it isn't my good-looking daughter-in-law come home from her spiritual hootenanny. I'm going to have to have a long talk with Raymond. He's got you believing in all that Blackfoot happy hunting ground stuff – it ain't healthy."

Lou ran up to me, his tail thrashing about. "Hey, there's my handsome four-legged bodyguard, did you miss me?" He jumped up on his hind legs and licked my face as if to say *I sure did! These guys don't know where you keep my treats!*

I reached into my jacket pocket and retrieved a dog biscuit. "Here you go, Sweetie. I missed you too."

Jameson pet Lou on his head. "Hey Lou buddy, did you miss me too?" Lou ran back over to me for another treat. *Hm, I guess not.*

Keough hugged me. "Hello, Darlin' how was the drumming circle? Did Raymond make you do the hokey-pokey and wear chicken feathers on your head?"

I chuckled. "No, he did not, but he did mention while he was in a spiritual drumming trance he saw a vision of you that made him shiver. He said you were clean, tidy and somewhat intelligent."

Kurt, Paul and Jameson laughed. Keough sneered at them and walked away. "You wait until I see that good-for-nothing Blackfoot. I got something special for him and it ain't pretty!"

"Oh, come on Keough I'm only kidding. He asked about you and I told him you were a Godsend because you've been so helpful around the ranch."

"Rose, you are an ornery woman, plain old ornery; shame on you for taunting me like that!"

Paul walked over and embraced me too. "Good to have you back home, Poppet. Dealing with this lot without you is bloody hard work! How on earth do you keep them in line?"

"I use a cattle prod. All they need is a friendly reminder on the low voltage setting. But enough of that . . . look at you, you look great! I never knew you had such cute dimples. Nice. Very nice! I like this new look a lot. No more covering up that handsome face of yours – deal?" Paul blushed and nodded.

Jameson looked around and asked, "Speaking of ornery woman and cattle prods . . . where is my mother? I've got some questions to ask her about my childhood."

Paul sarcastically mumbled, "Yes, don't we all."

Keough told him she'd gone to Dodson for the day but would return later in the evening. "I hope she finds what she's looking for. She had a handful of photos with her."

Jameson looked puzzled. "Photos? Where did she get photos? She didn't mention any photos of Dodson to me."

Keough pointed to the box on the floor. "When my wife Charlotte passed away, I found them in the attic. I thought Rose would like to thumb through them. Not many of me but dozens of Charlotte and the kids when they were little."

Keough's statement reminded me of the photo I saw of Charlotte with the two infants. I looked through the photographs, but it wasn't there. *I know I put it back in the box before I left for Raymond's place. Where could it have gone?*

Jameson excused himself and headed back to his truck. Keough watched him as he walked out. "Going out for a drink I suppose."

I thought for a minute and then realized he hadn't had a drink all day nor has he brought up the need for one. *Raymond, whatever you said to him – it worked!*

Jameson took something out of his jacket pocket and put it into the back pocket of his jeans then came back to the house. He reached back into his pocket. "Look what Raymond gave me before we left the cabins. It's a double owl totem. Two owls connected. He said he wanted me to have it as a keepsake of my first drumming circle. Hah, I guess he knew I'd need twice the guidance."

Jameson mentioned their lengthy chat before I'd arrived. "For once I felt as if someone was actually listening to me. I respect Raymond. He's a pretty awesome dude."

For once we all agreed on something. Raymond was the spiritual glue that held us together. Even though he wasn't pious about his beliefs, he always had the wisdom to motivate us.

I was exhausted from the previous evening's activities, but I still needed to finish revising Meryl's article. I put on a pot of coffee to keep me focused. As I was brewing the coffee, my mind wandered back to the voices at the circle. Was it really Joe's voice? Did I really hear him tell me to move on? All of it was upsetting, to say the least, but inevitably, it needed to be addressed. I knew at some point I'd need to move on and to let go of my grieving and continue living my life without Joe. *I will try Joe – I promise. However, would you give me another sign to move on – just to be sure? Maybe I'll need a little incentive like dangling a piece of cheesecake in front of me.* I chuckled at the image of me chasing cheesecake on a string. I was also puzzled by the disappearance of the photo. *Who would have taken it?*

I poured a cup of coffee and walked back into the living room. It was then I remembered Meryl had taken the article into the guest room to review it. I walked back to the guest room to retrieve it. Cecilia was changing out the linens and towels. I offered to take the towels in for her. I picked up the article from the guest room nightstand. While I was hanging them in the bathroom I saw the photo on the dresser. *Why would Meryl take this particular photo?* I'll ask her about it when she returns from Dodson.

Cecilia had Charlotte bathed, fed and dressed. She ran over to me with her stuffed Lou puppy. "Mama, Cecilia is taking us to a movie with doggies in it."

I scooped her up into my arms. "Really, and what movie would that be Baby Girl?"

"The spotty dog movie mama . . . the one with all the spotty dogs!"

Cecilia laughed. "She means *101 Dalmatians*, it's playing at the Main Street Theater, and I thought it would be a fun day trip for this lovely little girl who has been so well behaved while her mama's been away."

"But Cecilia, it's your day off. Do you really want to spend it around screaming kids?"

She smiled. "Why not, it's no different than listening to the commotion between Keough and Raymond. Only the kids are cuter and easier to please—a cup of animal crackers, and she's happy."

I thanked Cecilia for her selflessness. Giving up a day off on this ranch nominates you for sainthood. And she was indeed a saint. I must admit Joe had good taste and judgment when it came to women. He'd brag about it whenever we made love which led him to boast that he was hung like a horse as well. Always a gentleman, he'd say, "If it's true and you've done it . . . then it ain't braggin'."

Before they left, I asked Cecilia if she knew when Meryl was returning from Dodson.

"I believe she said late afternoon and she'd be home before dinner."

"How about I make dinner for us tonight? I've had a hankerin' for roast beef and potatoes."

Charlotte giggled. "Mama you sound like Pap-Pap!"

"Okay, Charlotte now you've insulted me. You and Cecilia have a good time at the movies. Come over here and give your mama a kiss and hug." She ran over and squeezed my neck then waved goodbye.

As they drove off, the phone rang – it was Meryl.

"Hello Rose, its Meryl. I wanted to give you an update on my return. I'll be back by 3:00 PM today. So many memories came flooding back, I guess I lost track of the time. See you soon."

She never gave me a chance to say anything. *I wonder what's going on.* "Oh well, I guess I'll find out when she returns."

I poured another cup of coffee and sat on the couch. The place was unusually quiet with Charlotte out of the house. I picked up the box of photos and spread them out beside me on the couch. Photos of Lash and his sisters on horses or playing in the hay loft–they were typical childhood photographs. I did notice there weren't many of Keough or Charlotte. I knew Keough wasn't the best of fathers and was often traveling with the rodeo. *But as a parent one would think he'd take at least a few photos with his kids. He must have been some drunken mess back then.*

I continued thumbing through the photos. Joe was such a cute kid. I was amazed how much he looked like his mother. She was such a beautiful woman. Why Keough preferred drink and rodeo over her was beyond me. One photo caught my eye. It was Charlotte when she was pregnant. From the date on the picture she must have been carrying Joe. It also had how many months she was pregnant on the back. Six months and she looked ready to deliver. She reminded me of my friend Cheryl in Manhattan and how big she was when she was having her twins.

I went into the guest room and brought the photo back to the living room to get a better look. There were definitely two infants in the photo. *But Charlotte didn't have twins; there were only Joe and his two younger sisters.* There was another photo of Charlotte hanging laundry and the same two infants in the photo.

Keough and Kurt must have smelled the coffee and came into the kitchen from the deck stairs.

"Hey, Keough come here for a second."

"What can I help you with Your Highness? Need your back scratched or someone to pour you another cup of coffee?"

"No Smart Ass; I want to show you something. Who is the other infant in these photographs? Was Charlotte taking care of another child? It looks to be the same age as Joe. Do you remember who it is?"

Keough stared at the photos for almost a minute. "Sorry Darlin', I don't know whose kid it is. Remember, I drank quite a lot back then. Hey Kurt, come here. You know whose kid this is?"

Kurt looked and shook his head. "I don't reckon I do – sorry."

A few minutes later, Jameson came in with his luggage.

"Rose, I want to thank you for your hospitality but I'm starting to feel like I'm wearing out my welcome. I'm going to go back to Raymond's' place and hang out with him. I've been two days sober, and I'd like Raymond's help in staying this way."

There was something else different about Jameson. Then it dawned on me – his eyes. I thought he had brown eyes and now their blue-green. I asked him about it.

"Yeah, I decided to take out my contacts. My mother and father have brown eyes and always felt weird having blue eyes, so I wear contacts just to fit in. But I decided its okay to look different. First step in my sobriety I guess. Anyway, would you tell Mother that I'll call her later tonight? And again, Rose thanks for your kindness and putting up with me. I know I haven't been the best of houseguests."

He walked over and gave me a hug then left for Raymond's. Keough looked surprised. "Well, I'll be damned. He finally decided that being a shit head wasn't the best of personality traits."

I was barely listening to what Keough was saying. I was still taken aback by Jameson's transformation. Then it dawned on me . . . he looked a little like Lash.

"Keough, is it me or doesn't he look like La . . ."

Before I could finish Keough said, "Lash, I was just thinkin' the same thing. Are we crazy Rose? How in the world can two people look so much alike and not be related. I saw the resemblance when he shaved off that God-awful beard. Now finding out his eyes are blue-green like Lash's." Keough shook his head in disbelief.

I ran out to the truck just as Jameson was pulling away. He slammed on the breaks. "What's up Amelia? Forgot to give me the bill for my stay? Just kidding, what's up?"

"I know you're going to think this is an odd question, but when's your birthday?"

Jameson laughed. "Yes, that is a weird question. Even weirder now that I stopped drinking but to answer your question it's August... August 18th to be precise...1951. I'll be 51-years-old this year. The funny thing is I was born at 12:08 AM. I was almost born on the 17th. Close but no cigar. Anyway, it's getting late. and I'd like to get to Raymond's before dark. You know how easily I get lost around these parts."

"Okay, but before you leave I'd like to show you something." I showed him the picture of Charlotte with the two infants."

"Yeah, I know her. She's mother's old housekeeper. Wow, haven't seen her in years! I wonder if she still lives in Dodson. Cute kids, are they hers?" I told him Charlotte was Joe's mother.

"Wow, so my nanny was the mother of the famous Montana Joe. Now, that's cool. I wonder if Mother knew who she was. I'll have to ask her later tonight. But Rose I've really gotta get goin'.."

I don't remember walking back to the house. *He was born an hour after Joe who was born August 17th at 11:07 PM. Jameson and Lash are the same age. Lash would have been 51-years-old this year. Charlotte worked for Meryl. She literally raised Jameson and Lash. This keeps getting stranger and stranger.*

Kurt and Keough met me at the door. Keough asked, "What's wrong, Rose you're as pale as a ghost."

"Keough did you know your wife Charlotte worked for Meryl?" Keough looked puzzled then Kurt spoke up.

"Yes, I can tell you she did. After this no-good-drunken twin brother of mine left her with three kids she needed to work to take care of them. No offense, Keough but it's the truth."

So Charlotte and Meryl knew each other well. Maybe that's why she had the photo in her room.

"Keough, do you remember anything about Joe's birth – anything at all?"

"I'm sorry, Rose. I'm ashamed to say I wasn't there when Lash was born. I just don't remember."

I could see Keough was becoming more and more upset by my questions, "It's okay Keough. You're a great grandfather to Charlotte, and you reconciled with Joe before he died." I hugged him and told him thank you.

I was still comforting Keough when Paul walked in. "Is everything okay? I feel as though I walked into an intense conversation. If you'd like me to leave I'll . . ."

"No, not at all Paul. It's a strange conversation for sure, but please don't leave. In fact, I need to get dinner started. I'll catch you up on things if you'll help me in the kitchen. The roast is already in the oven. I just need you to help me peel the potatoes. I'll shell the peas."

Paul grabbed a paring knife and began peeling. He knew his way around a kitchen. I'd never seen anyone peel a potato in one long skin.

"Okay, enough stalling. Are you going to tell me what's going on? Everyone looked rather stern and tense."

I looked at Paul, and for the first time I noticed how boyishly handsome he was. I guess I never let myself notice it before. *Why do good looking men always grow facial hair? I'm really glad he and Jameson decided to get rid of those ratty beards and mustaches.*

"Long story short, I think Jameson and Lash were raised by Charlotte Montana. I showed Jameson a photograph of Lash's mother and he instantly remembered her as his nanny. But that's not the kicker. Lash and Jameson were both born in the same hospital, same month and same year. Only Lash was born August 17th and Jameson August 18th an hour apart. How weird is that!"

Paul scratched his head. "Yes, that's weird indeed. But why is it of interest to you? My best friend in England was born the same day and year as me. The only difference is he's dreadfully ugly and full of rubbish and I'm unbelievably brilliant and remarkably handsome."

"Okay, Paul what do you mean by full of rubbish? Remember I'm not familiar with your slang."

Paul grinned. "You know full of rubbish or as you American's say full of shit, full of crap, shinola."

As if on cue, Kurt and Keough came into the kitchen arguing. "Kurt, as always you are dang wrong. I went eight seconds on a bronc named, *Red Demon* not *Red Devil!*"

"Aw, Keough you don't know shit-from-shinola, its name was *Red Devil* and you got bucked off in five seconds!"

- 152 -

The two continued their argument through the kitchen door and onto the deck.

Without looking away from peeling the potatoes Paul said, "I bet they're both wrong and full of crap! Bloody plonkers! "

I started laughing at Paul's ability to multi-task. "You're going to make me ask aren't you? Okay what's a plonker?"

Without cracking a smile, Paul nonchalantly said, "Plonkers—you know—dickheads!

I laughed so hard I slipped on a piece of potato skin that had escaped onto the floor and fell on my ass. With a gallant gesture, Paul helped me up. "Whoopsie daisies, up you go. Please try to stay on your feet until dinner is served. We wouldn't want you falling into the tatties."

I realized I hadn't laughed like this since Joe died. Afterwards, I began to feel guilty for feeling happy. I leaned back against the refrigerator and stared at the floor.

"Paul, is it wrong to feel happy? Joe was the love of my life, but he's gone. No matter how much I mourn, he's still gone and never coming back."

I couldn't hold back my tears any longer. I cried and cried until I couldn't cry anymore. Oddly, Paul didn't try to comfort me. He let me cry with no interference. I went into the bathroom and splashed water on my face. When I came out, I wasn't prepared for what Paul had to say.

"Poppet, are you okay. Please sit down and nod if you are because I'm only going to say this once so listen carefully. Joe is dead and that's a fact. It's dreadfully unfair, but he's dead. He was and always will be an amazing man. But he's gone Amelia and you are still here. You are vibrant, beautiful and a bit dodgy – but that's okay. I'm enormously proud to call you a dear friend. And as a friend I can't watch you do this to yourself, not to mention to Charlotte. She needs you. Keough and Raymond need you. But most of all . . . I need you. It seems I've fallen madly in love you Amelia. From the moment you stumbled into the path of my 18-wheeler spouting a load of rubbish about a fake illness. Nevertheless, you were hopelessly in love with Joe, and there was not a thing I could do about it. I'm sorry if this upsets you or changes the nature of our relationship, but I won't go on pretending I'm just your friendly-go-to-bloke when things go wrong. I love you Amelia, very much . . . and your roast is burning."

I stood up and walked over to Paul. He backed away. "You're not going to pummel me are you?"

"Nope"

"Aren't you going to check on your roast?"

"Nope"

"You aren't going to stab me again and again with a butcher knife and throw my body out into some desolate prairieland for the coyotes to consume?"

I gave him a look of sheer bewilderment. "You've been hanging out with Raymond again haven't you?"

"Perhaps a bit, but please stop pratting about. I want to know if you ar . . ."

Before he could finish his sentence I kissed him. The piercing beep of the kitchen smoke detector interrupted us.

Paul cleared his throat, "Eh, I'd better reset the smoke alarm and take the roast out. Perhaps we can salvage it. In fact, I prefer my beef to be a bit overdone – mad cow disease and all."

I blurted out, "The roast is the last thing I'm thinking about right now. You said you love me. How long were you going to keep your feelings to yourself?"

Paul walked over and took the roast from the oven. "I'd planned on taking these feelings to my grave as long as Joe was alive; however, his untimely death changed things. I knew as long as you were still grieving, I'd have to hold my tongue. I care for you too much to cause you more pain than you're already experiencing."

I didn't know what to think. Here's a man who loved me for years and a man who would have loved me for a lifetime had he not died.

"Paul, could you honestly love a woman who still had feelings for her dead husband? I don't think my heart could ever stop loving Joe. He was and always be the love of my life."

Paul let out a lengthy exhale. "Amelia, a wise and dear friend of mine once said that the heart has no boundaries or limits when it comes to love."

"And who is this sagely person?"

"It's a line from a book I recently read. You may have heard of it. It's called, *Lost Trails of Sweet Grass Canyon*, by some bloke named Montana Joe."

"Really, I didn't know you read any of Joe's books. I'm impressed."

Paul laughed. "Well, I must admit it was more like research. Be that as it may, I would love to continue this conversation; however, I'm bloody starved and I bet everyone waiting in the dining room is too. Shall we talk later perhaps over a glass of wine?"

"Yes, I'd like that very much. I want to know as much as I can about the man who loved me and never said a word. It might make a great article on unrequited love."

Paul flipped me the bird then kissed me on the cheek. "You're becoming quite cheeky you know that."

I turned towards him and whispered, "Oh, why don't you *naff off!*"

Paul raised his eyebrows. "Ooh, spoken like a true pub-bird! But enough of this British slang piss-off nonsense – I'm famished." He gave me a quick wink and carried the roast out to the dinning room.

I had started carving the roast when Meryl arrived. She looked exhausted. I told her we were about to have dinner and asked if she were hungry. She shook her head and went directly to her room.

Keough and Kurt looked at each other. Keough said, "Maybe she heard you were cookin', Rose and she lost her appetite."

"Very funny, Keough. How'd you like to have your dinner out in the barn?"

"I'm just kiddin', Rose; you're a good cook. Heck, a fella on death row would be honored to have you serve him up his last plate of vittles."

"Keough, since I'm not sure whether that's an insult or a compliment, I'm not going to comment."

After dinner, I went to check on Meryl. I knocked on the door. "Meryl, it's me Rose. Are you okay?"

The door slowly opened. She asked me to come in. It looked as though she'd been crying.

"Rose, please forgive my appearance. I must look a fright." She glanced in the mirror fluffing her hair. I told her she looked stunning.

"What's wrong, Meryl? Is there anything I can do? You look very upset and I've been told I'm a good listener."

She sat on the bed staring at a photograph she had clasped in her hand. "I love my boy so much. From the moment I saw him, I fell in love with those beautiful blue-green eyes."

Pretending not to know I said, "I thought his eyes were brown?"

She shook her head. "No, they're blue-green. Jameson wears brown contacts to look more like the rest of the family. Meryl eyes welled. "Such beautiful eyes he has. Speaking of Jameson . . . where is he? I need to speak to him."

I said he'd gone to stay at Raymond's place and also explained to her about the drumming circle and his spiritual awakening and sobriety. "It seems he's becoming friendly with Raymond. I guess if I had to pick a person for him to talk to, it would be Raymond. He's an amazing listener. Maybe you should talk to him too?"

"No, I would feel more comfortable sharing this with you. You are also a good listener, and I trust you Rose. I trust you not to judge me for what I'm about to tell you."

She walked over to the dresser and noticed the photograph was missing. I told her I'd put it back with the rest of the photographs. She asked if I wouldn't mind retrieving it.

"Not at all – I'll be right back."

I handed her the photograph. She held both photos looking at each one.

"Such beautiful babies they were. Charlotte was such a good mother."

Her statement puzzled me. "You mean nanny?

Meryl replied, "No, I mean mother – Charlotte is Jameson's birth mother. I'm Jameson's adopted mother. Jameson is adopted, and we never told him."

My research expertise kicked in. It was starting to make sense. The two children in the photograph were Lash and Jameson. Then it hit me like a ton of bricks . . . they were twins – fraternal twins.

"I knew it! I knew there was something very familiar about Jameson! Oh my God, Jameson is Lash's brother! Which also means that Keough is his real father?" *If finding out Jameson is his son doesn't kill him, knowing he's Joe's twin brother will definitely put the nail in his coffin.*

Meryl went on to explain how she and Mr. Wellesley couldn't have children of their own and when Charlotte found out she was having twins, she knew she didn't have the money to raise two infants. We offered to help and begrudgingly she accepted. She was so distraught over her decision and terrified to tell Keough that she'd sold one of his children.

"I can't imagine taking care of my own child and not being able to acknowledge him as my own. That would kill me!"

Meryl wiped her eyes. "She said it was for the best. With the money we gave her, Lash and his sisters were able to have a good life. For her own sanity, she eventually disassociated herself from Jameson. The fact that they weren't identical twins helped."

I told Meryl that from my research I learned twins run in the family. Keough and Kurt were twin brothers and Keough mentioned to me that his grandfather was a twin.

"I'm surprised I didn't have twins – being as huge as I was when I was pregnant with Charlotte, I looked like I was having triplets."

Meryl smiled. "Thank you for not judging me Rose. I feel so much better now that I've gotten that off my chest. For fifty-one years it's been gnawing at me and now I'm finally able to discuss it with someone. I'm very happy it was you, Rose."

I stood up and hugged her. "I'll be with you if you decide to tell Jameson." She smiled and nodded yes.

"Keough needs to be told as well. He needs to know, and he needs to know now. Jameson and Keough have more in common than they're willing to admit. The one thing is they both are alcoholics. You do know Jameson had an alcohol problem."

"Yes, I've known for years. I can't tell you how many times Mr. Wellesley has funded Jameson at those retreat centers. As he got older, his drinking got worse. I'm happy he's connected with Raymond. Maybe he can get through to him."

"He'll get through to him Meryl. Trust me if anyone can, its Raymond. But for now, you need to talk to Keough. He needs to know he has another son – are you ready?"

"Yes, I guess I'd better. I'm not sure how to start the conversation. What do I say, Rose?

Her eyes were beginning to fill with tears. I thought for a second then answered. "You'll know what to say. Remember he's lost one son. He needs to know he has another one who's alive and well."

Meryl nodded in agreement. "Okay, I'm ready."

Chapter 16

Paul was still on cloud nine knowing Amelia had feelings for him too. He never thought he would have an opportunity to tell her how he felt. He was interested in her from the moment they met. *What is it about American women that peak my curiosity. Maybe it's their straight forward attitude or the fact that I don't understand a bloody thing they say.*

Meryl and I walked into the dining room. Keough, Kurt and Paul were staring at the food as if it were their last meal.

Keough said, "Okay if you two are done with your gal talk how about we eat. There ain't nothin' worse than cold, overcooked, roast beef. Sorry, Rose but it ain't Cecilia's. Hey, how about you ask her to give you a few cookin' lessons?"

I frowned. "Okay and how about I give you a few lessons on bathing, Old Man."

"Aw, come on Rose I was just jokin'—no need to get personal. I took a bath last week just for you. And, it hasn't been a full week yet."

After dinner, Paul helped me take the dishes into the kitchen. I was about to put them in the dish washer when he stopped me.

"Oy, please let me do them. Being raised in a pub there is a rule. The one who cooks never does the washing up. And . . . I do them by hand. I never toss them in some bloody dishwasher."

"Hey, that's fine with me Paul. I hate to wash dishes. Knock yourself out!"

Paul gave me a bewildered glance. "And why would I want to knock myself out? Oh wait, yet another nonsensical American saying – am I correct?"

I smiled and said, "Yes, you are correct and I appreciate you doing the dishes – thank you."

Paul makes me smile. Come to think of it, he always makes me smile. Even in the most serious situations, he keeps a sense of humor. I find it an appealing quality in men. It was that same quality that first attracted me to Joe. Now that I think about it Joe and Paul are somewhat alike in many ways.

I told Paul that Meryl had something she needed to discuss with Keough, and we should give her some privacy.

Paul's eyes widened. "Oh God Amelia, she's not in love with him? Please tell me she's not romantically interested in him. That would be grisly."

"I'm afraid it's much more serious than that. It involves Joe and Jameson. Grab a beer, and I'll explain everything to you outside on the deck."

I proceeded to tell him about Joe's mother Charlotte having twins, Meryl adopting Jameson to help Charlotte financially and Keough not knowing any of this.

"The entire situation is mindboggling. Jameson doesn't know he's adopted and Keough . . ."

Paul stopped drinking his beer and sat down. "Bloody hell, he's going to lose the plot or as you lot would say go crazy when she tells him. I actually feel sorry for the poor sod."

I sat down beside him. "Paul, I'm scared that this will push Keough off the wagon. He's been sober since Joe's death and this could challenge both his sobriety and Jameson's as well. Strange how Jameson has issues with alcohol and Joe didn't. I'm just afraid this will destroy them both."

Paul put his arm around my shoulder. "Poppet, no matter what, I'll be here to support you. That's if you want me to stay."

"Yes, Paul I want you to stay. I don't think I can handle this on my own. I'd like your moral and physical support if that's okay."

He kissed me on my forehead and took another sip of his beer. "Then I'll stay."

Meryl slowly made her way to the living room. She noticed Keough had stepped outside with Lou. He needed some air, and Lou needed to pee. She walked outside and stood beside Keough. "Beautiful evening isn't it? I really miss these Big Sky evenings. There's nothing like them in New York."

Keough tipped his hat back. "Yep, nothing compares to a clear Montana evening. Look at all them stars. Before Joe died, we'd come out and stare at 'em. As his cancer got worse they seemed to comfort him." So what brings you outside?"

"Keough, there is something I need to tell you – it's about your wife Charlotte. Please let me finish what I have to say, and then I'll answer any questions you have."

"Meryl, this is startin' to sound serious. Is it about Amelia or did that bone-headed son of yours do something to upset you? With all due respect ma'am I can't stand that boy! He's a spoiled, over-privileged, reckless drunk. I'm a recovering drunk, so I know one when I see one. "

"Keough, please stop browbeating Jameson! He's not as horrible as you say he is. He's a good man."

"Good man, my ass! Lady, you are delusional if you think that kid is good, let alone a real man. Now my son Lash, he was a good man rest his soul. Jameson ain't half the man he was!"

Meryl yelled, "He's exactly half the man Lash was! He's YOUR son too. Jameson is your SON Keough!"

Keough shook his head in total disbelief. "Ma'am, I know I've lived out of a bottle for years and was a raging drunk for most of 'em, but with all due respect and as God as my witness . . . I don't ever, EVER remember havin' sex with you."

If the situation wasn't so intense, his statement would have made her burst out laughing.

"Keough rest assured, we've NEVER had sex. Charlotte gave birth to twin boys – fraternal twins. You were nowhere to be found. She knew with you gone, she couldn't take care of one child let alone two. Charlotte was a strong, brave woman Keough, but her decision was not made lightly. It was heart wrenching. She loved both those boys and she did what she had to do to survive. I couldn't have children and we were more than able to take care of a child, so we assisted her financially and adopted Jameson."

Keough took off his hat and ran his finger through his hair. "You mean to say I've got another son? I've had another son all these years and never knew it? She never said a word. My Charlotte never said a word to me. Then again why would she? I was a worthless, drunken rodeo has-been, believing I'd win the next big Wyoming-Montana rodeo championship. No wonder Lash hated me. Now I find out I have another son who also hates me. What kind of man does this to their kids? The girls never knew me because I was long gone when they were growing up. But Lash was old enough to remember me. Not very fond memories I might add." He paused for a moment and let it all sink in. "So Jameson is Lash's twin brother?"

Meryl nodded. "Yes, Jameson is Lash's twin brother but he was born officially a day later."

Keough squinted, "You mean Charlotte was in labor for two days?"

Meryl rolled her eyes. "No, Keough. Lash was born on August 17th about an hour before midnight, and Jameson was born a few minutes after midnight on August 18th.

"Ya' see what I mean Meryl? I couldn't even figure that out. What kind of father would I have been if I'd stayed? Maybe it was a blessing in disguise I wasn't there to influence them. There was one year I almost died due to excessive alcohol drinkin'. The doc told me that I was a lucky fella. I guess I was tryin' to kill the pain and almost killed myself."

Meryl walked over to Keough putting her hand on his shoulder. "Here's your chance to do it right. You're lucky you get to have a second chance – Lash didn't. Prove to him you can be a good father. I can already see you're a wonderful grandfather. Do you think you can share a little bit of that love with your other son?"

Keough pat her hand. "Is this what you and Rose were talkin' about?"

Meryl nodded.

"I'm lucky to have her in my life. She's the bright star of this family, and I'm so thankful for her believing in me when I couldn't. Lash loved her so. And as quiet as it's kept I'd die for that woman. I'll never admit it because we have way too much fun pretending we hate each other." How about we go back inside; it's startin' to get chilly. Could I convince you into having a cup of coffee with me? I know it's late but . . ."

"I'd love to Keough. And for what it's worth, Rose would die for you too. She loves you so much. Since Lash's death you are her only male tie to him she has. Now, she'll have another if both of you can accept him being a Montana."

Keough kissed her hand. "We'll cross that bridge when we get to it, but for now, how about that cup of coffee."

Chapter 17

"Okay, one more time Jameson. I'm Blackfoot. I'm not a wizard, or a Shaman, or medicine man. I can't make your craving for booze magically disappear. You need to take your addiction seriously, or I'm going to take you back to the Montana ranch."

"I'm trying Raymond. But it's hard. I wake up, and I want a drink. I go to bed, and I want a drink. It's like I have no control over these feelings. The strange thing is my mother and father don't drink that much. They'll have an occasional martini or scotch but rarely do they drink everyday like I do."

Raymond poured him another cup of herbal tea. "Maybe someone in your family drank. It's not uncommon for children to have the same addictions as distant family members."

Jameson took a sipped his tea. "That's another odd thing. I don't have any close relative at least any that I know of – weird huh?"

Raymond laughed. "Maybe it's because they know how aggravating a human being you are. I swear you remind me of my dear friend Joe. He was the most annoying man I'd ever called friend – you are the second most annoying."

"But I'm your friend, right? I mean, you wouldn't be doing all of this for me if you didn't consider me a friend?"

"Let's just say I might consider you a friend if you'd stop being such an asshole – now finish your tea. We have more work to do before the summer season starts."

"Sure thing, but I need to call Mother. I promised her I'd keep in touch."

"Okay, I'll be working in cabin 8 and when you're done chatting with your mother. Start cleaning cabin 12."

Jameson reached in his jacket pocket for his cell phone. He noticed two missed calls. One was from his father and the other from his mother. He deleted the one from his father. *I really don't want to talk to him right now. I don't need him telling me I need to sober up and take the business seriously.*

He redialed his mother. She picked up on the first ring.

"Hello, Son. Did you get my message? I left you a message last night."

"No I didn't, Mother. Raymond and I were up late getting the cabins ready for summer visitors. What's up? Is everything okay at the Montanas? Keough isn't giving you a hard time is he?"

"No, actually he's been quite pleasant. I left a message for you to come back to the ranch. I have something to tell you, and I must tell you in person. It's terribly important Jamie."

Jamie? She hasn't called me Jamie since I was in grade school. Something must be extremely wrong! Oh my God she's dying! Or worse she's staying in Montana!

"Mother . . . I'm on my way."

Jameson called to Raymond. "Raymond I've got to go right now. Something is wrong with Mother; she called me Jamie. She hasn't called me Jamie is decades."

"I'll come with you. If something's wrong, you'll need back up. Now where did I put my tomahawk? Hey, don't judge me. It might come in handy. Just give me a minute to lock up the place."

Meryl paced the floor wondering how she would tell Jameson he was adopted and Keough is his birth father. *Do I just come out and tell him, should I soften the blow and give him some agonizing, over-involved song and dance?*

Wringing her hands she glanced at the driveway. *I must get a hold of myself. He's going to be devastated no matter how I try to cushion this information.* The sound of the back door opening startled her – it was Keough.

"You didn't think I was going to let you go through this alone did you?" He walked over and held her hand."

"Thank you Keough for being here. I appreciate it."

"No need to thank me. I might have been a drunk, but I'm always a gentleman." He winked and kissed her cheek.

"I've got to be honest with you Meryl, he rubbed me the wrong way when we first met. Maybe it was because we're so much alike. It was like looking at me in a fifty-year-old mirror – not a pretty sight!"

Paul and I walked into the living room just as Keough hugged Meryl.

"Pardon us," I said. "I hope we are not interrupting you two. We came from feeding the horses to get some lunch, but we'll come back later. It looks like you guys were having some serious conversation."

Meryl explained she had called Jameson and he was on his way back to the ranch. "I need to come clean with my son. Things may get a bit tense. Keough offered to be my moral support."

"Hell, it's the least I can do; after all he is my kid. " Keough's face turned a deep shade of red. "I still can't believe it. But come to think of it once he'd shaved all that crap off his face he's almost handsome, but not half as handsome me."

Keough ran his hands through his hair and winked at Meryl, and the two exchanged smiles.

Paul whispered to me, "Is it me or is Keough flirting with Meryl? Randy old bugger isn't he?"

I was about to answer Paul when I saw Jameson and Raymond's truck pull into the driveway. Meryl's anxiety was palatable. Keough held her hand. I stood beside her and took hold of her other hand.

"We're here for you. Remember he's a Montana, and Montanas never run from a fight. We stick together."

Keough leaned in to Meryl, "Are you ready, Darlin?"

"I may not be a Montana, but I've never backed away from a challenge or a fight – I'm ready."

Jameson sprinted towards the house leaving Raymond behind. It startled him to see his mother, Keough, Paul and Rose all gathered in the living room.

Still panting from his sprint he asked, "Mother, what's going on? Are you okay? I drove like a maniac to get here. And by the looks on everyone's faces something is really, really wrong. Oh, my God you're not dying – are you?"

Keough looked at Meryl. She was about to answer Jameson when he screamed, "OH SHIT, you are dying."

Meryl walked over to her son and asked him to sit down.

"Jameson, rest assured that I'm not dying, but there's something I need to tell you. And please let me finish, and I'll answer any questions you might have."

Raymond finally made it to the house. "What's going on? Jameson said something was wrong with Meryl. He mentioned something about Meryl calling him Jamie? I still don't understand what's happening, but is everybody okay? Or is Jameson simply having one of his typical-Jameson-episodes-of-insanity."

Jameson asked Raymond and the others if they would leave and give them some privacy. Everyone began to file out except for Keough.

"I think I'd better stay if that's okay with you, Meryl."

"Of course Keough, in fact I would very much like you to stay."

Jameson looked puzzled. "Mother, why are you asking this jerk to stay? No offense Keough, but you have nothing to do with this. It's between me and my mother."

Meryl interjected, "Yes, it does Jameson. Please let me explain."

Meryl went on to tell him the entire story of his adoption and about his real parents. Jameson sat quietly listening to his mother and Keough. Jameson was incredibly calm while both explained their sides of the story. "Okay, so you're saying I was adopted and that I'm the nanny's son?"

"Yes, Charlotte was your birth mother."

"And Keough is my real father?"

Keough nodded. "Yup, I'm your pappy – crazy huh?"

Jameson stood up and looked at both of them. "Okay, cool, I get it. I never felt like I was a Wellesley anyway. Father never accepted me for who I was. He still doesn't. My entire life never made sense – now it does. So, what you're also telling me it that I'm a Montana? Now that's very cool!"

Meryl and Keough sat there in shock. They imagined him ranting, asking why he was lied to for years, stomping and screaming like a spoiled rich kid; but they never expected him to he so composed and calm about this life-changing news.

Keough asked, "So . . . you're okay with this news?"

Jameson shrugged. "I have to be. Staying with Raymond really helped me understand that we all have a mission in life. I'm still searching for mine, but he assures me I'll find it. And, if you haven't noticed I've stopped drinking."

Meryl hugged him, "Yes, we did and we're beyond happy for you."

"Yeah, Mother I'm happy for me too. But I have to give Raymond all the credit. When he's not trying to shoot you or scalp you he's a pretty awesome guy."

Paul and I asked if it were okay to come in. Jameson said yes and asked if we knew what was going on. We both nodded.

"Hey Rose, I'm a Montana, how sweet is that?" I hugged him and welcomed him into the family.

"But wait, if I'm Charlotte and Keough's son that would make Lash my brother, right?"

Everyone looked at each other as if to say, *Who's going to tell him the rest of the story? Obviously he hasn't connected the fact that he and Lash were born 30-minutes apart but one calendar date apart.*

Meryl asked him to sit down again. She sat beside him and said, "Not only was Lash your brother, you're his twin brother. You and Lash were fraternal twins."

Jameson's eyes widened. "Holy shit, this is surreal. Hey Raymond, I am ancestrally annoying. I'm the famous Lash Montana's twin brother, hah! This is some crazy shit!"

Raymond shook his head and muttered, "This must be what hell feels like . . . I'm in hell. Another annoying white man has come into my life. Good Lord! Karma's a bitch and I've got to start paying it back all over again. From beyond the grave you bug me still. Damn you Joe!"

Paul offered to make a pot of tea. The entire event took its toll on us, and we needed something soothing and coffee wasn't an option, especially Joe's coffee. I thought, *Joe if you're watching all of this I hope you're happy to know you have a brother – a twin brother. Oh my God . . . that would make him my brother-in-law!*

Keough called Kurt to inform him he was the uncle of a bouncing 175lb. nephew. Kurt congratulated him and said he was happy for both father and son.

"Tell my nephew I'll stop by tomorrow and we can get to know each other."

"I will. And Kurt . . . I love you. Thanks for being such a great big brother."

"Love you too Baby Brother. Now hang up before we both start singing show tunes."

Cecilia came in a few minutes later with a sleepy little girl in her arms. She said they enjoyed the movie and had already eaten dinner.

"It was late so we stayed in town overnight at my friend's house. Did you get my message?"

"Yes I did Cecilia. Sorry I didn't get back to you. It's been a mad house. I'll explain later."

We thought it best to put her to bed and she could have her bath in the morning.

I told Cecilia, I'd fill her in tomorrow morning and for her to take the rest of the evening off. Paul told her he'd clean up the kitchen.

"I won't argue with that. Goodnight to you both."

Before she left she offered in a hushed tone, "I know it's not my place to say but I really like Paul. And it seems he's quite fond of you too. Don't think I haven't noticed how he looks at you when he thinks no one is watching. Such a lovely accent he has. I've always been a sucker for a British accent. I could sit and listen to him talk for hours."

Cecilia winked at me, said good night and went to her room.

Does everyone realize Paul has a crush on me or am I the last one to know? I guess I was too involved with Joe's life and death to notice. I do like Paul a lot. I'm just not certain or ready to admit if I love him yet.

Joe, please give me a sign if it's okay to love someone again. I'm so confused and uncertain about this whole situation.

I told Paul I would pass on the tea and headed off to bed. I couldn't sleep. Then I remembered that when Joe had problems falling asleep, he would open the bedroom sky light. I opened it and quietly laid there looking at the stars. I tried to find the star Joe named for me. Honestly, he was much better at astronomy than I was. They all looked the same to me.

"Joe, if you can hear me tell me what to do. Tell me what you want for me and Charlotte." The sound of coyotes howling was strangely soothing. Raymond believes coyotes are the wise old spirits of the prairielands.

"Okay, coyotes I need your wisdom – help a sister out!"

They stopped for a minute then started up again.

"I can tell they aren't going to help me tonight."

My mind continued to churn. After tossing and turning for what seemed like hours, I decided to get up and go into the office and check my email. Since Joe died, I didn't get half the emails I once did. I clicked on my mail icon and noticed one from Joe's old account. These messages always gave me a little thrill, but my excitement quickly dissipated knowing they were sent after his death.

I immediately opened the one from Joe.

To: Amelia "Rose" Montana

Fr: Lash J. Montana

Subject: **Convergence by Jackson Pollock & other jokes of art, Part 5 of 5**

Hello Darlin'. This email will probably be my last. My heart is slowly giving out along with the rest of this ol' cowboy's body. I can't tell you how much I'm gonna miss you. And I know how you'll mourn for me afterwards. But I need to tell you this now while I still have the strength to write it.

Of all the things in my life that I'll always remember is your smile and them dang pointy elbows. You're smile melts my heart and them elbows . . . I wouldn't trade them for the all silver or gold in the world. I never thought in a million years I'd find a woman as loving, smart, giving and sexy as you. But, the thing I'll miss the most is your happiness. You're such a happy and fun loving woman. More than this aging cowboy deserves. Such a sweet young thing you are Amelia "Rose" Montana.

I know how much you love to argue. Heck, it's what you live for. But Baby please don't argue with my last request. I want you to move on. I want you to meet some fella who'll treat you like the amazing woman you are. Don't wait too long 'cause girl you are in your prime and you know it. Find a man who'll appreciate you for all of your charm and talent. That means no runnin' after horny old cowboys' Darlin'. One loony cowboy in your life is enough. Make sure he loves you and Charlotte. And if for some reason, you're uncertain about your judgment, ask Raymond. He's a great judge of character, and if he doesn't like 'em he'll just scalp 'em and send them runnin'. I love Raymond like a brother and more importantly, I trust him.

So my sweet, sweet Darlin' Rose, let me go. Box up my office. Store my things in the attic or take them outside and burn them – it's your decision, Baby. Promise me you'll continue to live life and not grieve yourself to death. I've got to stop now Darlin'. Tears are clouding my vision, and we all know cowboys aren't supposed to cry. We were two unique people bonded by an undying love for one another. Never forget that Rose. But please Darlin', move on.

Love, Lash

P.S. Oh and one more thing, always . . .

[End of email]

I sat motionless trying to wrap my brain about this last email. It wasn't like Joe to give up like this. No matter how sick he was, he was a fighter. I ran to Paul's bedroom and shook him awake.

"What's wrong Poppet! What's going on?"

"Come with me, *please*," I begged. He followed without hesitation. When we got back to the office, I pointed to the email and asked him to read it. Paul sat down and focused on Joe's message. After finishing the email, he stood up and gave me a hug.

"Amelia, as tough as it is to accept, it seems clear to me that Lash wants you to move on. I also find it extremely bizarre that this email comes after I've professed my love for you – don't you think? He's either ghostly psychic or knows you extremely well. And what's with the P.S. ending the way it did? Always what? What is the one more thing? Very peculiar I'd say – even for Lash."

"I have no idea what else he wanted to say. This is the fifth of the five emails, so I'm assuming it's his last one. But again – it's Joe. Who knows what he was thinking."

Paul scratched his head. "Well he was heavily medicated. Perhaps he just ran out of steam?"

"No Paul, I'm feeling this is typical Joe craziness. I'll call his lawyer in the morning. I'm sorry I got you out of bed. Please forgive me."

"Never feel the need to apologize when asking for my help. If I'm not mistaken, from the moment we met, you've been asking me for my help, and I like that you know you can depend on me."

I smiled and hugged him. "Then thank you for being my British guardian angel."

He kissed my palm. "That's from Joe." He leaned into me and gave me a warm and tender kiss on the mouth. "And that's from me – goodnight yet again."

I reached for his hand. "What happens if I need your help again? "

I glanced over his shoulder to my bedroom across the hall.

Paul smiled. "Are you asking me to come to bed with you Amelia?"

"I believe I am. I want to sleep with you Paul. And, I'm afraid. Does that make sense?"

"Yes, it does Amelia. If you're nervous, I don't want you to feel obligated even though you did rouse me from a deep sleep to come to your rescue..." I smiled at him comparing himself to a knight in shining armor.

"In all honesty, Rose, I've wanted to make love to you since the day we met at that truck stop. Something I never thought would ever happen. But it seems Joe had given us his blessing. Does that make sense?"

"Yes it does. It makes perfectly good sense. Joe wouldn't want me living the rest of my life like a reclusive nun. So . . . I believe I'm ready Paul."

"Are you sure?"

Yes, I'm sure."

I took hold of Paul's arm and we went back to my room.

The neighing of hungry horses woke me up. I glanced over at the clock it was almost 5:30 AM. Paul was sound asleep next to me. I crept out of bed, grabbed my robe and tipped out to the kitchen. I didn't want anyone to know that Paul and I had slept together. Walking into the kitchen, I saw Keough was already up and making coffee. *Oh shit he would be up!* I tried to slip back out of the room, but he'd already caught a glimpse of me.

"Well good mornin' Young Lady. Would you like a cup of coffee or would ya' prefer to sneak back to Paul and warn him not to come out of your room half naked?"

Not wanting to address the situation right then, I ran into my room, threw on a tee-shirt and jeans and then headed back into the kitchen.

"Keough I can explain. I . . ."

Keough put his coffee cup down and held my hands.

"Look Amelia, I was just pickin' at you. You're a grown woman and I love you like my own daughters. You don't have to explain anything to me. And if it makes you feel any better, I like Paul. He's a good bloke."

I grinned at Keough's attempt to use British slang.

"Yes, he is a good bloke Keough. He's always been there for me." I told Keough about an email Joe sent telling me to move on.

He leaned back in his chair. "Then I guess you have his blessing. Now it's none of my business but I've got to ask – does Paul make you happy?"

"He makes me smile, so I guess that makes me happy. But there's something about his eyes. They are kind and gentle. I swear if he were not from England, I'd say they're somewhat similar to Joe's – strange huh?"

Keough nodded then said, "You do realize that my great grandfather was from England."

It struck me as odd that he'd never mentioned it before. "No I didn't. Joe never mentioned anything about his family ancestry. I'd always assumed you all were native Montanans."

Keough walked into the living room and brought back a photo of his great grandfather, Reed Conwell Montana. I was surprised how much Joe, Jameson, Kurt and Keough resembled him. Even more intriguing he had the same gentle eyes as Paul.

"He moved from England to the United State in 1896 and settled here in Montana. It's been said that he changed his name to Montana. I can't find anything to prove it, but that's the rumor. It's also rumored that he was a twin. But the mystery and question would be why one would move and the other stayed? Guess we'll never know Rose."

"I bet he was running away from the law or something like that. Or maybe it was a woman. Now that would make a great article."

Keough shrugged. "More than likely there was some sort of scandal, but again I can authenticate it. And it wouldn't be the first time a Montana man's been chased out of town by a woman."

I laughed to myself with visions of Keough being chased by some gal with a horse whip. "Maybe Paul can help us, bein' he's from that part of the world."

"Did someone mention my name?" Paul came into the kitchen, rubbing his eyes, pretending to sleepwalk over to the coffee pot.

Keough chuckled. "I thought you folks only drank tea in the morning?"

Paul flashed a sleepy sarcastic smile.

He walked over to Paul and joked, "*I guess you really need coffee after all of that thumpin' and humpin' you two were doin' last night.*"

Paul's face went blood red. "You could hear us?"

"Hah nope, I was ten sheets to the wind. I just wanted to see you sweat."

"You are bloody evil you are! Now let me drink my coffee before I ask Raymond to scalp you."

Paul sat down beside me and smiled. "Hope you slept well."

"Yes, as a matter of fact I did, thank you." I glanced at Paul trying not to show how blissful I was.

Keough stood up and looked at both of us. "If you to want to be alone, I'll go feed the horses. I don't want to come between two budding love birds."

Paul shook his head. "You are so completely full of rubbish Keough."

"Okay, okay—I'm leaving... I know when I ain't wanted." Keough winked at me, grabbed his coffee cup and headed into the living room.

Paul exhaled. "I thought he'd never leave. But seriously, Poppet did you sleep well? I was hoping to bring you coffee in bed. Imagine my upset to find an empty pillow and a neatly folded quilt instead of a warm beautiful body beside me."

I slid closer to Paul's chair. "I'm still trying to accept the fact we slept together, Paul. I don't think I'm ready for coffee or breakfast in bed yet. I hope you understand."

"Of course I do. I totally understand. But think of it this way. You now have your own private English butler.

I chuckled at his attempt to make me feel less guilty. We enjoyed a sweet embrace.

He took our cups over to the sink. "Well, we'd better get cleaned up and ready for the day. I'm sure Keough will whine and moan if I don't help him with the horses, and I know the stalls need to be mucked."

He kissed me on my cheek and went to take a shower.

It was almost 7:30 AM., *time to get Charlotte ready for day school.* I went to her room to find her up and dressed. *Cecilia must have gotten her ready.*

She ran over to me, hugging my legs. "Look Mama I'm dressed."

"I can see that Missy. And who helped you?"

From the doorway, someone answered. "Who else would have the fashion sense to combine spring designer clothing with atrocious Montana cowboy attire?"

I whipped around – it was Jannine. I ran over and hugged her until she begged me to let her go. "Oh my God, when did you get here? I've missed you so much. Why are you here? Oh, it doesn't matter." I hugged her again.

"I got into Montana late last night so I stayed at a hotel. I don't know these roads well enough yet to drive at night."

I didn't see Morgan. "Where's Morgan? Don't tell me you two had a fight."

Jannine laughed. "No he's in Wyoming at some horse or cattle stampede extravaganza—a cowboy bonding thing I guess. Anyway, I didn't want to go, so I told him I'd hang out with my best friend in the entire world – if that's okay with you?"

"Of course it's okay. In fact I could use some of your famous moral support right now."

"Uh oh, nothing serious I hope."

"It's nothing serious Jannine, well at least not yet. I'll fill you on the way to the day school."

We were getting Charlotte strapped into her car seat when I saw Meryl and Jameson talking by the bunkhouse. They looked engrossed in their conversation, so I continued to get Charlotte settled in the truck and drove off.

Jameson tucked his cell phone back into his shirt pocket. "They said I can keep the truck as long as I need it. Don't worry, Mother I'll pay for the extended rental fee."

Meryl rubbed his arm. "That's not necessary. No matter what, I'm still your mother and I love you. Nothing will ever change that."

"Mother, if you don't mind, I'd like to stay in Montana for a while. I want to visit my mothe . . . Charlotte's grave and get to know Keough better. And from what I can see, he wouldn't mind if you hung around too."

Meryl blushed at the thought of Keough finding her attractive.

"I would love to Dear, but I'll be leaving for New York tomorrow morning. Your father's returning from Austria, and I'd like to be there when he arrives. I'd rather he heard all this from me."

Jameson agreed. "Hey, I was on my way to the cemetery. Would you like to come with me?"

"Yes, I'd love to Jamie. Charlotte was a wonderful woman and a good mother."

Keough walked over holding a potted plant. "Howdy Miss Meryl, how are you this morning?"

"I'm fine Keough. Beautiful flowers – what are they?"

They're prairie roses – Charlotte's favorite. I was headed to Dodson cemetery to plant them."

"What a coincidence. We're going there too. Jameson and I want to visit his birth mother's grave before I left for New York."

"You're leaving?"

"Yes, tomorrow morning. My driver will pick me up tonight, and I'm heading to Billings."

Keough appeared despondent by her announcement. "I thought you'd be staying a bit longer. But if you need to leave I understand. When are you comin' back?"

"I'm leaving, and I won't be back. Rose's article is finished and Jameson wants to stay and get to know you and the rest of his new family better. There's no reason for me to stay or return. I'm not needed here."

"I wouldn't say you're not needed and . . . well, what about me? I'd like you to stay. You're the only one close to my age to talk to around here. And to be honest – I'd miss you."

There was a brief silence then Jameson announced the time and gestured as to say, *let's get going, folks.*

"Do you mind if I tag along? I was headed there anyway and I don't see the need to waste more gasoline."

Jameson looked at his mother then at Keough. She said, "By all means come with us, Keough. You know these roads better than we do."

As they drove down the driveway, Kurt came out of the bunkhouse.

"Why is it every time them stalls need to be mucked, everybody leaves! I swear sometimes I think I'm the only one in the world who gives a shit about horseshit." He chuckled to himself and headed back to the stables.

Chapter 18

On the way back from the day school, I noticed a missed message on my cell phone. I didn't recognize the number. *I'll check it when we get home.* Before I had a chance to put the phone back in my purse, it rang again.

Jannine said, "Somebody wants to get a hold of you. You'd better answer it. It could be important."

In my crazy life, it could be a message from beyond the grave from Joe explaining the post script in his final email.

"Hello, Rose Montana speaking – who is this?"

"Hello Mrs. Montana this is the Montford-Wellesley Corporation. We've been trying to contact Meryl Montford-Wellesley; it's extremely urgent – it's about her husband." *I wonder what the hell happened.*

Jannine called the house. There was no answer. She called the bunkhouse phone, and Kurt answered.

"Hi Kurt this is Jannine Westone. Is Meryl there?"

"Well, howdy Miss Jannine. Nope, she ain't here. She, Jameson and that good-for-nothing-brother of mine took off somewhere a few minutes ago. Why, is something wrong? You sound upset. Is everything okay?"

"I hope so. The Montford-Wellesley Corporation has tried to reach her several times with no luck. They called Rose's cell phone saying it was imperative they get in touch with her."

I interrupted Jannine to tell her I had Jameson's cell phone number, and I'll try to get a hold of him. I called Jameson. He picked up on the first ring.

"Hey Rose, what's up. We're on our way to the cemetery to visit Charlotte's grave and . . ."

I cut him off. "Is Meryl with you?"

"Yes and Keough is with us too."

I told him to put Meryl on the phone – it was an emergency.

"Hello Rose, what's wrong?"

I explained that the Montford-Wellesley Corporation called about an urgent matter, and she needed to contact them ASAP."

She checked her cell phone and noticed there were four missed calls.

Keough pulled the truck over to the side of the road. "Sometimes the reception in these mountains isn't the best. They keep sayin' they're gonna put up more cell towers, but . . ."

Meryl stepped out of the truck and called the company. Jameson was going to follow her, but Keough stopped him.

"How about we give your mama some privacy; she'll fill us in when she'd done."

Five minutes later she came back to the truck with tears in her eyes. Jameson jumped out and ran towards Meryl.

"What's wrong? Talk to me Mother, what happened?"

Keough came running around from the driver's side. "What's goin' on Meryl? What's got you so upset?"

She could barely speak but managed to say, "It's my husband. He's suffered a massive heart attack – he didn't survive."

They helped her back into the truck. Keough turned it around and headed home.

Rose's cell phone rang again – it was Jameson. He told her they were on their way back to the ranch and would explain everything then.

The ride back was numbingly silent. Jameson stared out the window thinking, *I just met my birth father and less than a week later my adopted father dies. God, I'd love a drink right now. But I won't. I'll stay sober if for no other reason, to be there for my mother and respect for Keough.*

They arrived at the ranch. Jannine and I ran out to meet them in the driveway. Keough helped Meryl out of the truck and took her directly into the house.

"Jameson, please tell me what's happened. Is Meryl okay? Are you okay?"

He leaned against the truck taking a deep breath. "It's my father, my adopted father. He suffered a massive coronary. Mother's still in shock. Thank God Keough was with us. I don't know what we would have done without him. I'm proud of him. And my brother would be too."

It took me a minute to remind myself that Joe was his brother. Jannine walked over and hugged Jameson.

"I know we didn't hit it off when we first met, but I'm so sorry about your father. And it just dawned on me that you and I have something in common. We're both Montanas. Well, I'll be an official

Montana when Morgan and I get married, but I already consider myself a Montana. You're now part of a freakin' amazing family my friend."

"Yes, I'm beginning to realize that – loyal and fierce."

He thanked Jannine for her condolences and for welcoming him into the family.

"I'm going to go check on my mother. Again, thanks Jannine. You're a good friend. No wonder Rose loves you so much."

"She'd better. I'm the only best friend she's ever had. If I didn't tell her what to wear she'd live in denim and khaki."

"Or even worse . . . brown corduroy," Jameson added.

"Okay Jameson, you are officially a smart-ass Montana. I'm impressed!"

Cecilia offered to make an early supper. "It's important you all eat and keep your strength up. I'll also go pick up Charlotte. I think they need you here, Rose."

"Thank you Cecilia. That would really help me. I want to stay with Meryl. She's going to need lots of support right now."

Meryl had her bags packed and by the door. Her driver was on his way to pick her up and take her to Billings. The corporate jet would fly her and her driver back to New York. Keough came into the living room with another bag.

"Keough, I don't think that piece of luggage belongs to me."

"Yeah, I know it doesn't . . . it belongs to me. I'm goin' with ya'. You don't think I'm going let you go through this alone do ya'? Don't bother answering, 'cause I'm goin' whether you like it or not."

We all looked at each other in disbelief. I think it even took Meryl a few seconds for it to sink in.

Keough walked up to Jameson and put his hand on his shoulder. "Jameson – Son, I need you to stay here and take care of our family. Can I count on you to do this for me? When everything is settled, we'll call and let you know all the details. But for now I really need you here, Son."

Jameson nodded and hugged Keough.

Jannine came over to me and said, "Rose, did you ever in a million years think you'd witness this kind of love between Keough and Jameson? It's fucking unbelievable. It's like we've been sucked into some sort of bizarre-O, mid-western Lifetime movie."

Lou was the first to hear the limo coming up the driveway. He raced to the door and sat in front of it. He sniffed Keough's luggage and looked up at him as if to say, *are you leaving without me?*

Keough knelt down and scratched him on his head.

"You've got to stay here boy and help keep things in order until I return." Lou looked up at him, whimpered and then walked back over to me.

"We'll be okay Keough. Call us as soon as you get to New York."

"We will Rose. But we've got to leave now."

He took hold of Meryl's hand, "Are you ready?" "Yes, Keough I'm ready – let's go."

I watched the car until it was out of sight. I knew exactly how she was feeling. It wasn't that long ago I went down that same road to say goodbye to my husband. I had Paul to lean on. I'm happy she has Keough. I looked over at Jannine. She had the strangest look on her face.

"What's up with you, Jannine? You're acting weirder than normal."

"I just thought of something, Rose. Has Keough ever been in a jet before?"

I thought for a while. "Come to think of it, I don't think he's even been on a plane, let alone a small jet."

Jameson overheard our conversation and added, "If it's our company pilot, he's in for a treat. This guy is like the Mario Andretti of the Learjet. He'll have Keough tossing his Cheerios over Kansas."

We all laughed so hard we had tears in our eyes. I snorted so bad Lou started barking at me. Jannine asked if they had an in-flight camera on the jet. Jameson lifted his eyebrows in such a way that his face emitted a momentary flash of evil. Then he nodded.

Jannine was holding her sides from laughing so hard. She said, "I'd pay big ass money to get that footage. We could show it over and over at family dinners and holidays.

Chapter 19

Last night's moment of laughter soon turned to quiet morning sadness. The only father Jameson had ever known died only a few hours after he learned that he wasn't his birth father, and in the ultimate ironic twist, his birth father was traveling with his adopted mother to New York to support her with the loss of her husband. The whole chain of events made the entire Montana family shake their heads in utter disbelief. I thought about Joe's last email. Meryl was going to handle her husband's affairs and that's exactly what I needed to do. I needed to start packing up Joe's office.

I told Jannine about Joe's final email. "I would so appreciate it if you would stay and help me? I don't think I can do this alone."

"Of course I will. It's going to be sad for both of us. But at least we'll have each other to lean on. I'm a pretty good packer. I packed up your condo in less than 24-hours and you know how much of a pack-rat you were."

I laughed because I was always accusing Joe of being the family pack-rat. Paul stopped by the office to ask if I needed his help.

"We are good. Jannine will be helping me. However, we will need boxes. Could you bring us some? They're in the storage shed next to the barn."

Paul returned with a stack of folded boxes and left them outside the office door.

"I'll be back in a few. I'm going to check on Jameson and Kurt."

I walked into Joe's office and looked around. Funny, I still referred to it as, *Joe's Office*. Jannine started on one side packing all of his books from the shelves, off the floor and desk. A knock on the office door startled us. It was Raymond.

"You need me for anything, Rose?"

"Knowing you are here, Raymond, is help enough.

"It's hard to pack up a lifetime Rose. And Joe had a lifetime of joy with you. This is the first time I've ever been in here – what a shit hole! I knew he was a hoarder, but I never thought he was this bad."

I didn't think I could laugh or even smile while completing the task I dreaded for more than two years. *Leave it to you Raymond to lighten the mood. Joe would have laughed too. He saved every shredded note paper that had a story idea, interesting quote or research factoid he used for novels – you name it, he kept it. He never wanted to forget a possible storyline.*

Raymond started packing the files from his manuscript file cabinet. I began packing his cowboy memorabilia which included spurs, rodeo buckles and team roping trophies. I opened the small closet behind his desk. There was a pair of tan chaps hanging inside with a pair of his boots. He told me they were Keough's old branding chaps. There were some other odds-and-ends stored in boxes including a couple of old rodeo shirts, a collection of bandanas and two large manila envelopes tucked underneath the rodeo apparel. Both envelopes had my name hand-printed on them.

I sat on the closet floor and laid them across my lap. *What could be in them? And why were they hidden away underneath all this stuff?*

I opened one envelope and took the contents out. I could not believe what he saved. In that envelope was every one of the emails we'd written to each other. There had to be at least one hundred sheets of paper. The second envelope held even more memories. There were postcards and souvenirs from our honeymoon in Italy and pictures of us from every place we'd been together. I pulled from the envelope, tissue paper held together with a ribbon. When, I untied the little bow, there were the two daffodils I carried at our wedding. I never knew happened to them. Jannine must have given them to Joe after the ceremony. He saved them. He'd saved everything. Our entire life together was in these two envelopes. I was about to put all of it back into the envelopes when I noticed a smaller white envelope inside with "Rose" hand written across the front of it. It was in his handwriting. Joe never wrote me anything in cursive because he could type much faster than he could write. Plus his penmanship looked like the scratching of a squirrel on acid. I tucked the envelope in my pocket to read later in private.

After three hours, we'd finally finished. Seven large boxes of Joe's extraordinary life were now housed in the attic. I couldn't bring myself to burn it or throw anything away. Paul stayed behind and swept the floor while Raymond asked if he could sage the room.

"It will bring new energy into this space and kill any prairie fleas Joe left behind." I was lost in thought and didn't respond. "Aw, come on, Rose that was funny, right?"

I snapped back to reality and smiled. "Yes, of course it was, Raymond but I have to ask, am I doing the right thing? This was Joe's entire life. Everything he was, everything he did, everything he wrote was in here. Now it's all stored away in a dark attic."

He sat on the floor with me. "Rose, remember when we were at the drumming circle? You felt Joe there didn't you? And when we first met, you felt his presence in the cabin at my place he used for research. All of that stuff in the attic is WHAT Joe was, not WHO Joe was; does that make sense?" Raymond paused to see if what he was saying was getting through to me. "Joe was a writer and a celebrity. Who he was – well, he was the man who loved you from the moment he met you in that Currysville library, Rose Montana. But he's gone, and it's time you let WHAT he was go. You see that man over there sweeping the floor." He pointed to Paul. "He's nothing like Joe, and he loves you for who you are; a grieving woman who was crazy in love with a man who was larger than life. I'd say that takes pretty huge prairie oysters. It's okay to let him love you Rose. Now, take this last box up to the attic so I can sage the office. Because whatever Cecilia's cooking for supper is making me hungry. So get going."

I carried the box to the attic. I had to move the other boxes around a bit to make room for it. I thought about everything Raymond said. *Paul is a good man and I'm happy to have him in my life.* The attic it was filled with so many memories of Joe. Two of his prize saddles sat covered in one corner; a trunk filled with his research journals sat in another corner. *Am I doing the right thing by saving all of his things?* I keep telling myself that someday when she's older I'll let Charlotte go through all this stuff so she'll know who her daddy was and how much he was adored by the millions of devoted readers and fans.

The sound of footsteps and Charlotte's unmistakable calling for her mama brought me back to reality. Jannine stepped through the attic door with her in his arms. She wiggled out of her arms and came running over towards me and sat down on one of the boxes. Charlotte picked up one of the photo albums and started thumbing through it.

"Look Mama, it's you and Daddy. She kissed the photograph. I love my Daddy – he's a hottie." I was totally taken aback by her description of Joe.

I said, "Yes he was Baby Girl and where did you learn the word *hottie*?" She giggled, "From Aunt Jannine. Morgan's a hottie too – right Aunt Jannine?" Jannine turned away pretending not to hear her. *She's growing up way too fast.*

Jannine sat beside me. "Are you okay, Sweetie. You've been up here for almost forty-minutes. Paul and Raymond sent us up to make sure you didn't get eaten by killer mice or even worse . . . giant Rose eating beetles. All joking aside, they wanted us to tell you that dinner is ready."

"I'm okay Jannine. I just needed a moment alone to say goodbye."

"Understood, it's just that we were worried . . . and hungry. Take your time. We'll see you downstairs – when you're ready."

"Thank you Jannine. I love you."

"I love you too, Amelia."

"Come on, Charlotte, let's get cleaned up for dinner." When Jannine picked her up I noticed she still held onto the photo of us. I could almost hear Joe telling her, *"Hold on tight to your daddy and mama, Baby Girl. We'll always love you."*

When I stood up, something fell out of my pocket. It was the white envelope I'd found earlier addressed to me from Joe. I started to open it – then stopped.

"It'll read it later tonight, but right now Joe, our family needs me." I tucked it back into my pocket, took one final look around and closed the door.

Dinner was quiet. Meryl and Keough had arrived in New York and said they would call us when funeral plans were finalized. We decided to make it an early evening. The day's events were extremely exhausting to say the least. Charlotte fell asleep on the living room rug and Jannine was curled up on the couch. I took Charlotte into her room and tucked her in without changing her into her pajamas. No reason to wake her up. She can have her bath in the morning.

Jannine stumbled to the guest room waving goodnight to everyone. Kurt and Raymond headed back to bunkhouse. Jameson was too stressed to sleep and decided to go out for a drive. I asked him if he knew the roads well enough to go out at night.

"No I don't, Rose. However, if I'm staying in Montana I'd better start learning them."

"What do you mean staying in Montana? What about your job, your friends, your mother?" He asked me to step outside on the deck with him.

"Rose, all my life I've never felt connected to anything—not my job, my friends or my family. I never fit in, so I drank. Now I know why. I wasn't born to be a New Yorker or the CEO of a corporation. I was born in Montana. My birth family is here in Montana. My brother and mother lived and died in Montana. So, if it's okay with you I'd like to stay for a while."

It took me a moment to wrap my brain around his request. "Absolutely, you are welcome to stay here if you'd like. It's not like we don't have the room in this six-bedroom house. Or you can stay in the bunkhouse which is more like an apartment suite. Plus when Keough returns, Meryl may come back with him, and I can't see her camping out in the bunkhouse."

Jameson laughed, "Neither can I, but don't let Mother fool you. She's Montana tough through and through."

He looked up at the night sky. "This is where I wanna be, Rose. Ain't that the prettiest sky you've ever seen? There's nothin' like a big Montana sky to humble a man."

I thought, *oh my God he sound so much just like Joe!*

We walked back to the house. I told him to be careful. He said he would.

"Goodnight Rose."

"Goodnight Jameson."

He got into his truck and drove off.

It was 9:00 PM, and the house was quiet. I couldn't remember it ever being this quiet so early in the evening. I was covered with dust from the attic and decided to take a quick shower. I'd just turned on the water on when Paul knocked on the door.

"I just wanted to say goodnight. I'm going to stay in the bunkhouse tonight if that's okay? I thought it best to give you some time alone. It's been such a dreadful day."

"Paul, you can sleep here with me, if you'd like. It's not like anyone will be up before noon, so we'll have plenty of time to ourselves."

"Poppet as much as I would love to, I think its best, you get some much needed rest. I'll see you in the morning."

"Are you sure Paul?"

"Yes, Rose I'm sure. Oh, and, don't forget your letter." He pointed to the floor. "It may be important. Goodnight Poppet."

I picked it up from the bedroom floor. *Should I read it tonight or in the morning? No matter what I do, it'll keep me up all night.*

I peeled back the flap and opened the envelope. The letter was two pages long. *Of course it was. Joe never wrote anything under two hundred words in his life.*

My darlin' Rose,

You know I'm no good at handwritten letters. Typing is more my strong suit. When I sat down to write this letter to you, I thought you'd appreciated it more in cursive. Not that you'll be able to read my chicken scratch anyway, but I'm willing to give it a go.

I want you to know how much pleasure you've brought to this old cowboy's life; more than I expected or deserved. You see, when I first saw you at the Currysville Library my jaw dropped and my heart soared. I thought, "How is it possible for a woman to create such a range of emotion in a man. My palms started to sweat and I felt like I had a bag of gravel in my throat, I was so choked up. It was as if the Prom Queen asked me to be her first dance. I was terrified. I'd never felt like that before. When I jumped from behind the table, I knew I couldn't pass up the opportunity to meet you. And in that same moment when I asked you to marry me, it wasn't a joke – I knew you were the one. How – I don't know. You'll have to talk with Raymond. He's the one who believes in this soul mate stuff.

Something else I never told you. Before I arrived at that Currysville book signing, I had a dream about meeting a beautiful woman. Now I don't usually remember my dreams but this one was so vivid I wrote down all the details. That woman was you Rose. Now you understand why I couldn't let you leave. Call it fate, a spiritual connection, or just plain old fashion luck. I know now that it wasn't luck. Some people are destined to be together. And yes, I knew I was dying and I should have been honest with you, but Darlin' the time we shared was worth every bit of pain I'm feeling now. You were the ride of my life. And I wanted to share it with you for as long as the good Lord would let me.

My beautiful sweet Rose, I know you'll eventually find this letter. More than likely after I'm gone I suppose, so read it, keep it or destroy it. Either way I want you to know our meeting wasn't by chance. We were meant to be Darlin', and you were meant to be a Montana. I love you Rose.

Joe

P.S. Oh and one more thing . . . Always expect the unexpected, "wink"

www.ingramcontent.com/pod-product-compliance
Lightning Source LLC
Chambersburg PA
CBHW070020260626
47159CB00005B/1896